MW01052501

Just Holler
BLOODY MURDER

A NOVEL BY DERSHIE MCDEVITT

ISBN: 1477555986
ISBN 13: 9781477555989

for Larry

My heartfelt thanks go out to our friends on Dewees Island, where this book is lovingly and deliberately set. That means you Judy and Reggie Fairchild, publicists, photographers extraordinaire, and selfless promoters of our shared special island. And you, Brucie and Lo Harry and Barbara McIntyre for your genuine encouragement. And thanks to Albert, the fourteen foot alligator who has shared his fresh water pond with us for over ten years and behaved so normally that my readers now get to peek into his unique world through the eyes of Callahan Banks.

Thanks to my incredibly supportive writing group, P.B. Parris, Annice Brown, Ellenberg, Nancy K. Hayes and the late Elizabeth Daniels Squire for patiently reading and rereading, always with tact, wisdom and insight. And I must mention Gracie, the writing group cat, who purrs moral support from our laps and inspires us all.

To my uncontaminated first readers, Sheri Groce, Jasmin Gentling, Mary Hood Pearlman, Ann H. Howell, Joel Cole, Martha Satterwhite and Sandy Holder, thank you.

And to our family, I'm grateful for your forbearance when I missed precious hours with you in pursuit of this dream. Without my techno-angel Trent, all would have been lost. Thanks to Inez and the late Bruce Bridgford, to Brandon, Trent, and Kendal McDevitt, our talented, brave and riotously wonderful kids, and thanks to our sons-in-law and grandchildren who have added such spice and vinegar to the Circle McDevitt: Larry, Travis, Tara and Audrey Hinton, Patrick and Harper Beville. I love you all.

Finally, and most importantly, to Larry McDevitt, my first, second and forever husband, best friend, financial supporter, and dearest life partner, I dedicate this book.

What a blessing to have shared the path with each of you.

Just Holler

BLOODY MURDER

Prologue

THURSDAY, JULY 3

Nothing seems amiss to Callahan Banks. A full moon lights the wide expanse of secluded South Carolina beach at low tide. Sand dollars litter the beach, a long-ago wealth of shell money for a little girl's play. A transparent ghost crab skitters nervously into the dunes. It's one a.m., but the water still holds warmth from the sizzling July day.

Her bare feet sink into silver sand, newly dampened on the outgoing tide. Callahan's so close to the water's edge that frothy bubbles coat her toes. At least the lazy hush, hush of wave against shore doesn't induce the agonizing grief it did when Lila died three months ago.

Mother and daughter shared an idyllic existence in this isolated place for eighteen years until Callahan left for college and, then, grad school. Now, she's an Assistant Professor of biology at UNC-Asheville, only a four-hour's drive from Charleston, plus a twenty minute ferry ride to this barrier island called Timicau. But it's the first time she's been home since Lila died, a house without her mother impossible to fathom.

Out where the water darkens in its depth, about forty yards off shore and unseen by Callahan, a woman's limp body momentarily rides the crest of a moonlit wave before slipping beneath it and disappearing.

Pungent beach-scented air–a hint of fish? Eau d'-moldy clams?–evokes memories of Callahan's thirteenth birthday and a midnight walk with Lila, when children with proper mothers had long since been tucked in their beds. Dripping wet from skinny-dipping, the sounds of their laughter muted by the vast space of the deserted beach, mother and daughter had emerged from the water to walk side by side on the hard, flat sand.

"Look, Callie B." Lila's firm body glistened with salt spray as she pointed at their moon-made shadows on the shore ahead. "Look at that. You've outgrown me, you Wonder Woman, you!"

Since Lila had decreed that no house of hers would ever have a mirror–"a waste of time and a distraction from what really matters"– Callahan stared in amazement at her own long-legged shadow, stretching an exaggerated foot beyond her mother's there on the sand.

"Don't get cocky now." Lila's teeth flashed happy white. "I'm not exactly the hardest person to outgrow."

Lila Banner Boone, barely five feet tall, with olive skin and the dark unfathomable eyes of a mystic, was a contrast in every way to her delicate, pale-skinned daughter, whose aristocratic features and sea-green eyes hinted at distant blood lines and a long-lost English father.

Her mother's exuberance embarrassed Callahan in those early teenage years but never overshadowed her. Buoyed by Lila's approval, Callahan had slipped easily through adolescence and emerged with a confidence unusual in a girl so young.

Maybe we were too close. There were just the two of us. It makes adjusting to losing her all the harder.

Though a savvy thirty-two now, Callahan still pictures her mother as part sea nymph, part Lilith. Her mother planted the seed for those images on this very beach when Callahan was four. "I walked out of the sea right here, and two smiling gray dolphins delivered you into my arms." Lila extended a tanned finger towards a large sand bar fifty feet off shore. 'This is the place,' I said to you. 'We will live here like gypsies and never tell anyone who we are or why we came.'"

The slap of a rogue wave against her ankle brings Callahan back to present.

A true gypsy would have had some potion up her sleeve, some artifice for sustaining life against all odds.

But the Bohemian mother she'd believed immortal had been slowly eaten away by the cancer.

While Callahan's lost in thought, the body in the ocean lifts over the sandbar on a large outgoing wave. There's the sound of one distinctive slap from the wave's direct hit—something Callahan normally would notice—and the body bobs over the bar and out to the darkened water beyond. It floats aimlessly there in charcoal shadows of deeper water, occasionally knocking against that very sand bar where the dolphins are said to have delivered Callahan to Lila.

Callahan senses the movement of Timicau's tides like a yogi, loves the reversal of force that follows the ebb. Tonight, though, it brings scant comfort. She mouths a quiet plea, "Please give me some sign you're out there somewhere, Lila. Just let me know I'll see you again . . . someday . . ."

She thinks the breeze may have grown a little stronger. Another ghost crab skitters across the sand. Behind Callahan on the Island, a Great Horned Owl whispers its haunting whoo-whoo-who-who-whoo. But here on the beach, this place above all others that has been sacrosanct to Lila and Callahan, nothing, absolutely nothing of significance seems to be happening.

Wait a little longer

Moonlight silvers the full length of an incoming wave.

Wait and listen for the signs. Some sigh from the wind, some change in the tenor of the owl's hoot, some disturbance in the cadence of the waves.

She gazes out over the sea as a lacy cloud crosses the moon.

Everything feels meaningless.

Then, she turns from the ocean, suddenly too miserable to stay any longer. Slipping on flip flops to avoid sand spurs, their barbs a painful menace to bare feet, she heads for the path that leads through the dunes back to the middle of the island and Lila's vacant little stilt house on an inland pond.

It's then that she senses it. Not on the sea or in the sand or wind, but beneath her own skin. At first, it's just a familiar whisper. Then, an internal rush of air, the flutter of a bird coming home to nest. The joyful life force of Lila Boone fills Callahan's body and turns her skin to gooseflesh. She whoops out loud, "MOTHER! Thank God! I knew you had to be around here somewhere."

Seconds later, still trying to take in the sensation of being filled with Lila's energy, Callahan realizes why her mother had picked *this* night to return.

How could I have missed it? It's early, but there's a turtle nest hatching. We have work to do, don't we?"

The assurance of Lila's presence propelling her back to the beach, Callahan quickens her steps, running giddily up the moon-milky expanse of deserted sand. At this north end of the island, everything is eerily bleached, flat and colorless. Something small and dark wiggling across the dull white surface of a dune to her left catches her eye. Callahan's smile is sheer bliss.

I knew it.

In a second, the one small creature becomes the many as tiny turtle babies who've hatched under the sand and waited, stacked together, for this perfect moment to boil out of their nest high up in the dunes, swarm towards the beach ahead of her.

She frowns uneasily. Predictably guarding the shoreline, their shadows casting spidery images on the sand, are the ghost crabs, large claws waving in fiendish anticipation.

It surprises Callahan each time she does the brutal thing she's about to do. She races for a crab that has seized the lead turtle, reaching it before it can pinch the little turtle's flipper and turn it on its back. She seizes the crab from its backside–her own gesture of self-preservation– and wrests free the baby turtle, its soft body no bigger than an Oreo. Its four flippers race on in the air till she places it on the sand. Holding the crab so she's out of reach of its pincers, she grabs a piece of driftwood, drops the crab to the beach, and smashes the life out of it. Squash!

Even the sound is satisfying.

The little turtle is paddling frantically towards the water now, its head popping skyward when the first wave washes over it.

He's home. Lila's husky voice says the words in Callahan's head.

The little creature is swimming with purpose straight into the lapping surf. The next wave hits it head on but doesn't wash it back to the beach as usually happens.

A strong one.

Callahan can still see its small head raised, a bump on the water, where it swims out beyond that first breaker.

Headed for the Sargasso Sea.

It will swim frenetically for the next forty-eight hours, trying to reach the protection of the huge mass of seaweed that travels the currents of the Atlantic Gulf Stream. In twenty years, one out of ten thousand of these babies will return to this very beach, a species virtually unchanged over two hundred million years of evolution. Thrilled beyond measure that it's launched, she turns to rescue its fellows.

In fifteen minutes, it's over, the beach's surface covered with the tiny dimpled tracks of the hatchlings. Callahan's grateful that none of the detestable new houses being built along the beach have been sited here. No bright lights yet to confuse the babies, attracting them from moonlit ocean to arid death in dry dunes. At least a hundred baby loggerheads have followed the moon's reflection on the water to the ocean tonight. Four–she counts them now–ghost crabs are dead by her hand. She feels the surge and return of her own life force.

Thank you, Lila. I know now you're out there somewhere. You and your turtles have brought me back.

Sighing with a contentment that's been lost to her these past three months, she throws an idle kiss to her mother somewhere in the sea vapors and wonders how murder can be so satisfying.

Unseen, far out beyond the breaking waves where the water holds black shadows in its depth, the opalescent body still bobs and rolls in the quiet surf. It's a ghoulish place of first rest now for the turtle babies tired from their long beach crawl and frantic first swim.

Seaweed being their natural realm, they instinctively cling to floating strands of long blonde hair when they reach it. Ten cling there while others crawl on the vacant-eyed face, its contours providing safety for three and then three more. The lee side of one curved arm shelters a latecomer. Half opened palms on both hands–their red-lacquered fingernails catching the moonlight–teem with baby loggerheads.

The little turtles linger there, crawling across and rearranging themselves on angled pelvic bone, tanned bare belly, mounded breast, over swollen lip and upturned lash until the path lit by the moon across their ocean home seduces them seaward. Then, one by one, they slide from their island of flesh back into the sea, leaving the blonde in her indigo-blue bikini awaiting the incoming tide to move her landward.

At high tide early the next morning, the body beaches itself and is discovered by Timicau Island's first morning walkers, John Culpepper Dade III and his loose-boned hound dog, Nadine. The dead woman is Victoria Weatherly, thirty years old, a former debutante, and the event planner at the Charleston Museum of Art.

Later, when Callahan hears about the body and remembers the direction the turtles were swimming, she muses that maybe the last thing–and from her perspective, one of the best things–Victoria ever did was provide an interval of rest for the tired and vulnerable little loggerheads.

Chapter One

There's something about looking at the world upside down that actually helps me see things more clearly.

Callahan's been balanced on her head now for almost two minutes.

Blood to the brain? Or maybe it's reconnecting with Mother on the beach last night.

Early morning sun filters through the screens of the second floor porch that surrounds all four sides of Lila's little tree house on stilts, bringing pleasant warmth. A flicker lands on a live oak limb, not two feet from the screen, a flash of yellow feathers and the formal black "V" on his breast identifying him as one of Callahan's favorite woodpecker species. Pavorotti hits a perfect high note on Lila's old CD player. Callahan knows it's time to call Lila's accountant. She came home to face reality, and it must be done.

When she finishes her yoga practice, she'll call for an appointment. With his help, she'll assess the limited resources her mother left and force herself to decide whether to rent or sell this house. They're the only two options she can afford. That much she knows for sure. And then, her cherished home since childhood—her eyes mist—this place of escape and refuge, will be her retreat no more.

Still upside down, she consciously redistributes her weight on her wrists, pushing both forearms to move her shoulder blades deeper into her back, and extends her bare feet towards the lazy fan turning above her.

The last headstand she did on this deck was on April tenth. Lila was lying nearby in the hammock, a quilt tucked around her wasting frame. "Watch out, my tall and elegant daughter." Her voice was weak, but her mouth creased into a wry smile. "You're about to trim your toenails on that fan blade."

Callahan had instinctively jerked her feet down though she was five foot six, and the covered roof rose ten feet above the deck. Lila cackled in delight.

"Gotcha, didn't I?"

"That you did, Mom, but, then, you always do."

Lila lived in that hammock those last weeks of her life, absorbed as always in the behavior of the wildlife teeming around the swamp pond thirty feet below: a thirteen foot male gator, his mates and offspring, egrets in full breeding fettle, newly arrived, raucous, squawking moorhens with their flashy red facial feathers. Lila could identify them all and recognized many as individuals, even some of the migratory birds that summered on Timicau Island and wintered farther south. Soaring ospreys and hunched nocturnal black crowned night herons were some of her favorites, but a curious, destructive coon or a retiring bobcat she found equally fascinating. And for over thirty years, she'd logged her observations of them all.

The heavy black leather-backed record book, connected to pen-on-a-string—its fourteen earlier incarnations all stacked on a bookcase in the house—lay open beside her that day on the hammock. "April 10: Good news! The painted buntings are back, two in and out of live oak west of porch all day..." The pen line trailed off the paper. Drugged by pain medicine, she'd fallen asleep. It would be her final entry.

Tears fill Callahan's eyes, overflow her eyebrows, and drench her forehead. A weird sensation.

I've never cried upside down before.

"Yoo hoo." At first, Callahan thinks the shriek is a flaw on the Pavarotti CD. "Hello up there. I'm coming uhhhuuupppp." But Pavarotti sings on, and the voice comes again from the bottom of the stairs, two stories down. "It's real important, honey. We have got us one hell of problem." A pause. "I know you're home. I can hear that smarmy Italian warbling clear down here."

Maybe if I'm quiet, they'll go away.

Callahan lowers her knees to her chest, her feet to the floor, and lies still, her back absorbing warmth from the floor of the deck. Her tears, geographically reoriented but still flowing, now wet her cheeks and pool under her ears.

Bam! Bam! Whoever's down there is assaulting the sliding barn door which secures the steps at the bottom from the incursions of scavenging coons. "Sweetie pie." The voice becomes louder and more insistent. "My, Gawd, Callahan"–then, raises an octave—"that gator's gotten huge. Why hasn't somebody shot him? He's swimming straight toward me. No kidding, he's not fifteen feet away."

Callahan's face clouds unhappily. She now recognizes the sultry drawl that holds the same exaggerated alligator fear it did when they were children. Albert, the gator down there, is more curious than predatory when it comes to humans. All these years he and Lila have coexisted easily, keeping respectful distances from each other.

Callahan sits up and mops her face on the tail of her tee shirt. "Come on up, Francie," she yells over the side of the house. "It's not latched. It never is."

What could possibly bring Francis Dade clear out here?

Seven other people live on Timicau Island, all of them in the Dade compound around Twelve Oaks Plantation. Three of them are Dades, the four others, their servants. And none ever voluntarily leaves beachfront breezes in summer heat to come to the mosquito-infested center of the island. Reluctantly, Callahan finger-combs her tear-damp hair, stands and reaches for the pull to turn the overhead fan on high.

Francie will be unbearably hot and bitchy by the time she climbs two flights of steep stairs.

At the bottom of the steps, Callahan hears her frantically jerking the heavy barn door, trying to get it to slide open across its track. The trick is to pull it out slightly, but Callahan's not inclined to offer any advice. In fact, she's rather savoring the image of Francie Dade–probably in impractical, open-toed sandals and a thin, sherbet-colored, clingy cotton dress that makes her white skin a mosquito magnet–struggling with the door while keeping a terrified eye on the biggest gator on the island.

It bothered Lila not at all that the stairs from the ground twenty feet below the bedrooms on the lower level of the house were precariously precipitant. Nor did it bother her that the steps up to the second floor with its great room, kitchen and sweeping porches were even steeper. There was no money for gradually curving steps, not enough square footage inside the house to accommodate a staircase, so the two levels of the house are connected only by the outside steps from ground to lower deck and lower deck to upper. "Climbing's good for the heart." Lila had said it more than once. "Besides,"– twinkle of dark eyes—"it discourages casual drop-in visitors."

As if living on the edge of a swamp doesn't already do that.

Callahan finds herself smiling as she pictures Francie, an indolent, Marilyn Monroe look-alike right down to her peroxide blonde bouffant hairdo with its perennially retouched roots, flailing away at mosquitoes.

Something's definitely up. She hates coming out here so this isn't a social call.

Callahan wonders, as she often has before, how such a trampy woman could be John Dade's daughter. She still misses John terribly, the only father figure she ever had. Lila would never take John up on his open proposal to marry him, but a thirty-two year friendship between Lila and John had anchored and enriched Callahan's life in countless ways. His unexpected death of a ruptured cerebral aneurism on his sixty-sixth birthday two years before had been a shock and jarring loss to her and her mother.

John's only son, Francie's older half brother, Pepper, John Culpepper Dade III, moved back to the island within weeks of John's death, and the contractors came close on his heels. *And that's when the trouble began.*

First, Pepper built Francie her own mansion a quarter of a mile up the beach from Twelve Oaks. Then, he completely remodeled the south wing of the old plantation house for Honey, his nineteen-year-old other half sister. And now, he's hawking beachfront lots, like Mexican blankets in a roadside stand—albeit a little more pricey. A half million dollars, she's been told, is the starting price.

Down below, Callahan hears the sound of the door rolling open at the foot of the stairs. Francie's gotten it open. She's on her way up.

You have to face the truth, whether you like it or not. What *the Dade children—at least Pepper and Francie—seem to love most about Timicau Island is the money they're making selling it off in lots.*

She's glad John didn't live to see this happen. It's probably just a matter of time till Pepper tries to buy her house and its ten acres, the only property on the whole island he doesn't now control.

I'll fight to keep him from getting it. At least, there will be one place on the island where Lila's birds and beasts can live in peace. Oh no.

Callahan swallows hard.

He's probably sent Francie out to soften me up for the sale.

The screen door on the first floor level slams, and Callahan sighs. She dreads any and all encounters with Francis Dade who, she long ago decided, must have been born feral.

If Francie's here, she wants something.

Callahan tries to anticipate what to protect today. Early on, it was the one-of-a-kind doll clothes Lila made for her that disappeared. Later, a favorite stuffed bear with brown leather button eyes from John. Then, a ten-year-old's collection of delicate jingle shells, a filmy red scarf. By the time Callahan, two years older than Francie, became a teenager, Francie came calling only if she needed Lila's help on a science project. Until Callahan turned fifteen, when Francie returned, and, this time, the reason was boys.

What was it John had so tactfully said about his daughter? "She's one of those girls who ripen early."

Callahan had little exposure to or use for boys in her early teenage years, but a few took an interest in her. Her favorite? It takes her a minute to even remember his name now.

Tim? Slim Tim Hubbard.

He of the first kiss, those first sweet physical explorations. The bliss had lasted for six months with hand holding in darkened movie theaters and idyllic moonlit beach walks. Lasted until a well-"ripened" Francie went out of her way to offer Tim something he found considerably more interesting.

Francie's on the upper landing now. Callahan hears the sound of her steps and tries to twist her unwilling mouth into a civil smile.

Protect yourself.

For the sake of conversation, she tries to recall if Francie's been divorced two or three times in her thirty years of living, but for the life of her Callahan can't remember.

A gasp from Francie precedes her around the corner of the porch, then her scent, a blend of something like Victoria's Secret perfume and cigarette smoke. "Thank you, Jesus," Francie says it out loud as she comes into view, "for letting my heart survive this ordeal."

Callahan stares in disbelief. Francie's not swathed in gauzy sherbet colors. Nor is she clawing at reddened mosquito welts on flawless white skin. She's completely covered in a pajama-like outfit made out of camouflage-patterned tent screening. She's also clearly hot, miserable, and furious at Callahan.

"Why in the hell, when we have an emergency like this, would you turn off your cell phone? I've been desperately trying to call you for at least an hour." She begins unzipping zippers, body parts emerging one-at-a time from the mosquito protective gear.

This is a bit like watching a butterfly emerge from a chrysalis, though in this case, I think the best I can hope for is a worm.

Francie's voice, though still irate, drips with self-pitying sugar syrup. "I could have been eaten alive by that gator, Callahan. Surely he's not the same one I hated when we were kids. Don't they ever die?" The jacket falls to the floor, and Francie fumbles into her lower recesses, produces a lace hanky, and begins wiping down her arms.

Callahan fights a smile.

This may be the first time I've ever seen Francie perspire. She's actually glistening with sweat.

She's tugging at the helmet now, stretching elastic around her neck out and up over her head to reveal a badly tousled, beauty parlor do. "No thanks to you, I have survived a golf cart ride in the steam heat of summer, a near alligator attack, and a climb that Sir Edmund Hillary would find challenging. All just to deliver somebody else's bad news."

Two more zips and pant legs fall away with waistband. The cocoon becomes a heap on the floor. So far, Francie–completely focused on her chrysalis operation–has neither looked at Callahan nor seemed to expect a response to her questions or complaints.

After more huffing and mopping, both her hands go to her head in a familiar hair-arranging motion that Callahan remembers from their teenage years. Front to back, lift, bottom back to top, lift, squeeze two handfuls on top and pull gently. Miraculously, Francie's hair springs back into place and looks completely normal now.

The wonders of hair spray.

Beneath her mosquito netting, Francie is, after all, predictably clothed in a coral-pink, form-fitting, low-necked, cotton tee shirt with the word YES prominently outlined in turquoise rhinestones, aqua linen pants, and Italian soft-leathered sandals, their toe thongs a pink daisy that matches her toe nail polish and the tee shirt. Two pink sequined flamingos with turquoise toes dangle from her ears though at the moment, one flamingo's hanging a bit lopsidedly after being temporarily hooked on the mosquito helmet. A diamond tennis bracelet and a sundry collection of gold and diamond rings drip from wrists and hands to complete the accessorizing.

"Well, Callahan." Francie finally makes eye contact as she collects the mosquito gear and drops it in the middle of the teak picnic table. Thick blue eye shadow accentuates her eyes, the single facial feature that keeps her from achieving the innocent blonde look. Her eyes, heavy lidded and too small for the scale of her face, slant upward at their outer corners, giving her features a foxlike cast. Callahan remembers their color as dull tobacco brown, but today, they're a startling shade of turquoise. "The long and the short of it…"

"God, Francie." Callahan interrupts her. "Are you coordinating the color of your eyes with your outfits these days?"

Francie's a little taken aback. "Well, yes. No. Not always. They're just colored contacts. I feel more like myself with blue eyes. That's all. Besides, JP likes them, and I'm picking him up for an early lunch and a little nooner." She smiles, unselfconsciously contorting her upper body like her bra strap is too tight. "He's the single best fuck I've had in years. Haven't you noticed, Callahan?"

Callahan's brow registers confusion. "Noticed what? I neither know who JP is, nor have I fucked him if that's your question."

Francie puffs her generous breasts a little huffily.

At least they're the real thing.

Callahan's seen them sprout, expand, and seduce many more males than innocent Slim Tim Hubbard over the years.

Francie shimmies them subtly. "I didn't mean that." She's petulant. "No reason *you* would know him. He's James Peter Mellinkamp, the foreman on the Pasquini House. I thought maybe you'd picked up on what a hunk he is on the ferry. I tell him his mama sure knew what she was doing when she stuck that Peter in his name because he has the biggest, prettiest one I've experienced in a long, long time."

"Do you mean to tell me"–Callahan's thinking how little small talk ever passes between them before they got down to brass tacks–"that you meet him on the job site and do it right there?"

Francie's lower lip droops into an offended pout. "Of course not. There are other workmen there, though none of them"–her nose wrinkles mischievously–"are any where near as well endowed as JP is."

She's probably polled the whole delegation.

"We just take a little golf cart ride up to my new house," Francie says. "You do know that Pepper kicked me out of Twelve Oaks and built me a place of my very own, don't you?" The pouting lip slips farther from its mooring, something new displeasing her. "Pepper, that reminds me. I can't stay a minute longer because he has ordered us all to be at Twelve Oaks at one today to talk to Cole. You, too. I'm your messenger boy."

"Cole? Cole Hunnicut? The Sheriff?"

"Yes, maam, one and the same. He told Pepper to round us up for an incest. No,"–she laughs easily and self-corrects–"don't I wish it? Inquest, I think that's what he called it. Or to collect information for one. Whatever. He's trying to figure out what killed Victoria."

"Killed Victoria? Victoria who? What are you talking about, Francie?"

Francie's eyes widen blankly. "Well, I think that's what I've just been trying to tell you." She frowns. "Victoria Weatherly, that predatory girlfriend of Pepper's, that's who. Who took it upon herself to get drowned out here yesterday and ruin the whole day today for the rest of us." Francie's eyes stray over Callahan's head to the clock inside on the kitchen wall. "It's ten thirty. Damn. This is taking way too long. I'm supposed to be picking him up at the Pasquini's right now." She reaches for the netting and, pink lacquered nails flashing, begins reinserting and zipping herself back into the chrysalis.

"At least, I cooled off a little. These mosquito things will cook you alive." The netting muffles her words as it slides over her face. She stretches the elastic band over her chin and down around her neck. "It's too bad you can't understand plain English, Callahan. Let me try again. Pepper's snooty girlfriend is dead as that tree." A long nail directs Callahan's gaze to a lightening-scarred palmetto trunk just off the porch. "She spent Wednesday night at Twelve Oaks with Pepper and stayed on after he left to go to the mainland yesterday morning, you know to catch a few rays." Francie slides one sandaled foot in a pant leg and zips it up. "She was supposed to go back on the ferry whenever she was ready to leave, so Pepper had no way of knowing she never did. She must have floated out there in the ocean all night long like some gaffed flounder." Francie begins the same process with foot two. "I was working with Wallace"–Wallace has been the Dade's handyman as long as Callahan can remember–"separating some irises and moving more of my mother's perennials to my new house." Zip. She reaches for the top and begins similar maneuvers with her arms. "Do you have any idea, Callahan, how hard it is to give up mature camellias and gardenias, not to mention herbs when you planted them with your own mother? Well, it is unfair and a trial." Zip, right arm. Zip, left. Zip, front. Fully suited up, she turns towards the top of the stairs, then pauses. "They're investigating it as a possible murder. Victoria, I mean, but she was a diabetic, and my guess is she just O-Ded or U-Ded. Get it? Under dosed? Cole has to go through the motions to make it look right since he and Pepper go back so far." She casts an uneasy look towards the pond and seems reassured at the sight of Albert on the far side. Then, waving a mitten-netted hand in Callahan's direction, she turns, walks to the stairs, and begins descending, pausing again after the second step. "Oh, crap, Callahan, I forgot something else. Pepper said he'd like to talk to you after Cole gets through. Something about your house."

There it is.

Francie accomplishes her leaving more efficiently than her coming. Callahan hears the door roll closed at the foot of the steps, the backup beeps of the golf cart, then watches it fly across the yard, on to the path and disappear into the dense maritime forest in the direction of mid-beach and the Pasquini house. All transportation on the island is by golf cart, and from the speed of her departure, Francie really is anxious to get to JP.

"So," Callahan says out loud, "I am commanded to be present in two and a half hours to discuss the death of a woman I don't even know. Nor do I know how she died, where they found her, or rat shit. I can't go see Mom's accountant now, and"–her jaw muscles tighten–"Pepper Dade thinks he's going to steal your little house from me, Lila."

She balls a fist in the air and startles herself by screaming out loud. "Pepper Dade!" Two roosting egrets on a nearby bald oak limb fly squawking into the air, spooked. "You don't know it yet, but you and your trashy sister have got a fight on your hands!"

Chapter Two

Callahan hasn't been back to Twelve Oaks since John's funeral two years ago because she can't stand the thought of the place without him. Her breathing goes shallow when she turns Lila's rickety green golf cart off the crushed oyster shells of Pelican Flight on to the drive that leads to Twelve Oaks. Though no cars are allowed on the island, Pepper seems to be making plenty of exceptions when it comes to construction vehicles these days. The once meandering path through oak trees heavy with Spanish moss is now rutted in hardened gouges from heavy equipment and twice as wide, a remembered musty-earth smell of pine needles and bay noticeably absent.

They've cleared all the undergrowth.

She slows for a better look. Palms, pines, myrtles, wild blackberry, even the popcorn trees, those invasive Chinese tallows with their shiny leaves and fluffy white blooms, all are cleared back from the path. Only the twelve massive live oaks that line each side of the drive still stand, their gnarled-arm canopy darkening the way ahead.

They must be two hundred years old. This hard-packed dirt over their roots will probably kill them all before they're done.

"Shit." She says it out loud—"Shit"—twice. It doesn't help. Nose wrinkling in distaste, she drives on, dreading what lies ahead. They've built a complete compound here since Pepper moved back, garish metal sheds to store machinery visible off to her right through the trees, these surrounded by stacks of lumber, a swale cart full of construction debris, and a pile driver tall as an oak tree.

A veritable termite colony.

Her eyes fight tears as she nears the clearing where a plush two-acre lawn surrounds the white-columned plantation house.

Now let's see what they've done to screw up his house.

She looks for the new wing Pepper added for Honey, unsure if she can endure another blight on the place. It takes her a minute to spot it on the right side of the house which, she realizes, must have originally been disproportionately shorter than the left.

If you didn't know there was an addition, you'd never suspect. It gives nice symmetry.

She swats a mosquito that lingers too long on her hand–they seldom bite her–and considers turning the cart around and going home.

I wonder what Pepper would do if I just didn't show up today.

All she'll be able to tell Cole about Victoria Weatherly is that she saw her once or twice this past spring from a distance on the beach. A leggy, glamorous, longhaired blonde draped over Pepper like Spanish moss on an oak.

But she decides to stay. A congenial relationship with Pepper could make things easier if she has to sell Lila's house. She's had only a howdy relationship with both Honey and Pepper for many years. Callahan was nine when Pepper left for The University of North Carolina in Chapel Hill and twelve when Emma, nicknamed Honey, was born to John's second wife, Ruby. Callahan drives the cart to the front of the house and brakes to a stop on the parking pad. In fact, she knew so little about Pepper that at first she was naïve enough to be pleased when she heard he'd sold his beachfront house on Sullivan's Island to move back to Twelve Oaks.

He looks so much like John, I thought he'd be like him.

Undetected on a bench behind a low hanging oak limb, Callahan had actually watched Pepper direct that move from the mainland to

Timicau as she waited for the ferry. It was a trying experience for him, and she'd admired the way he conducted himself.

That day.

The Aggie Gray, Timicau's little ferryboat, only had room to haul passengers, their groceries, and a few belongings. So apparently, Pepper had hired a large barge to transport his fully packed moving van the twenty minutes up the Intracostal Waterway to the island.

An obviously frustrated Pepper, in khakis and a blue cotton button-down shirt, both sleeves rolled up to the elbow, was standing on the ferry dock next to the boat ramp that gradually sloped from a gravel driveway into the water. It was noon, the hottest time of the day, and the summer sun was brutal. His shirt drenched in perspiration, both hands overhead motioning, he was yelling encouragement to a small, sallow man at the wheel of an unwieldy barge near the end of the ramp. This was the man's third unsuccessful try at negotiating the barge straight enough and far enough up the ramp so the driver of a yellow moving van waiting at its top could drive it on.

"You've got to give her more gas, Percy." Pepper yelled at the barge captain. "Really gun the motor." He checked a dive-watch on his left wrist and scowled down at the receding seawater on the lower half of the ramp. "This tide's doing its damnest to strand us. What have we got? About ten minutes to get her loaded, or we'll have to wait till midnight to have enough draw for the barge with the weight of the van."

His resemblance to his father was striking. More slightly built than John, and not as tall–barely six feet she estimated–with sun-streaked tightly curled blond hair, he still radiated the Dade aura. Her eyes kept returning to him on the dock there like he was stage-lit.

Something amused him just then. He threw his head back and laughed out loud, the firm lines of his chin in profile so like John's. And he kept laughing in that way John had of finding things funny sooner and longer than other people.

Just hearing him laugh was a gift.

"Hold up a minute." Pepper yelled at the barge captain. "We're coming in crooked again. Anybody know how to jack a ramp sideways?" He grinned at this own joke. "I'd like to get this truck on the island before Christmas."

Clearly out of patience, Pepper motioned the barge driver to stop, emptied his pockets, unbuttoned and took off his shirt, and deposited everything on the dock. Then, he walked around to the front of the ramp and down it till the water was up to his waist. He collected both tie lines off the sides of the barge and carried them back up the ramp.

Doesn't hurry. Acts like he has all the time in the world. Just like John.

He tossed the starboard rope to a man wearing the green shirt of the moving company on the far side of the ramp and told him to wrap it round a nearby live oak and hang on tight. His pants dripping, Pepper emerged from the water and wrapped the port rope twice around a tree on the opposite side, not fifteen feet from Callahan, keeping that end for himself. "Start over Perce. Back out and we'll help you guide her in" They were going to use the ropes to guide the barge up the ramp to the van at its top.

At first, the barge knocked against the end of the ramp and turned clumsily. Pepper shouted encouragement. "Don't let up on the gas. Keep her coming, Perce. Now, pull. Pull." The muscles on Pepper's back bunched as he and the moving man leaned backward, straining at the ropes. Suddenly, the barge seemed to divine its purpose and slid, like a race horse into a starting gate, straight up the ramp to the back of the waiting van.

Pepper's shoulders sagged in relief. He released tension on his line and tied the barge to a piling. "That'll do, Perce. Good work." To the driver of the moving van, "Back her on the barge, and let's get this show on the road."

He's competent and can relate to all kinds of people, the same way John could.

Pepper followed the moving man into the shade of the biggest oak in the parking lot, then only about six feet from where Callahan sat. She was surprised he didn't notice her, but he was absorbed in pounding congratulatory thumps on the back of the dark-skinned man, whose face was actually dripping sweat. Pepper pulled a handkerchief out of his pant's pocket, wiped his own face, neck and chest and offered it to the man, who took it. "Jesus H. Christ," Pepper confided to him, "I do hate work."

She'd forgotten, if she'd noticed before that day, that Pepper's eyes were the same salty turquoise as John's. You couldn't help but stare when you first saw them, their bleached color incongruous in so masculine a face. No doubt about it. Pepper bore enough resemblance to John that she had longed to know him better.

Till I figured out what he was up to on Timicau.

"Callahan, are you planning to sit in that golf cart all day, or are you waiting for an invitation to dismount?" The sound of Pepper's voice rattles her composure and brings her back to his front yard at Twelve Oaks.

Where is he?

She spots him, finally, off to her right and just behind her, lying in a Pawley's Island hammock that's strung between two huge trees on the shady edge of the yard. He must have been there when she pulled up and watched her this whole time. A once-familiar warming tingles her cheeks.

Oh, double shit. Why would I blush now when I haven't in years?

She wishes that she hadn't chosen the V-neck white tee when she put on her favorite calf-length gray skirt. She'll turn ruby red and blotchy from the bottom of that V to the top of her forehead.

Pepper makes no effort to get out of the hammock. "I'm the appointed gate keeper. Seems Cole wants to interview us one person at a time. He's in there talking to Francie right now. Come over here, would you, and act neighborly. Haven't seen you since Lila's funeral. I do miss that woman, and, besides, I've had a hell of a morning. I seriously deserve some sympathy."

"I bet." Callahan wills the blush to recede, pushes a shock of loose hair back from one eye and shoves her toes deeper into her Birkenstocks. She fumbles in the golf cart like she's left something there.

Breathe.

Conscious steady breathing used to help dispel blushing back when it happened too often. "Hang on," she tells Pepper. "I'll be right over, but this cart's a little finicky. If I don't cut it off just right, I'll run the battery down." That much, at least is true.

Breathe. Breathe.

The prickles, mercifully, do begin to subside. She wiggles the key till she's satisfied the cart is turned off. Then, composed–well, more composed– she takes her time walking across the carpet of manicured lawn towards Pepper.

Why would I blush after all these years? Probably because he startled me.

She's more ill at ease than she appears. Or at least she's pretty sure that's the case. She's been told that she projects an aura of tranquility even when she's flummoxed.

Horn-rimmed reading glasses sit low on his nose, and a copy of *The New York Times* lies open on the ground under his hammock. A glass of something yellow–lemonade? beer?–sits on a small wicker table beside the hammock. He's giving her the old male-female once-over as she nears him, a bemused expression on his face as his eyes move from ankles to knees, knees to thighs, thighs to breasts and finally settle on her face. The prickling threatens to return.

"It's been one hell of a morning." His pleasant, easy smile doesn't match the tone of what he's saying at all. "About as bad a day, I believe, as I ever want to live through."

"I was so sorry to hear about Victoria, Pepper." She's reached the hammock. "Though I didn't know her, and I can't see what help I can be to Cole." There are those eyes again, less striking behind glasses, their color like some distillation of the sand, sky and sea. In spite of herself, she's fascinated.

He throws one foot, then the other, over the edge of the hammock and sits up, looking more rumpled child than lord of the manor. "I don't know any more than you do." His voice is aggrieved. "I told Cole you wouldn't have anything to tell him, but he insisted. Maybe he just wants to see you all grown up after so many years. You remember he used to hang out with me here? We've been friends since grade school. I told him nobody on this island has any cause to hurt Vicky. It has to be her diabetes or just some damn rotten luck while she was swimming." He reaches for the glass and takes a sip. Ice tinkles.

So it's lemonade.

"But for some reason"–Pepper scowls–"Cole says till the autopsy results come through, he's got to handle this whole mess like it could be foul play. Actually, though"–his eyes crinkle in a slight boyish grin– "I've been needing to talk to you anyway. I didn't even know you were on the island till Francie told Cole this morning. When'd you get here?" He sets the glass down and motions her to a white wrought iron chair near the hammock. "Sorry I don't have an extra glass, or I'd offer you some lemonade."

She sits in the chair, taking time to arrange her skirt around her legs, still uneasily conscious of his eyes upon her.

Is he toying with me?

She's sure she'll start to blush again if she looks directly at him. So, she pretends interest in a cardinal over her head in the tree. "I got here about lunchtime yesterday, Pepper. Drove down from Asheville and caught the eleven o'clock ferry. It's great to have it run regular hours, nice to be able to depend on it even if it is just for the few of us on the island."

"Well, it won't be just the few of us for long. People started fighting over the best lots out here the minute I put them on the market."

Pepper reaches in the pocket of his rumpled tennis shorts, pulls out a handkerchief, takes off his glasses and mops his eyes and forehead. Then he folds it in quarters and stuffs it back in his pocket, leaving the glasses on the wrought iron table with the lemonade. "I hope you'll stick around a little longer this time." His voice is warm and genuine. She relaxes a bit.

He needs a haircut. John would never let his hair get that shaggy around the edges.

"I'll be here for a least a couple of weeks." She forces a smile. "I'm not looking forward to it, but I've got to go through Mom's things."

Trickles of sweat dampen his hairline and bead his forehead. This time he uses the tail of his yellow golf shirt to wipe his face. "You have my total sympathy. I've still not gotten Daddy's estate sorted out, and it's been almost two years." His eyes without their glasses radiate a dull misery. She can't help but feel a little sorry for him.

Someone with eyes that sensitive could never hurt Victoria, could they?

She's reminded of Ted Bundy. Most of his victims had completely fallen for the handsome psychopath by the time he killed them. She purposefully thinks about Bundy, in an attempt to break the spell of those mesmerizing eyes.

I know this much. They're the eyes of a man who'd rape an island.

"I found her." Pepper's morose voice interrupts her thoughts. "Found Vicky this morning about six o'clock. Well, Nadine did first, and then me." At the mention of her name, a doleful brown hound lying in the shade of Pepper's hammock raises her head and wags an economy size tail, if not enthusiastically, at least cordially.

Callahan extends her hand, and the dog languidly lifts herself to walk towards it.

Either she's assumed Pepper's tempo, or she's imprinted hers on him.

Nadine gives Callahan's hand a cursory sniff before bestowing a slobbery lick. Once begun, Nadine seems to warm to the task, progressing from Callahan's fingertips to her wrist and then to a thorough swabbing from forearm to elbow. Callahan stifles a giggle. The long wet tongue tickles.

Pepper's watching with amusement. "Well, I am pleased to inform you that you are only the third woman Nadine Dade has ever shown an interest in. And that's in three long years of dog life, which would compute out to…what?…twenty-one years human? The first, being my sister, Honey—not I might add, Francie, whom she detests—and the second being Varina, who by nature of being in charge of the kitchen garners an unfair advantage over the rest of you." The smile he angles Callahan's way turns down at the corners. It says, I may or may not be teasing you.

She puts her cleansed right hand on Nadine's bony back and works the muscles along the vertebrae, her fingers comfortably at home in the plush loose yardage of the dog's extra skin. Nadine moans, collapses, and rolls over to proffer a sandy belly. Pepper's smile this time turns up at the corners.

"She's a wonderful dog." Taking Nadine's cue, Callahan moves now to stroke the velvety underbelly. "But I'm not here to talk about Nadine. I…"

He interrupts her. "If you're one ounce your mother's daughter, you think every dog is wonderful, so I'm going to counsel you, Nadine, not to get the big head."

"You're probably right about that." Callahan gives the soft tummy a last pat and stands up to appear more business-like. "Francie said you wanted to talk to me about something besides your girlfriend. What's up?"

Cole Hunnicut steps out of the French doors onto the patio just then, whistling to get their attention as he motions them up to the house. Pepper stands. "Vicky wasn't my girlfriend"—Pepper's gruff voice is low—"anymore. That's what's making it look so bad. I broke up with her when she came out here night before last." Frowning, he shakes his head like he's trying to clear fuzz out of it. "She was a little torn up, but it was the right thing to do, and by yesterday morning, she was fine." Pepper runs a hand through his hair. "If I hurt Vicky enough for her to do something stupid like kill herself, I'm a worse judge of character than I think I am. She just wasn't that upset, I'm…"

"My darling, oh my darling boy!" *This* time Pepper's interrupted by a tiny woman who's seated behind the wheel of a three seated, gold, stretch golf cart that's barreling up the driveway.

It's Irene Pasquini and her dog.

Callahan met her on the ferry last April.

"What a terrible thing for you and your family." The tiny woman with her silver-white bob is a dead ringer—albeit a miniature—for Carol Channing. She continues to jabber condolences as she drives across the grass and brakes to a stop near them. "That beautiful girl, so tall and elegant. I am coming back that tall in my next life." She attempts a smile, but has so clearly gotten her money's worth from a zealous plastic surgeon that it comes out only a cheery grimace. Tootsie, the white Maltese in her lap, interests Nadine. She gets up and meanders toward them.

Irene jumps from the cart and rushes across the grass towards them on high-heeled red sandals, somehow managing to keep the tiny dog in her arms—its hair the same white-blonde color as her own—out of the reach of Nadine's long inquisitive nose. She embraces Pepper, her free arm circling him somewhere about mid chest.

Then before Callahan can think how to defend herself, she finds herself quasi-embraced as well. "Callahan, I didn't know you were back on the island."

Callahan's been trying to work up a healthy resentment for this woman ever since she met her, because Irene and her husband are the first off-islanders to begin building on Timicau's pristine beachfront.

She manages a perfunctory hug back and a scratch to the topknot of the dog. "Good to see you, too, Irene." In the interest of civility, she's hoped to ignore this gregarious woman, but—as this hugging just proved– ignoring Irene's a bit is like trying to ignore the squirming Tootsie in her arms. In truth, it's been hard to even develop a healthy disdain for the woman because Irene Pasquini loves everything.

She's ecstatic about her face lift, which she feels will last her way into her seventies, about her third husband, their new house–now that the steps have been framed in–her wealth, her gluten-free diet for celiac disease, and obviously, even about Callahan.

She releases the one-armed hug. "Welcome back, Callahan. I'm getting geared up to share this island with you before much longer. I sit up there on the third floor–now that they've got the platform built–and feel like a queen surveying my kingdom."

Her kingdom!

Callahan fights an impulse to gag.

"Robby's ordered me a special new pair of binoculars for that very purpose."

That would be Robert Pasquini, her latest husband.

"The finest binoculars money can buy, so now I won't miss a thing that's going on down below me. There's so much to see, the boats, the birds, the dolphins. I hear your mother left books of her observations. I want to pour over all of them once we get moved in."

Callahan manages a smile, then surprises herself with an interesting thought.

Why should I care?

"Mrs. Pasquini," she says quietly, as Pepper motions her to follow him across the lawn into the house. "Were you by any chance up on your third floor yesterday afternoon when Victoria disappeared? I wondered, with your wonderful new binoculars, whether you saw anything."

Irene, still clutching Tootsie, has climbed back into her golf cart, is about to drive it up to the parking pad besides Callahan's cart when she turns to Callahan with eyebrows raised mischievously. Tittering naughtily as the golf car jerks forward, she says, "I wonder if Sheriff Cole will think to ask me that question."

Chapter Three

With his hand on the crook of Callahan's elbow, Pepper steers her towards the expansive patio on the west side of the house, where Cole Hunnicut stands, squinting into the sun, under two hanging ferns. His sturdy legs are planted wide in a stance reminiscent of the high school quarterback he was. His broad tanned face looks momentarily puzzled as they walk up the steps towards him.

"Cole, you remember Callahan Banks." Pepper releases Callahan's arm. "Irene Pasquini–she and her husband are the ones building that house north of Francie's on the beach–will be along directly. She went to park her golf cart."

Cole's smile is genial, his big teeth even and white. "Callie Banks, my gawd, that really is you." He looks her up and down. "For a minute there, I had to wonder. Left my specs back in Pepper's den. This one's done a little growing up on us, hasn't she, Peps?"

He's still likeable.

Tall, athletic, and good-humored, Cole was nice to the little girl Callahan when Pepper's other friends teased or ignored her.

"She has done that." Pepper pats her shoulder. "And a credible job of it, I'd say."

Egotistical bastard.

Callahan scowls, but Pepper, behind her, misses it.

Cole does not. He extends a calloused hand a bit tentatively when she reaches him, his large, sweaty fingers swallowing hers in a handshake. "Sorry to get reacquainted this way, honey." His wide shoulders shrug emphasis to his apology. "I heard you were back on the island. In fact, Missy was pretty sure she spotted you yesterday in the check-out line at The Pig, but Cole Junior threw a tantrum, so she had to drag him out."

Callahan grins. "It's good to see you, too, Cole. So that was *your* little boy at the grocery store? He wanted a Hershey Bar, and when his mama said no, he almost flipped the cart trying to get one on his own." Cole releases her hand, and she tries to be subtle about wiping her damp palm on the nubby weave of her skirt. "He's a handsome little boy. Come to think of it, he really favors you."

"That's my son, all right. A real chip off the ole block, I'm afraid." Cole looks down at what must be at least size twelve shiny black boots. "Trouble is, he's such a handful I'm not sure I'm gonna be able to talk Missy into another one. I keep telling her she needs to get her a little girl."

Mrs. Pasquini rounds the end of the patio then, her high-heeled red sandals clicking on the flagstone as she nears them. The perky dog clasped in her arms is doing its best to wiggle free and join tail-wagging Nadine, who's close upon their heels.

Dogs are so deliciously impervious to pretense. Under pink satin bows and that rhinestone collar, you have a Maltese with just one thing on her mind, getting loose to play with Nadine.

"Here I am at last," the little woman trills as she bestows another almost-smile upon the trio on the veranda.

"Good," Pepper says to Cole. "That means we're all accounted for but JP and Robbie, Irene's husband. He was here till late yesterday afternoon but had to fly back to Atlanta, so you'll have to catch him when he comes back." Pepper pulls his handkerchief out of his pocket and mops his forehead again. "JP is Francie's latest, shall we tactfully say, love interest? Since she still conducts her love life like a praying mantis, we expect he won't last long, but he *was* working on the island yesterday, so I knew you'd want to talk to him."

Impressive. Pepper must know that praying mantis females eat their mates.

Pepper inserts himself between Nadine and Mrs. Pasquini when she reaches them, places a protective arm around the little woman's bony shoulders, and guides her to the open double doors that lead into the house. "Let's get out of this heat. JP will know where to find us, and Honey's agreed to run you down to the ferry, Irene, after you talk to Cole."

Pepper blocks Nadine's entrance to the house with a leg maneuver that appears well practiced, and the four of them troop into the welcome cool of the air-conditioned west side sunroom. Callahan remembers this room fondly from childhood. It's one of the two least formal rooms in the house, its three French doors hung with creamy floor-to-ceiling sheers that filter the afternoon sun. The walls of the room are papered in pale yellow, and the two over-stuffed love seats are slip covered in a lemon chintz that's the color of early morning skies over a springtime sea.

"Let's see." Pepper sighs like the work of sorting this day is about too much for him. "Cole's through with Francie so, Irene, why don't you and your little dog–Tootsie, is that right?–go on back to my study with him next. Oh, and Cole, Irene needs to make the next ferry. She's flying back to Atlanta for a party, but she and Robbie will both be back in Charleston late tomorrow afternoon."

Cole nods and extends a hand to direct Mrs. Pasquini, dog still in arms, out the door of the sunroom into the central hall of the house. "Let's get you going then." Irene has struck up a conversation with Cole by the time they turn into the hall, her high-pitched chatter, the words undecipherable, drifting back to the two of them.

"And now, as for you, Miss Callahan." Pepper's shoulders straighten like the burden has lifted some. "You're coming with me. Honey's in the east room, and she and Vi will have my head if they don't get to eyeball you."

Callahan nods and follows the sweaty back of his yellow golf shirt across the thick carpet. He pauses at the door and motions her ahead of him into the moss green hall. The deep crown molding, elegant wainscoting and beautiful plaster detailing throughout the house always wow her. This is a house built to stand on its own, nothing like modern wood and glass beach houses purposefully designed to draw attention from themselves to ocean views.

Pepper's grandfather's exquisite attention to scale and detail has survived the whims of the house's three mistresses and now the indifference of his playboy grandson. He lets her go ahead of him into the east room. Architecturally, it's a cool green mirror image of the yellow room they just left on the other side of the hall.

Connecting to the dining room, behind which is the kitchen, this room, not the massive living room that spans the entire front of the house, is the heart of the house. Honey, all five feet seven inches of her, puts down her *Cosmo* magazine, unfolds herself from the sofa, and hurries to hug Callahan. A sunny blonde with long legs and a relaxed manner, Honey's unstudied athleticism would make her a perfect model for a Patagonia catalogue. Callahan can picture her running across a sweeping lawn to catch a football or tilting precariously from a sailboat in a high wind, her long sun-streaked hair whipping behind her. Her eyes are the gold-brown of tanned leather, not so different a color from Francie's, but with a liquid depth that made you want to trust her.

"Callahan, oh my gosh, I cut short my run on the beach when I heard you were coming. I wanted to tell you how sad I was about your mom. I was still at Salem when she died, cramming madly for exams I'm ashamed to say, and I didn't even know about it till I got home. It must have happened fast." Her cheeks still hold a hint of roundness, vestiges of a chubby little girl who wouldn't spend a night away from home without a zip-lock bag of butterscotch candies and a suitcase full of teddy bears.

John got this daughter away from her mother in time.

He'd finally kicked Ruby out of the house when Francie was eleven and Honey only a year old, gaining full custody of them both by exposing Ruby's many dalliances. It was a humiliating and unpalatable thing for John to go through. By then, Francie was too old to avoid contamination, but Honey was not. Emma had the natural goodness of her father. It was no wonder the nickname Honey had stuck.

"I could have come, would not have missed the funeral, had I known." Honey pushes a hank of heavy blonde hair back from her face. "I told Pepper just yesterday I haven't forgiven him for not calling me. We all loved Lila on this island."

"Don't worry about it, Honey. I was so upset I can barely remember who was there and who wasn't."

Pepper holds up both hands. "I am guilty, guilty as charged." He points at one of the four chairs slip covered in an airy green paisley that surround a light oak coffee table in the center of the room. "Have a seat, Callahan." There's a large gray beanbag dog bed on the floor nearby, so Nadine must pass time in this room, too.

All three of them drop into the downy comfort of the chairs, and Pepper stretches like he has a kink in his back before easing his feet up on a matching ottoman. The coffee table is cluttered with newspapers and magazines, *Field and Stream, The New Yorker, The Wall Street Journal, Time, USA Today, Vogue* and even last February's swimsuit edition of *Sports Illustrated.*

"I really debated whether or not to call Honey when Lila died," Pepper tells Callahan. "I finally decided to wait till the last minute to tell her, because I knew she'd be upset and was in the middle of studying for exams. Then the day I intended to call, the pile driver broke down on the Applegate's house, and all hell broke loose because their contractor was ready to get started."

The Applegate's house? Another one?

A pained expression crosses his face. "I feel rotten about it. I'm no contractor, as you know, and managing all this development is nothing but a headache for a man who enjoys daily naps and long periods of uninterrupted quiet."

"Oh, my darling child." Varina bursts through the door from the dining room, balancing a tray with a pitcher and three tall frosted glasses. She sets it down on the coffee table and pulls Callahan up into the embrace of two thick, brown arms. The large-boned woman must be taking dead aim on seventy, but she's still so strong that she's hugging the breath out of Callahan.

Dear, dear Vi.

"Varina, how are you?"

"Pretty good"–Vi releases Callahan and plants a noisy kiss on her cheek–"for somebody who keeps having birthdays."

"And Wallace?" Callahan has equal affection for the Twelve Oaks' handyman, with his powerful square body and gap-toothed smile.

Smiling resignation, Vi registers her perennial complaint. "Well, he'll do as husbands go, but I still can't get that man to take me dancing. If I'd a'known I'd be staying at home every night for fifty years, I'd never have married his sorry ass." Her eyes sparkle with humor when she adds, "he's pretty good to have around the house ever now and then." Her face clouds then, her lower lip jutting forward in mock anger. "You haven't been to see me since Mr. John died. Whatta you mean by that?"

"I was planning to come this trip, Vi. Like I told Pepper, I'll be here several weeks this time, sorting out Mom's house, and I only got here yesterday."

Even Varina's smells bring comfort, the moist, earthy sweetness of her and always a hint of something home-baked. She radiates the big-hearted kindness of one who's managed to love her way through three generations of Dades. "Well." Vi heaves a massive sigh, her large bosoms trembling in its aftermath. "I gots my hands on you now."

There's something so wide open about the way Vi loves her that it almost makes Callahan uncomfortable.

"You go on now and pour you some lemonade." Vi motions to the tray. "Because Mr. Cole is going to wear you out with questions. You know, he even wanted to talk to me, old Varina? 'Vi,' he says to me, you knows what goes on here, but you is always keeping it under your hat. Today, you just maybe oughta take off'n that hat and give me a peek beneath of it.'"

"So?" Pepper reaches for the pitcher and starts to pour a glass of lemonade, "Did you, Vi?" He hands the first glass to Callahan, pours another for Honey, and gives it to her. "Did you take off your hat and let him have a peek?" He pours the last glass for himself. "What do you have under there that's worth keeping secret?"

Varina doesn't speak for a moment. Then, she folds both arms across her chest. Callahan remembers buying Vi a red lacquered bracelet for Christmas one year, but Vi's hands were so large she couldn't get the bracelet over them and on to her wrist.

"Well, even though he's our Cole, he's the Law now, too." There's a hint of anger in her voice.

Or is it resentment?

"So I done what he told me to."

Pepper is nodding encouragingly. "And...?"

She frowns, the upturned lines etched around her mouth resisting a down-pull of displeasure. "And I tells him true how sweet that dead woman was on you, how she was hoping for an engagement ring just like all them others before her. They come and they go, but they never gets to stay." Vi's voice rises with emphasis the longer she talks. "I tells Mr. Cole, I says, 'Too bad Mr. Pepper can't find him a Missy. Ain't a woman born good enough for him to marry. He'll, by jiminy, do what it take to hustle them down when they catches his eye, but then he'll run just as fast to the other way when he decides it's time to get shed of them.'" Her brown eyes flash an anger that surprises Callahan and, from the looks of Pepper's face, him too.

He puts down his glass without taking a drink and shakes his head like he doesn't understand what Vi means. "Varina." His voice is husky. "Varina, surely you don't think I'd have done anything to harm Victoria."

Vi's bosoms heave in two more deep breaths before she speaks. Her nostrils flare. "What I am saying, Mr. Pepper, is that what this house needs is a man who knows how to love a woman decent and a woman who knows how to love the same. Ain't been a'one of you, since your own mama, Mignon, broke your Daddy's heart and died, that's got the loving right." Vi looks directly at Emma. "And you is my last hope, Honey Bear." She turns back to Pepper, her voice softening a little, her eyes locking into his. "We all gotta' turn up our toes one day, but if you asks me, you plumb broke that poor woman's heart. She ain't the first woman to get a heartbreak at Twelve Oaks, and she probably ain't a-gonna be the last."

"And that is, in fact, exactly what she said." Cole startles them all when he speaks from the hall door where he's been standing unnoticed. "Mrs. Pasquini and Tootsie"–Cole shakes his head in obvious amusement–"send their regrets. She had to hurry to make the ferry and didn't have time to say goodbye." His tone becomes businesslike. "Callahan?" He motions her to follow him into the hall. "Guess you're up."

Glad to be out of the crossfire between Pepper and Vi, Callahan hurries to follow Cole down the hall. His khaki uniform shirt stretches taunt over the muscles of his back, and he's wearing the thick black gun belt of a law enforcement officer over his lightweight khaki pants, but no gun. "What ever became of that orphan coon you and Lila adopted?" He speaks to her over his shoulder.

"Charlie. His name was Charlie. We kept him about ten months and then set him free, but he showed up off and on for several more years and never developed any fear of us. He'd always take treats straight from our hands. His favorite was fish-popsicles."

"Cute little booger, but, man, that was one mischievous animal." Cole pauses in front of the library door, turns, and smiles. "Do you know, Callahan, I still have a nightmare every now and then about that time you dived in front of Francie's bike to save that turtle." He's shaking his head as he walks through the library door. His hair is buzzed to his scalp. "You could have broken your neck."

Callahan remembers her fury at Francie that day. "It was a diamondback terrapin, Cole, not a turtle. Diamondbacks are endangered, and she was laying her eggs in the dirt along the trail. Francie aimed for the nest on purpose, just to upset me." She follows his sturdy, erect frame from the hall into the library, then across to the dark oak door of the office on the far side of the room, loving the musty familiar smell of so many books gathered together. "I'd do it again in a heartbeat."

"Well, she about endangered you in the process." Cole opens the door into the office that was John's and steps back for her to walk in ahead of him. When she does, her eyes unexpectedly mist. The masculine browns and greens of duck prints, books and leather swim before her. John's scents still linger here, too evocative for her senses to ignore, pipe tobacco, old books, spent ashes in the grate of the little square fireplace under its carved walnut mantel. Callahan swallows twice, then again, struggling for control.

First, I blush, then, I cry. I'm an emotional wreck today.

"Callahan, are you all right?" Cole's professional voice has gone soft.

"I will be in a minute." She wipes tears under each eye with an index finger. "I'm mostly embarrassed. Have you ever had something like that take you over when you didn't see it coming? John Dade was like a father to me."

He nods and waits.

"See, I passed a lot of wonderful hours in this room when he was alive, and it all just hit me when I walked in here." She takes a recovery breath. "I...I'm okay now. Frankly, I don't see how I can help you in your investigation, but at least it's been great to see you after all these years." She brushes the palms of both hands up her cheeks to remove the last vestiges of tears and sits down in the captain's chair he's indicated by John's—*now Pepper's?*—beautiful antique desk. A large lamp on the corner of the desk casts a puddle of yellow light on a single spiral notebook lying there. "Okay, Cole, go ahead, shoot."

Brother, I could have come up with a better way to begin a possible murder interrogation.

Cole doesn't seem to take notice. He sits down across from her at the desk, his professional demeanor returned as he picks up and opens the spiral notebook. He puts on a pair of wire-rimmed glasses that look hilariously out of place on his big features, moistens his pencil tip between his lips, and speaks. "Let's begin with the obvious. I wonder if you were on the beach at all yesterday."

"Well, that's easy. Yes. I took a walk after I got settled in at the house, maybe around noon, and then another late last night, around midnight. I found a turtle nest hatching up on the north end."

Cole scribbles something in his notebook and then looks up. "The north end's less help to me than the south end unless we had a crazy riptide or current that could carry the body that far up the coast. I was hoping you might have been farther south on the beach, below Twelve Oaks or near Francie's house on one of your walks."

"Let's see." Callahan's still fighting a flood of memories. John taught her how to build a fire in that little fireplace across the room. "The first time, on my day walk, I did walk the full two miles of the beach, but not the second time. Last night I put in across from our house, about half way up the beach, turned north and stayed north looking for loggerhead nests."

Cole chews the corner of his lip, his eyes narrowed in concentration. "Well, one pass is better than none. Did you notice anything, anything at all, either when you walked on the beach past Francie's or Twelve Oaks? Were there footprints leading down to the water from that picnic table up there under the trees? It had to have been pretty close to low tide then, wasn't it?"

Callahan's positive she didn't see any footprints. "No. I didn't see any. You're right. It was a really low tide, you know, with the full moon last night, so the water was way down. I'm sure I'd have noticed footprints if anybody had walked into the water there."

Cole nods and asks if she saw either Pepper or Victoria or, for that matter, anyone else on the beach.

"I've been trying to remember that myself. I saw them together last spring, or I'm assuming Victoria was the tall blonde with him. Yesterday, there were two people sitting up there at the picnic table. I heard them talking, but I was barefoot in the surf clear down at the edge of the water, so I was too far away to know who it was or understand what they were saying. I'm fairly sure that at least one of them was that same woman because I saw her stand up once. She was wearing an electric blue bikini."

"You didn't hear anything they were saying?"

"No, and I hesitate to even mention this because I'm not positive about it, but I thought at the time that the woman might be crying. I was too near the water to hear much."

Cole writes in the notebook again and then asks. "How about this? Did you see anyone in the area around the Pasquini house, the house about a half-mile up the beach from Twelve Oaks, next door to Francie's? It's about half built."

"No."

"Well then, how about anyone at Francie's house or around her gazebo just south of the Pasquini house?"

"Sorry, I'm not more help, Cole, but no, again."

"You're doing fine, Callahan. Think hard on this one. Did you hear anything, ANYTHING, unusual from the time you arrived on the island until you left the beach last night? Yells? Loud exchanges? Specifically, did you hear Pepper's voice?"

"I didn't, Cole, nothing unusual except for maybe that woman crying up by the picnic table."

Cole stands up, walks around the perimeter of the small room and sits heavily back down in his chair.

He's too big for this little office. Bet he's feeling claustrophobic.

"Try this, Callahan. Do you know anything that might be unusual or helpful about Victoria? For example, did you know that Mr. Pasquini and Victoria worked out at the same health clubs on the mainland when the Pasquinis were in South Carolina? Have you ever noticed Victoria engaged in a conversation with anyone on the ferry, Mr. Pasquini, JP, or any of the other carpenters that ride back and forth to the island?"

"To the best of my knowledge, I've never talked with Mr. Pasquini, though I think I know who he is. I have met Mrs. Pasquini, but not JP, Victoria, or any other workmen. I've only just come back to the island and haven't been here since April."

Cole sighs, drums the end of the pencil on the desk's ink blotter. "Well, even if you don't know any of the construction workers, have you ever seen a stranger in a place where he shouldn't be? Off the work site? On the beach? Elsewhere? Have you seen Victoria, or the girl you assume to be Victoria, with any other men besides Pepper?"

Callahan hesitates.

Pepper's already told Cole that Francie and JP are an item, though he may not know they're meeting all over the place for sexual liaisons.

She decides to go ahead and tell him about that, anyway. She doesn't know from Cole's reaction whether it's important or not, but he does pause again to write in his notebook. It's his next question that really throws her.

"This question's a little more ticklish, but would you have any reason to suspect that the relationship between Pepper and Francie is anything but platonic, a typical brother-sister relationship? In other

words, have you ever seen anything that suggests to you there might
be something sexual between them? They're only half siblings, you
know."

Callahan is sure she looks startled, hopes she doesn't look horrified.
"No, definitely not."

But why would he ask that?

"Final question. Do you think either Pepper or Francie is capable
of incest?"

*Francie used that exact word this morning, didn't she, when she joked about
a possible inquest? Is that telling?*

Callahan squirms at this second mention of the issue, tells Cole he
knows Pepper lots better than she does. And as for Francie, anything is
possible with Francie when it comes to sex.

Cole nods, makes some more notes in his notebook and closes it, so
she takes it they are through and stands to leave.

"Oh," he says, "one other thing. Pepper tells me you still roam the
island like a native and would know better than anyone if anything suspicious is going on in the swampy, uninhabited interior of the island.
Do you ever make your way up to that deserted shack on the north side
of the island, where Ruby once had her studio?"

Surely Cole knows the truth about the "studio."

Lila told Callahan about it years ago. Under the guise of being an
artist, Ruby had talked John into building her the one room shed, saying she wanted to paint in seclusion. Then, she used the building for
her many assignations, safe from the prying eyes of Vi and Wallace,
John, the children, and the house servants. To Callahan's knowledge
no one has used the house for anything in almost twenty years except
to store fishing gear. John had refused to maintain it after the divorce,
purposefully letting the elements take their toll on the shabby monu-
ment to his even shabbier second wife.

"Well," Callahan tells Cole, "the last time I was at the shed was in
April, shortly before Mom died. She was too weak to monitor a bald

eagles' nest in that tall oak near it, so she sent me to see if the nest was still active. And it was. There was a rowboat pulled up on the mud bank of that tidal lake in front of the studio. At first, I figured it was Pepper's. I've heard he's a good fisherman, but there was no one there."

"They say, Callahan, you could track a vole through a swamp if you took a notion to. You notice things other people don't. So besides that boat, did you notice anything else unusual?"

"This probably doesn't mean anything either, but there was a smoky smell about the place that day, like the old fireplace might have been recently fired up. Since John had died and Pepper moved back into Twelve Oaks, I just figured he was using Ruby's place for a warming shed after fishing in Lake Timicau or that tidal creek there between it and the ocean. One thing about my theory didn't hold up, though." Callahan pauses, moistens her dry lips with her tongue. "The footprints around the boat were those of a smaller lighter person than Pepper. Probably someone five foot ten or a little shorter, wearing cobbled boots."

Cole stands up then, reaches to shake her hand and thanks her. "You've been more help than you know. I may want to talk to you again. I do need to remind you that this is a potential criminal investigation, so please don't share our conversation with anyone, Pepper, Francie, even Varina."

Callahan promises. As she leaves, Cole sits down behind the desk and begins to scribble in his notebook.

Why does he consider this a possible criminal investigation, and why did he ask me that incest question twice?

Deep in thought, she walks so quietly across the library's thick beige carpet that when she steps out into to the hall, she startles Francie, who's standing just outside the door.

Francie's changed outfits and added more perfume since she saw her this morning.

Something oppressive like "Breathe No More."

She's wearing gold high-heeled mules, tight gold capris, a pale purple scoop-necked sweater she's managed to slide off one shoulder, and enough gold bracelets and necklaces that she tinkles when she moves. Which she does, as her hand goes to her hair. It's now teased into a new large-haired style.

Not a pageboy exactly, not a French twist. Maybe you'd call it flying buttresses.

"Well, hi there," Callahan greets her. "Are you waiting for me or just passing your time doing a little recreational eavesdropping?"

Francie seems edgy, her voice sharp. "Is Cole still in there?"

Callahan nods yes, and Francie elbows past her into the library, her gilded tail section twitching as she makes her way towards the office, which she enters without knocking. "Cole, I can't find JP anywhere." She doesn't close the door, so Callahan overhears without trying to. "I know I promised you that he'd back up everything I told you, but"–she throws both hands in the air, bracelets knocking together noisily–"no JP. Maybe we had a misunderstanding. I gotta go anyway, or I'll miss the ferry. I have what you might call an important engagement in town tonight. He'll turn up tomorrow, and I'll send him over to talk to you. Okay?"

Callahan, unable to hear Cole's response, is pleasantly distracted by a whiff of butterscotch. She turns to see Honey walk up behind her. "I didn't hear you coming, but I smelled you. You must still love butterscotch."

"I do." Honey's smile is sheepish as she sticks out her tongue to show Callahan a half-melted yellow candy. They both laugh. "I guess some things never change, Callahan. Listen, I'd hoped to catch you before you left to ask you a huge favor. Pepper and I are taking his boat out tomorrow night into Charleston harbor to watch the Fourth of July fireworks. He's a lot more beat up by all this than he's showing. I wondered, I mean, it would do us both a world of good if you'd come along and keep us company."

Chapter Four

SATURDAY, JULY 4TH

"*You're* Callahan Banks, or I'll eat my sombrero." The thirty-something, redhead with small, even teeth smiles enthusiastically as Callahan steps from the noon day sun on the Timicau ferry dock into the damp cool of the *Aggie Gray's* boat cabin. The woman's green eyes twinkle as she points over her shoulder at a wide-brimmed orange straw hat hanging from a cord round her neck.

Callahan nods understanding.

The sombrero.

"Good thing I *am* Callahan Banks. That's a lotta straw to eat in one sitting."

New leather-cushioned benches encircle the ferry's oval cabin, and four more form a square central island in the middle. Rick, the Boat Captain, and his mate are engrossed in making entries into a logbook balanced on the dash near the wheel. As her eyes adjust to the dim light, Callahan looks for any other passengers who might be riding the private ferry to the mainland, in hopes of avoiding an extended conversation with this one, but the other seats are all empty. The boat smells different today, something mildly fishy.

The chatty woman–she can't be over five foot two–is looking at Callahan expectantly. In the crook of one freckled arm, she's balancing a yellow plastic bucket full of brackish water and the strings from a net bag stuffed with big whelk shells. There's a canvas bag overflowing with brightly colored clothing on the other. She extends her left leg to pull two more canvas bags of soggy towels out of the aisle. A snorkeling device falls out. She grabs it and shoves it back into the overflowing bag. "Irene Pasquini has told me all about you." The bucket with the brackish water is clearly the source of the fishy smell though Callahan can't see what's in it.

The woman motions Callahan to sit across from her on a bench on the center island and begins rearranging floor paraphernalia to make more legroom. "'Annie,' Irene says to me, 'you won't want to take your eyes off this woman, features as classic as a cameo, flawless skin.'–those were her exact words, flawless–'and the thickest chestnut-brown hair you've ever seen.'"

Callahan sees no alternative but to sit where she's being directed. Dressed in white shorts, rubber sandals, and a pink tee shirt for a late morning milk run to the mainland, she squirms under the frankly appraising stare of her cabin mate.

There's nowhere to hide on a ferry.

She planned to use this time on the trip to the mainland to call Honey on her cell and get out of going for a boat ride in the harbor tonight with Honey and Pepper.

"And Irene is right." The woman's probing eyes are fixed on Callahan, like an ornithologist's on a rare bird.

Callahan feels her face prickle and prays this is not going to be another blushing day. "Well, hey, thanks for the compliment, but I'm not sure there's a thing on Timicau Island that Mrs. Pasquini doesn't find beautiful. Tell me who you are and what brought you to the island."

The chubby hand that reaches to squeeze hers is at least ten degrees hotter than her own. "Oh, my goodness." The woman's drawl is very

Southern. She releases Callahan's hand and throws one hand in the air apologetically. "I *was* being rude. Forgive me for not introducing myself. It's just that I've been dying to meet you." She leans towards Callahan. "In fact, I decided this morning that the survival of my progeny on this island may depend upon you. I'm Annabelle Applegate, but everyone calls me Annie. I'm Wharton's wife. We, Whart and I, bought the lot next to the Pasquinis, and I came over to the island early today to meet with Pepper Dade." Her voice lowers conspiratorially as if she doesn't want the boat crew to overhear her. "I'm sure you know how picky Pepper is. Whart sent me out on a recon mission to get as much skinny as I could before our architect submits the final details on our house plans for Pepper's approval."

Her orange-red hair, dark at the roots from perspiration, is an unmanageable halo around pink cheeks. Her ears are apparently attached to her head at close to a ninety-degree angle because their outer edges stick out through the hair ever so slightly, giving the impression of slipper shells hidden within the halo.

Callahan's distracted. Slipper shells live their lives stacked together like poker chips. The bottom one is always the female, the rest are male. If something happens to the female, the male next in line changes into a female. It's all Callahan can do to keep from picturing a frenzy of hermaphroditic sexual activity under the flaming mane across from her.

Clearly unaware she's also being scrutinized, Annie pulls a bright purple cotton-jersey sweater out of the large canvas bag and mops beads of perspiration off her face.

Callahan suppresses a smile.

At least our new island residents are proving to be colorful.

Returning the sweater to the bag, Annie begins anew. "Pepper Dade, my goodness, the man is a saint. He's promised to teach our triplets how to fish, but, according to him, you are the expert on birds and snakes and gators and such. And if Harry doesn't learn the difference between a water moccasin and a corn snake fast, I may soon be just the mother of twins." Annie's smile at this prospect seems almost cheery. She points to the fishy bucket. "He had a baby water moccasin in here this morning. Are you really a biology professor?"

Callahan nods yes.

"Well." Annie shakes her head in a way that makes both ears poke through a little more. "You don't look old enough to me. I was telling Whart the other day..."She talks on as the mate passes them, winks hello to Callahan, closes the doors, and motions to Captain Rick that the boat is ready to leave the dock. Rick blows the outside whistle to warn off latecomers, and a whiff of diesel fuel fills the cabin. As the boat backs away, the dock slips out of sight behind the last window of the ferry.

Another talker like Irene. At this rate, we'll have a monkey colony on the island, nothing but nonstop chatter.

Callahan knows she should be listening, but finds herself absorbed in just observing the woman. Annie's wearing elastic waist camouflage pants, the kind whose legs are ready to zip off above the knee into shorts at a moment's notice. Her collarless white cotton blouse, simple but expensively tailored, is sleeveless and so spare that it crimps her chubby upper arms at the shoulder. The thin material of the tail of the blouse is tucked into her pants, accentuating a jolly round belly and a spare tire below. Weary of dieting, body-obsessed college girls, Callahan appreciates the unselfconscious practicality of Annie as well as her clothing.

As the ferry pulls from the Timicau Island Inlet into the Intracostal Waterway, a small brown-haired, freckle-faced boy–Callahan estimates his age at about nine–careens into the cabin through an open door that leads from an outside staircase to the deck above. His hair sticks up from his forehead in at least two cowlicks, and the way his ears protrude from his head leaves no doubt as to his maternal ancestry. The child shrieks, hit from behind by a flying body and, then, another. Before Callahan can sort which gangly arm, freckled nose, or skinned knee belongs to which, the boys are on their feet again, war whooping as they chase each other with jury-rigged shell tomahawks in a circle around the central core of seats where she sits.

Captain Rick turns once, twice, and then a third time, to frown irritably, reminding Callahan of a sign she recently saw in a coffee shop in Asheville. "Please supervise your children or we'll give each two cups of espresso and a puppy." She has a feeling that no threatening sign or disapproving boat captain will take the wind out of these children's sails.

Once this gang moves to the island, nothing will be the same.

Two of the boys circling her look remarkably alike.

Identical twins, same zygote.

Squarely built and redheaded, they wear khaki shorts, obviously soggy sneakers whose heels light up with each step, and turquoise tee shirts with the message, "Timicau Island. A private island to call your own." written in large black letters across the back.

So now, Pepper's hawking clothes to sell the island?

The backs of their necks above the turquoise tees are badly sunburned. The third boy, the freckle-faced, brown-haired one, is identically dressed but is not sunburned. At the moment, he is doing his best to outrun his brothers.

Obviously the biological outlier.

He has the round chocolate eyes of a waif and is a full head shorter, probably five pounds lighter than his brothers. Barely able to stay out of their clutches, so far defying all laws of gravity, he again rounds the central island of benches where Callahan sits, but this time loses his balance and crashes into her knees. He slides across the aisle against the water bucket whose slimy contents slosh out on the floor on him as well as on his mother's and Callahan's feet.

"Sorry."

" Harry!" Annie grabs for him, but he's already up and running. She dives into the canvas bag, comes up with a sand-gritty green Turkish towel, drops to her knees and begins mopping Callahan's sandals, the floor, and, finally, her own soggy pants and tennis shoes. "I am so sorry," she repeats as she sops, wrings out the towel in the bucket, and sops again.

The boys race out of the cabin then, the brown-haired triplet dragging his two brothers with him as they cling to the elastic back of his shorts. The air seems to clear a bit.

Less rubber and moldy canvas.

Seconds later, they thunder up the stairs to the upper deck. The pounding of their feet is right overhead now, and an occasional thud or crash makes the boat shudder.

"Don't think a thing about it," Callahan tells Annabelle. "Rubber sandals are made to get wet." She stands and walks to the end of the aisle to recapture two fiddler crabs that washed out of the bucket and skittered away. They're both males, their front claws overdeveloped for grabbing mates. They click the pincers on these claws angrily, unable to reach Callahan because she picks each up from behind. She carries them to what's left of the water in the bucket and drops them in.

Annie's apologetic voice is barely audible over the din above. "Well, that's not the best introduction, but there you have them. Those are our triplets. Conceived in a petri dish and dedicated to the proposition that no pregnancy should ever go unpunished." She points to the spare tire that bulges below her belly, then stands up and settles herself on the bench again. "I call it the Applegate sub-continent." She gives a hearty laugh. "You know that old saying about worrying over a man with no shoes until you meet one with no feet? Well, I had a fit over this first belly of mine before I had the triplets. Then, I found out what real bodily change can look like."

"Tom, Dick and Harry," Annie says. "Tom and Dick are identical, and Harry, the one that just spilled his bucket, is our little scientist. We gave them names everyone could remember." Her voice is round and warm. "But Whart says we missed our cues. They should have been Curly, Moe and Larry. They are that funny. Harry's also the one you've got to help me save. Anything that creeps, swims, or crawls, he'll get his hands on it. These are his conch shells"–Annabelle inaccurately identifies the bag of whelk shells in the mesh bag–"and this whole bucket of goo is on its way home to his aquarium." She sighs, her eyes lifting towards the sound of a particularly loud boom overhead. "Be quiet up there, boys! Settle down!" Her admonitions go skyward with no noticeable effect. She tries again, a bit louder. "These people will think we are a bunch of savages."

A mind reader comes to Timicau Island.

She returns her attention to Callahan. "Oh, well, what can you do? Boys will be boys." She rearranges herself in a way that says, "Let's ignore them, shall we, and talk girl talk?"

"Wasn't that just the worst thing, Victoria Weatherly? She was such a beautiful girl. Have you heard anything more about what happened to her? It surprised me just a little that Pepper didn't seem more upset. Someone said they'd broken up before she died, but still… don't you think his reaction was a bit off?"

Callahan stretches a cramp out of one wet foot and notices Annie's appraising stare of her long leg. "Actually, I don't live on the island anymore, so I don't know Pepper well enough to have an opinion about how he reacted or should have."

"I probably shouldn't be telling you this." Annie's voice lowers conspiratorially, "but the autopsy results are a bit troubling."

Callahan frowns, confused. "I thought it would be several days before they released any results. They just found her yesterday."

"It *may* be several days before they release a full report, you know, getting lab reports back and everything," Annie says, "but my Whart's a pathologist, and his partner did the post on her last night. What they found was puzzling because they found nothing at all, no problems with her blood sugar, no circulatory compromise, nothing. About all they know is that she didn't drown." She casts a guarded look in the direction of the mate, who's standing on the open stoop outside the door, staring uneasily up the stairs towards the sounds of the boys on the top deck, and lowers her voice to a near whisper. "Victoria's lungs had no water in them. None! And that means that whatever happened, she was already dead on the beach before she washed out to sea. Did you know her?"

"I didn't." Callahan's increasingly uncomfortable receiving these confidences. "I'd seen her a time or so on the beach, but I didn't know her. Did you?"

"Oh, honey." Annie rolls her eyes. "Of course, I did, but I'm the kind who would find out even if I didn't know. We live in Charleston, you see, so you can count on the help of your friends to fill the gaps in your knowledge." She flashes that easy, small-toothed smile again.

"What I've heard," Annie says, leaning closer to Callahan, "and what I've seen, make me think Victoria was no one-man woman, if you know what I mean." She mops her face with the sweater arm again and leans across the aisle towards Callahan, her large warm bosoms brushing Callahan's knees, a hint of the moldy canvas smell hanging in the air as she whispers. "You know JP? Well, I think, I mean, I'm pretty sure, those two were carrying on."

The infidelities of the Dades and their various significant others is *really* more than Callahan wants to discuss. "It might make sense to share that information with Cole." The water outside the window behind Annie is a sparkling blue. An American flag, whipping in the wind on the boat's stern, reminds Callahan that it's the Fourth of July, and she still hasn't called Honey to get out of tonight's boat ride. She wishes she could extricate herself from this conversation as well, and, miraculously, her wish is granted.

Rick's cell phone rings, and a piercing shriek issues forth from the upper deck. Annie races for and reaches the door to the stairs with surprising alacrity and disappears behind it. When she returns with a red-haired Tom or Dick, she unearths the green towel again and holds it against the wailing boy's bleeding mouth, rocking him as she does. "Another tooth," she shrugs her shoulders philosophically. "We'd hoped to keep these permanent ones a few years longer."

Captain Rick waits till the boy stops sobbing to speak. "That was Francie on the phone. Have either of you seen JP Mellincamp? She says he's not at the job site today, and nobody can find him anywhere."

Chapter Five

Three great white egrets, prehistoric in their awkward grace, fly silently past the upper deck of Lila's porch in the dusky twilight, their silhouettes outlined pink by the setting sun. They land clumsily on the top branches of a huge live oak near the porch's screen and jockey for positions with the fifteen or twenty other egrets already there. Their squawks, that garrulous and guttural quark, quark, always strike Callahan as incongruous in a creature so outwardly elegant.

She turns her green porch rocker slowly for a better view, her back now to the stair entry at the other end of the deck. The friendly old rocker creaks as she settles into it.

"Reason number one." She says it out loud to the egrets and holds up a finger for emphasis. "I didn't *want* to go out in a boat with Pepper and Honey tonight because I get sea sick too easily." Saying it out loud does nothing to ease her guilt about asking Vi to deliver a last-minute regret message.

Well, maybe it was rude, but I just didn't want to go.

The birds, preoccupied in their nightly grooming, seem oblivious to Callahan and her justifications. They extend long fringed wings and crane necks into unimaginable curves, their black beaks preening the length of each tail feather, one at a time. When she was a little girl and they were taller than she, the egrets were bird people to her. Bird people who performed their hygiene rituals nightly at the same time Lila was plunking her into the bathtub. The slightly altered nursery rhyme Lila chanted as she scrubbed Callahan's hair comes back to her now. "Rub-a-dub-dub, three men in three tanks, and none of them dirty as Callahan Banks."

Callahan smiles, the silly memory evoking another more serious bathtub time discussion. Lila was scolding her for wandering off alone into the woods after she'd been told not to go to the beach. "Maybe when you're five..." Her mother's voice was atypically stern. "But you're too young to walk to the beach by yourself yet, Callahan. It's not safe."

"But, Mama." Callahan remembers a caged feeling of abject despair. "When you're four, you're four for a very, very long time." Lila had smiled then and given her a hug.

Man, I miss my mother.

Callahan reaches for her wine glass on one of the orange mini-step ladders Lila painted, christened "end table," and placed between the five rockers on the porch. Hints of grass in the New Zealand Sauvignon Blanc cool Callahan's tongue and throat.

I do love a good wine.

Though her mother lived frugally, she never scrimped on wine, so Callahan has the developed palate of a connoisseur without the income to support it.

"Reason Number Two." She speaks out loud again. "I didn't want a gourmet picnic dinner." Her mouth waters at the thought of a baked potato stuffed with broccoli, tomatoes, and plain yogurt, her favorite at-home meal. "And..." She interrupts her soliloquy to watch thin ripples of water behind Albert's tail as the huge gator silently crosses the pond. "I'm just more comfortable with critters than with people, so why not stay home?" She sighs contentedly, noticing in spite of the camouflage of its coloration the silent, almost illusory movement of a small deer approaching the pond.

Are Pepper and Francie capable of incest?

Cole's last question pops into her consciousness as it has several times since yesterday, its implications so repugnant that she tries to dismiss them. "Well, that's another reason," she complains to the egrets. "I'd sure rather be here than dealing with the Dades and all their complexities." She takes a very deep breath, exhales, and sets the wine glass down, feeling both relaxed and relieved.

"Well, I wouldn't say we're all *that* complex." A deep, male voice from behind completely startles her. The egrets in the tree erupt like popped corn, squawking raucously.

Callahan's on her feet, fists clenched, heart pounding, before she recognizes Pepper Dade standing in the shadows at the top of her stairs.

"How long have you been there?"

"Long enough."

He looks so much like John as he ambles out of the dimness towards her that it's disorienting.

Even his clothes.

He's wearing white duck pants, bleached gray-brown Docksiders without socks, and a blue knit golf shirt that's so faded it looks twenty years old.

It may be John's shirt, but it isn't John. Remember that.

"Well, you startled me."

She smells something light and lemony, more soap than aftershave, as he comes closer. There's an uneasy quiver in her chest. She can't sort whether she's afraid or just really, really embarrassed.

"You know"–his right hand is buried deep in his pants pocket up to a brown leather wristwatch band–"we may have had us a murder on this island, Miss Banks. You ought to exercise a little more caution up here all by yourself. You're mighty easy to sneak up on."

When he nears her on the porch, that right hand comes suddenly out of his pocket towards her face, and she jerks away, fearful, before seeing it's empty. He extends his index finger to the tip of her nose and raises his eyes towards the ceiling in a parody of deep concentration. Confusion and trepidation freeze her beneath his touch. He holds it there for several seconds so she smells his clean lemon scent intensely now.

"Umm," he says at last, withdrawing the square-nailed fingertip from her nose. "Dr. Dade here with a reliable diagnosis. Cold nose, healthy dog. In Nadine-language, you're not one bit sick." His hand drops to his side, and his mouth droops. "So you just didn't want to come with me tonight, sugar, is that it?" He shakes his head forlornly, then seems to notice her fear. "You don't need to be afraid of me, Callahan." He leans closer. "I was just pointing out to you that somebody who wanted to do you harm wouldn't have to go very far out of his way to get it done." His voice is old shoe easy.

Studied or natural?

His face and arms are badly sunburned. When she speaks, she knows her voice betrays apprehension. "I didn't exactly say I was sick, and, by the way, my name's not Sugar. I just said I didn't *feel* like coming." She had been deliberately deceptive, she knows, carefully choosing her words so that she didn't actually lie to Vi. She looks away from him, feeling as muddled as the river currents at the confluence of the Ashley and the Cooper. "Why didn't you tell me you were standing there? You scared the hell out of my birds, too." A few of the egrets are still circling the pond.

"I *am* sorry."

He has a deeper, richer voice than his dad's.

"You don't sound sorry to me."

"Frankly, I'd just paused for a minute to admire the scenery when I got to the top of the steps. You've grown into a fine-looking woman, Callahan. All those white egrets there in the tree and you in that clingy white shirt giving them some kind of lecture. And the sunset reflecting pink off of all that whiteness. It was something to behold." His eyes crinkle at their corners. "I didn't mean to scare you, honey."

"My name's not Honey, either. That's your sister's name." She points at the wine bottle sitting next to her glass. "Well, you're here, so would you like a glass of wine?" She doesn't sound as shaky as she feels. "Or there may be some beer left in the fridge. Corona, I think."

He picks up the wine bottle, peers at its label, then smiles. "Well, matter of fact, yes, I would love a glass of *this* wine. It's one of Lila's New Zealand Sauvignon Blancs, isn't it? She about had me weaned from martinis with this stuff by the time she died." Those pale eyes of his that hold the color of the sea are flat and mournful when they raise to hers. His voice goes husky. "I miss your mother."

She'd have taken him for a beer man.

How does he know Mother's tastes in wine?

Callahan ignores the moment of softness in him. "Well, we're even." She makes a point of not meeting his gaze, turns and walks to the kitchen for another wine glass. "Because I miss your father, too, desperately."

She's intensely aware that he's watching as she passes him. She showered and washed her hair before coming back upstairs. In cadence with the egrets, she supposes, and their evening grooming rituals. Dressing for comfort not company, she'd pulled on a favorite pair of faded red shorts and a thin, scoop-necked cotton tee shirt. She is both barefoot and braless.

I bet he's not missing that little fact.

Earlier, she lit a lamp inside on the end table by the couch. She feels his eyes on her back, the skin across her shoulder tingles, as she walks through the open French doors past that splash of light into the kitchen.

He isn't on the porch when she comes back with the wine glass and a bowl of unshelled peanuts. She's thrown a gray sweater she keeps on a kitchen peg over her shoulders for modesty's sake since her bra is one flight down in the bedroom. Her hand shakes as she pours his glass half full of wine.

"Thanks."

She jumps again because this time he's directly behind her. He's walked out of the living room with the familiarity of one who knows the place. She hands him the wine glass.

"I helped myself to your facilities. Always thought it was clever the way Lila nestled that half bath there behind the bookcase." He moves a rocker across from hers so that his back is towards the pond and slides a stepladder table between them before he sits down. So she sits, too. Without asking, he reaches for the wine bottle, fills her glass and his own.

"You know," he takes a long slow sip which he obviously savors, "*you* are a lucky woman. On another night, I might have taken this much harder, your standing me up and now acting about as welcoming as a Soviet border guard. Generally speaking, I'm not a man who takes rejection well, but tonight I've decided to forgive you. First of all, this wine helps a lot, and, as fate would have it, I've already spent way more time in my boat than I wanted to." He points at his face. "I burned the shit outta' myself out there all day, trying to help Francie find JP." He takes another drink of wine, sits the glass on top of the ladder, rubs the top of his ear, then flinches in pain like he's forgotten it's sunburned. "They found his sunfish floating in Lake Timicau, so Francie decided. that if his sailboat's there, her precious boyfriend is, too, and drowned."

The egrets are gradually flying back into the oak trees, their territorial protestations muffled as night descends. Far out on the skyline over Charleston, the first Fourth of July fireworks light the sky. Her heartbeat is more regular now. She feels safe enough to sip her own wine. "Well, did you find JP?"

This is wonderful wine.

It softens the very sinews of her body, makes her almost glad Pepper stopped by. There's a tension between them she finds exciting in spite of herself.

Sexual tension?

"Nope." He shakes his head in the negative.

What a paradox it would be to be attracted to a man you basically detested.

She tugs the bottoms of her shorts a little lower on her legs.

His lips twitch into a slight smile, his eyes lingering for just a minute on her ankle before lazily traveling the distance of her to where shorts meet leg. "No JP. We're not going to find him on that water no matter how hard we look. The man's like a buzzard off a guts wagon. He's had enough of Francie, so he's flown away to—metaphorically speaking—feed off some new woman. I've gotten to know his type supervising construction this past year. They have zero allegiance to the job. I'm guessing that the only thing JP Mellincamp would readily pledge allegiance to is his own pink pecker." This time, Pepper rubs his ear so hard it makes him wince.

Sort of an endearing mannerism. He rubs his ear when he's uneasy or frustrated.

She tugs her sweater forward to cover more of the front of her blouse.

"My sister sails dangerously close to the wind, Callahan, and she has miserable taste in men. Her first husband was a fertilizer salesman, one of those bill-backward hat wearers. Counting the teats on a milk cow was enough to make the man horny so he was ill designed for the faithful husband role. She went the other way with her second one. He was a trip without a suitcase, an up-tight accountant. I'm guessing he was the virgin bride on their wedding night, so you can imagine how long that one lasted. After him, and before JP, there was a long string of nameless, faceless, creeps, each enjoying the pleasure of her boudoir for a month or two. JP's no different, just another kind of trouble, but for some reason, Francie's crazy about him."

Callahan remembers Annie Applegate mentioning something on the ferry about Victoria and JP.

Maybe Pepper's right about JP.

Another thought strikes her.

If JP had anything to do with Victoria's death, then he'd really have a reason to disappear.

Some swallows out over the pond begin doing touch-and-goes into the water. A spray of colored lights brightens the far horizon, then disappears to be followed by a muffled pop, pop, pop. The theory with the swallows is that somehow they collect enough water in this way to make the adobe mud for their nests, but Callahan's never quite believed it. "Didn't you hire JP to work here?"

Pepper leans back in the chair, both hands behind his head, and stretches. The old rocker cracks under his weight. She wishes she'd thought to point him to a newer chair, but it's probably too late now.

"Well, yes, but working's one thing. Balling your sister's an entirely different one. How was I to know she'd take up with him?"

Callahan smiles ruefully, shaking her head. "Francie's a handful, alright."

"'You don't know the half of it. You know what, Callahan, you ought'a smile more. You've got a smile like sun through storm clouds, but you don't do it enough for my taste."

She takes two more sips of her wine and tucks a piece of hair behind her ear.

He doesn't miss a thing I do. It's like being under a microscope.

"Mind if I change the subject a minute?" Pepper leans forward, takes some peanuts and begins shelling them. "I want to give you a little unsolicited advice."

She feels an internal sap of stubbornness rise. Lila worried about this quality of obstinacy in her daughter, considered it about her only flaw. When people tell Callahan what to do, she feels inclined to do just the opposite. "You can give me all the advice you want, but I'll probably ignore it."

Pepper's mouth is full of peanuts. For a minute, she thinks he's going to choke on them, his eyes widening in surprise. "Well," he says when he gets through chewing and swallowing, "let me put it this way then. If I were you, I wouldn't go tramping all over the island by myself for a while. Especially stay away from the north end till we find out what's happened to JP." His sun-bleached brows pull together in a frown.

What business is it of his where I go?

It's the very same battle she's fought with her mother since she was four years old. Callahan's perfectly confident that she can take care of herself. "The north end? And why's that, Pepper?"

"Because first there's been Victoria, and now, this JP-missing thing. If I'm wrong, and JP hasn't just run out on Francie, I'm thinking we could be back to dealing with Juby T. Roy again. You do remember Juby T., don't you?"

She chews her lower lip, folds and tightens both arms around herself. She remembers him alright. "He's Ruby's older brother. Mama said their daddy named them Ruby and Juby, which always cracked me up."

"You got it." Pepper nods. "Except he was my dear stepmother's older half–not whole–brother. They both had trashy mothers, just different ones, and their mutual father had the penchant for a rhyme."

The memory of Juby's sallow face, rodent-like eyes and thin black moustache makes Callahan involuntarily shiver. He had an evil smile and a way of looking over his shoulder at you like he was hiding something. "Every time John got him arrested and fined for illegally clamming and oystering on Lake Timicau, he paid his fine, and then, came right back, didn't he?"

Lake Timicau is an inland lake on the north end of the island, whose fishing waters are legally accessible to non-islanders through a small deep creek of ocean water that flows in and out with the tides. But, its oysters and clams are off limits for harvesting because to dig them, one has to step onto the mud flats and the private property of the island.

"Yup. He's always insisted that he has a right to be here. Says his family's been digging clams there for four generations and no Johnny-come-latelies like three generations of Dades have the right to deny him that privilege. His good friends call him Bulova. Did you know that?"

"Bulova? No, why?"

Pepper helps himself to some more peanuts. His wine's almost gone. She debates whether to offer him more.

"The story goes that he stole a Bulova watch off of a corpse he found in an alley, wore it for years, and bragged about it. Anyway, Callahan, I have an idea that Juby T., Bulova, whatever you want to call him, could be more violently staking his claim this time. You know he's been threatening to get even with us for years." Pepper drains his glass and helps himself to more wine. "He doesn't take kindly to interference when he's liquored up. Ruby always joked he substituted whisky for syrup on his pancakes, her way of saying he had a snootful most days. He's a dangerous character."

Callahan remembers the hobnail footprints she saw by the water when she went up to Ruby's shack to check the eagles' nest in April.

They could have been Juby's.

Pepper scratches his ear and winces again. "Juby and Ruby," Pepper's saying, "are the only two people I can come up with that hate us enough to want to harm us, and they're both crazy enough to do it. My stepmother's had no use for me since I encouraged Daddy to divorce her and fight to keep the girls. Their whole marriage was just one massive misalliance. Daddy should have been married to Lila." He takes another sip of wine, closing his eyes as if to better savor it. When he reopens them, his voice goes deep and serious. "I really don't want you going up there to the north end, Callahan. Do you understand how dangerous it could be?"

Callahan feels her jaw set. "I understand everything that needs to be understood." Her voice holds as much steel as his does. She looks past him, over his shoulder towards the mainland at a brilliant flash of white from a skyrocket.

He shakes his head, obviously not reassured, and shifts in his chair towards the pond. For a few minutes, they both sit in the quiet of the darkening porch. The swallows have come back. "They're gonna sodomize themselves on those cat tails if they fly any lower."

She smiles at his joke, glad to leave the unpleasant subjects of Juby T. Roy and where Pepper thinks she should and should not go on the island.

Pepper surprises her then by standing up. "Well, I probably ought to head home. Really, why I stopped by here is to warn you about Juby." He reaches out to scoop her hand into his. "I'm feeling a little protective of the women on this island. After all, it was my fault Victoria was out here." His hand is big in proportion to the size of his body and surprisingly leathery.

She nods—"Thanks, then"—and reclaims her hand.

He shrugs, turns, and walks towards the top of the stairs, stops. "Oh, forgot to tell you. I fixed your wobbly toilet seat. Tightened down the lug nuts like I told your mama I would. Hope you don't mind." She can't see his smile there in the shadows, but she doesn't miss the irony in his departing comment. "Happy Independence Day, Miss Banks." And he's gone.

She does mind. She knew the toilet seat was loose and had planned to tighten it herself. "Happy Independence Day yourself." Come hell or high water, first thing tomorrow morning, she will be taking herself up to the north end of the island.

To hell with you, Pepper Dade.

Chapter Six

SUNDAY, JULY 5

When she awakes Sunday morning, Callahan's cell phone message light is blinking, its ringer still off. It's another blissful part of living in Lila's house. With no landline, a person can go days without having to field a call.

Unenthusiastically, she punches in her code, scrolls through the numbers and listens to the last three calls. The first is Patsy Hunt, a real estate agent and fun new friend from Asheville, with glowing reports of a Chopin concert at the Brevard Music Center last night.

The second call is Evan Brame–*Evan again*–his third call this week. She's only dated him four or five times over the last couple of months, so his voice seems ridiculously possessive. "Can't imagine why you haven't called me back. How long are you going to stay down there?" Long-fingered Evan, a tenured physics professor at UNCA, whose students appropriately rename him Dr. Brain each new semester for good cause. She pictures his intense, deep-set nut-brown eyes, his overdeveloped brow ridge, his ponderous mannerisms and yawns.

She wishes the men in her life attracted her more. She's found a few interesting enough to sleep with, but the magic soon fades, love's soaring arias sadly lacking.

Is it them or me?

She's never sure which. Like her mother, Callahan's decided that men are essentially good accessories but can be burdensome if they hang around too long. She doesn't recognize the third phone number with a Charleston area code.

"Good morning!" She *does* recognize the voice.

Pepper!

"Thought I might give you a chance to repair your tarnished reputation."

It's barely nine a.m., and he's already called her. "How about dinner tonight?"

Shit!

"I still want to take you for a ride in my boat. Let's head over to the Morgan Creek Grill. I can tie the boat up on their pier."

Where did he get my cell number?

"Hope you don't mind my calling your cell. Your mama gave it to me once. I'll pick you up about seven in my golf cart, unless I hear otherwise."

Why would Lila give him my number?

Dealing with him first thing this morning feels daunting. She's focused on heading to the north end of the island for a look around. She'll worry about Pepper Dade later. By the time her coffee's brewed and poured into an insulated carrying cup, Callahan's thrown on last night's red shorts, a beige tee shirt, and her best swamp-walking, two-strap rubber sandals.

The little golf cart seems friskier in cool morning air under a cloudless sky. Exhilarated, she turns left, away from civilization, and heads for the narrow sandy trail that leads to Ruby's shed on the east bank of Lake Timicau. Huge live oaks darken the path ahead, their twisted branches and dense foliage blocking the sun. An osprey shrieks protests as she nears its nesting platform twenty feet high in a slight clearing, then, angrily goes airborne when Callahan slows the cart for a look.

Pepper placed three such platforms around the island in February, and the heads of two baby ospreys are visible now above the messy sticks of the massive nest. Remembering Pepper, his unannounced arrival last night, his presumptuous, overbearing behavior, and the final straw of the tightened toilet seat, momentarily darkens her mood.

I'll give myself a couple of hours to calm down and call to regret when I get home.

The rest of the trail, a quarter mile further down the beach, grows only narrower and darker. "The Hundred Acre Wood" Lila christened it when Callahan was little, the moniker straight from *Winnie the Pooh*. This is the least accessible part of the island, totally undisturbed by humans, the place where snakes and coons, rabbits and deer, bobcats, ospreys, and Great Horned Owls live undisturbed.

And it's here, too, that the sinuous panther, a subspecies called Eastern cougar declared extinct a hundred years ago, continues to live its remote and shadowy existence. Callahan can count the number of times on two hands that she or Lila actually saw the long, thick, black-tufted tail, the lush tawny coat, the graceful whiskers, or the mesmerizing yellow-green eyes. The animals, always one graceful bound from deep cover, have survived in this isolated pocket of habitat solely because of their wariness. Like domestic cats, wild cougars still liked catnip, though. Twice, she and Lila left a large pile of it on a raised pine stump and were rewarded with a bounty of cat tracks in the sand around the stump the next day. Both times, the catnip was gone.

All cats, even house cats, are stealthy hunters, placing their feet so carefully that they avoid even the crackle of sticks or leaves, so Callahan has never heard the panther in the bush nearby even on those rare occasions when she's comes upon one. It's the cougar's tracks, sometimes four inches across, that betray where it's been, a large pad half-circled with four toes, no punctuation from retractable claws, the front tracks noticeably bigger than the rear. And their scat. She's seen it often here on the north end of the island, larger and more curved than the small nugget-like scat of a bobcat. Occasionally, a male's territorial marking mound can be found, sand pulled into a pile and sprayed with the distinctive essence of urine.

And there are the victims. Cougars kill about one deer, their favorite prey, a week. Both the deer and the cougars swim between barrier islands. A few days after a kill, the presence of circling turkey vultures on Timicau or on Caper's Island to the north often leads Callahan to the spot where a carcass was dragged into cover. Deep claw marks on the deer's back and a surgical bite at the base of its skull leave no doubt as to its predator. Today, hoping to spot another cougar as she nears the north end, she feels that heightened sense of anticipation she always feels.

Hurricane Hugo cleared the northernmost tip of Timicau of all its trees over ten years ago. Still, it's a bit of a shock to emerge from the moist, yeasty woods onto the pluff-mud shores of the lake with its stark little shed and fishy, half-stagnant smell of oyster beds. Callahan's pulse quickens, her eyes taking in the detail of what lies before her. In a general sense, nothing looks different or disturbed. The rusted tin roof over the covered front porch of Ruby's little gray building lists on the far side, where a support beam has begun to give way to rot. Slimy gray mud at the edge of the lake is cluttered with dead and live oyster shells, an occasional spurt of water issuing forth from a live one. A beat-up rowboat is tied to the weathered twenty-foot pier that sticks out into the water.

Probably an old fishing boat of Pepper's.

In fact, except for the oysters and the frenzied, scurrying of fiddler crabs on mud flats, there's no other sign of life or movement.

She pulls the cart to a stop on a grassy mound several yards from the back of the shack, climbs out, and heads across the mud towards the shack, up the two steps, under the sagging roof of the porch, to the front door. Heavy dust on the floor in front of the door and on the two wooden porch rockers has been disturbed.

Juby?

A seagull screams behind her. A wave crashes behind the dunes to her right as she turns away from the door. The spit of land between Lake Timicau on her left and the beach to her right is probably no more than five hundred feet wide.

Unexpectedly, the hair at the back of her neck tingles. Something—or someone—is watching her. A panther in the woods? A dolphin fishing the lake waters at the end of the dock? The prickling intensifies and spreads to the hair on her arms. She tries to swallow but finds it difficult. She spins away from the lake back to the two hollow-eyed windows on either side of the front door. Something moves behind the left one just as she turns. Or does she just imagine it? She steps closer to the window, tries to peer into the house, but the glass, pitted from sand and coated white with salt from sea spray, makes it impossible.

Callahan feels rooted in place as she examines the door. Two double bolt latches on the outside of the door, important for securing it in high winds, are always kept locked, but today neither is engaged. She reaches for the rusty door handle, gritty in her hand, and turns it. It moves reluctantly, sand in its works providing scratchy resistance, but the door doesn't open. She puts a shoulder to the wood, twisting the knob as she throws her weight forward against the door. It doesn't budge, almost as if it's locked from the inside. She tries the maneuver again and, then, again, her sense of urgency rising as she becomes more convinced that there's someone inside the shed. The door groans. A screw falls out of a top hinge, but still it won't open.

Callahan stops short, her left shoulder going numb.

What am I doing? If someone's hiding in there, do I really want to get in?

She thinks of JP, of Juby T. Roy, even of Ruby. Not one of them would she want to face alone on this isolated spit of land.

Her breath becomes shallow, the pounding of her pulse rising in her ears. She's suddenly very ready to leave, almost panicky in her urge to flee. But she forces herself to pause. For reasons she can't explain, she takes the time to refasten both of the exterior bolts. Only after sliding the protesting cold metal of each across its metal slot on the weathered gray frame, does she give herself permission to run.

And run she does, her rubber sandals slapping the mud as she fights for balance, slipping and tripping erratically back to the golf cart, a sense of self-preservation now propelling her away from the place. When she reaches the cart, she throws herself onto the seat, gasping in relief, and floors the accelerator pedal. She is aware–not for the first time– that it's impossible to make a golf cart go fast.

I might be better off if I just ran.

But her sandals aren't running shoes, and she'd have to come back sometime to get the cart, so she stays in the cart.

It isn't until Callahan finds herself deep in The Hundred Acre Woods and nearing the osprey's platform that her breathing grows normal and the frantic pounding in her chest recedes. She reaches for her coffee cup and takes a drink. Thanks to the insulation, the coffee's still warm. She drains the cup, keeping the accelerator pedal pushed to the floor. The rickety cart rattling along is reassuringly cheery now. But she can't relax, can't shake the feeling that she was in real danger on Ruby's porch.

Maybe Pepper's right. There is something frightening happening on Timicau Island.

Chapter Seven

Her fear subsiding and curious about the Pasquini and Applegate houses, Callahan makes a snap decision to pass the turnoff to her own house. She drives her golf cart south along Pelican Flight Road—or so Pepper has recently christened this path down the east side of the Island—and turns left into the woods on a construction road.

No one ought to be around building sites at ten o'clock on a Sunday morning. I'll just have a quick look around.

Wrong!

Irene Pasquini and Francie, lounging in vinyl beach chairs atop the unroofed second floor of the Pasquini house, spot Callahan the minute she pulls into the clearing. Francie squeals and waves. "Well, if it isn't Miss Banks, herself, come to pay us a call. What a coincidence. We were just gabbing about you."

About me?

Since they've already seen her, Callahan realizes she's probably trapped.

But what on earth are they doing up there?

The Francie Callahan knows would consider it a colossal waste of her time to ever "gab" with anyone as old as Irene Pasquini. Both women stand as Callahan pulls to a stop below them, and Francie hurries to the edge of the bare platform where she teeters precariously some fifty feet in the air. She's wearing a fuchsia strapless top that bunches together in the front around a gold ring suspended from string ties around her neck.

"Climb on up. We're higher than the mosquitoes." Francie's voice is animated.

Could she be drunk at ten o'clock in the morning?

"We were just admiring Mrs. P's magnificent views. Not only do you have a complete ocean vista up here, you're so high you can see every inch of my little plantation." She circles her shoulders excitedly, bosoms bobbing like balloons under the thin jersey fabric.

She's her usual tawdry self.

Callahan takes in the tight white jean shorts and dangly earrings.

Does she lie awake nights designing these get-ups?

With dread, Callahan gets out of the golf cart, promising herself that she'll only stay for a few minutes and quickly invent an excuse to leave.

"Be careful, dear." Mrs. Pasquini, holding Tootsie, has joined Francie as Callahan climbs the roughed-in pine steps connecting the ground level to the first and, then, second floor. The older woman's wisely standing a full foot back from the edge with a steadying hand on Francie's shoulder. "The stairs were just framed Thursday." Delight glosses her voice. "So there's no railing yet, but I'm *so* glad you came. Robbie toted four chairs up just in case we had callers." Irene's smile is beatific. "Tootsie's the most delighted because I couldn't for the life of me figure a way to carry her up the ladder when I had to go up and talk to JP."

The little dog's tail wags agreement so extravagantly that her hindquarters bob independent of the rest of her body.

Her head swimming from the heat, height, and climb, Callahan pauses at the top of the stairs to give the silky-haired dog a friendly behind-the-ear scratch. "Hi, Toots. I like your topknot ponytail." The corners of the dog's mouth actually seem to pull back in a smile.

The view is three-sixty and magnificent. "Wow! You *can* see the whole world." Callahan circles slowly, fascinated with the bird's eye perspective of the island. She notices a cleared area up the beach to their left with pilings sunk at intervals throughout the space.

The beginnings of the Applegate house.

She's surprised at how exposed Francie's compound down the beach to their right is. The shiny white-pillared mini-mansion is surrounded by what appear to be newly planted formal English gardens, and a path towards the beach beyond leads to a green-roofed gazebo nestled into the trees where the maritime forest meets the sand. Farther south, beyond Francie's compound, Callahan can see the beach in front of Pepper's house though the huge oaks block any view of the house except for its slate gray roof. Two container boats from the Charleston harbor sit on the horizon so far out in the ocean that they don't appear to be moving. The beach slope is gradual, long and inviting, a squadron of pelicans in V formation patrolling the skies above.

"We designed the house to maximize this view." Mrs. Pasquini, in a pink cotton blouse that exposes her pale thin upper arms, pats Callahan's shoulder excitedly. "We're putting our living room on the top floor to take maximum advantage." She insists that Callahan walk the perimeters of the platform to see the views in all directions.

Francie, still seemingly oblivious to any danger, leads them, mincing ahead in raffia wedge sandals that are laced around her ankles, up her legs, and tied mid-calf.

The theme today must be bondage.

She points towards a red tin roof. "There's your house, Callahan." Callahan's already spotted the roof standing out from the dark green canopy of the forest like a cheery kite lodged in the trees. The few egrets still roosting in her trees are wisps of tissue paper at this distance, and the pond, a shining mirror. Even Albert looks benign, a toy alligator placed by a child's hand on the mud bank of a pretend pond.

Callahan's relieved to see that the Pasquinis will not be able to peek in at her covered porch or even see the sheltered path to her house. Unlike Francie, her privacy's not compromised by this behemoth of a house. She lets out a breath she didn't realize she was holding.

"Look at our view of Lake Timicau." Irene lightly touches her arm, and Callahan pivots a half turn, then freezes.

"Something wrong, Callahan?" Francie moves uncomfortably close to her on the northern rim of the platform, following her gaze to the dock in front of Ruby's studio.

Is she crowding me on purpose?

"No." Callahan's searches the shoreline of both lake and beach, questioning her sense of perspective, looking again for what should be there but is not. The rowboat that was tied to the dock less than twenty minutes ago is nowhere to be seen. "No, Francie. Nothing's wrong."

Was the boat's owner inside Ruby's studio? If so, how did he get out? What other explanation can there be? I didn't see anyone clamming at Lake Timicau or pass anyone going the opposite way on Pelican Flight. Somebody could have been fishing behind the dunes on the ocean side. That's probably it.

Callahan forces herself to turn away from the view and smiles weakly at Mrs. Pasquini. "Wonderful views!"

"Sit down, dear, and get out of the sun." The little woman steers her to a shaded beach chair under an overhanging oak. "You look a bit pale."

Stepping over a pile of net fabric she recognizes as Francie's mosquito gear, Callahan gratefully lowers herself into the chair.

"All I have to offer you is coffee." Mrs. Pasquini points to a mechanically complex thermos made of chrome and black enamel. "It's probably getting a little too hot for it now, but Francis wanted to see my views early to beat this heat. It did taste good an hour ago, didn't it, Francis?"

Francie nods yes as she settles herself into a second nearby chair, tugging down her tight shorts when they ride up her thighs. Her eyes stray in the direction of the dock, and her forehead creases in a puzzled frown.

She knows something upset me, and she doesn't know what it is.

With her legs crossed dramatically above her knees and one sultry shoulder thrown back, Francie manages to look cheaply seductive even when there's not a man in sight to seduce. She runs both hands through her hair. "I was just about to fill Mrs. P in on the latest Applegate-triplet-brat news. I caught the two bigger ones down at the main dock shelter yesterday, shooting their water pistols at that huge wasp's nest in the ceiling, which, incidentally, I've asked Pepper to get rid of about six times. Anyway, when I asked them what the hell they thought they were doing, one of the little monsters said they were doing an experiment to see if the wasps would treat it as an attack or just think it was raining." She shakes her head in obvious disgust. " I still can't believe Pepper sold them a lot, let alone so close to you, Irene."

Instead of responding to Francie, Mrs. Pasquini turns to Callahan. "Are you sure you won't have some coffee, dear?"

Callahan decides to follow her lead and ignore Francie, too. "No coffee, thanks. But I am curious if there's any news about JP, and why you were just talking about me?"

Francie's hand goes to her blonde hair in a practiced brush-hair-out-of-one-eye maneuver that's of habit, not necessity. "It is worrisome, Callahan. We know nothing more about JP." She raises the palms of each hand to her eyes and rubs in a circular way that doesn't smear her dark mascara. Her purple lacquered nails are accented with tiny rhinestones. "I've had a sick headache all morning from worrying about the man. I'm subject to them, you know, just like Mama. Whatever would possess him to leave me this way I cannot imagine."

Mrs. Pasquini, with her dog still draped over one arm, manages to pull another beach chair across the platform into the shade before Callahan can get up and help her. She sits down beside Francie, pats her shoulder, and speaks in a small, kind voice. "Now, now.

Don't get yourself in a swivet yet. He'll probably turn up for work tomorrow. Workmen do this kind of thing, you know, go off on a toot for a holiday weekend and, then, pretend nothing extraordinary has happened."

Francie seems unaware of Mrs. Pasquini's ministrations. "Even though I always told him I'd leave him for Garth Brooks, I didn't *mean* it." She pulls a cigarette pack out of a purple string purse, extracts a long, thin cigarette and lights it with a jeweled lighter, sucking the smoke hungrily. She closes her eyes in obvious relief. "Well, I can't be entirely sure about Garth. I mean, I've always questioned this preoccupation people have with fidelity in relationships. Monotony I call it, not monogamy. So…if Garth Brooks *was* to happen into my life, I couldn't say for *absolute* sure I'd be true to JP." She smiles weakly. "But it *would* take somebody as sexy as Garth to tempt me. JP was the best I've ever had, and that man was hung like a whale."

Should I tell her that whales have remarkably small penises? Probably not.

"Let's change the subject." Irene's voice, betraying embarrassment, becomes a tactful, solicitous coo. The dog has flattened itself on her lap now, its head completely hidden in the crease between bent knees and thighs so it looks like nothing but a skein of expensive knitting yarn. "We were *not* gossiping about you, Callahan. I'd just asked Francis for a little island history lesson, since we're all going to be neighbors." She hands Francie a used Styrofoam coffee cup for her cigarette ashes.

Francie knocks a long ash into the cup and turns to Callahan. "And so I was telling her about your English ancestry and Lila and the process she used to acquire *our* property on Timicau Island and all." The smile on Francie's face reflects none of the edge in her voice.

"And"–Callahan works to keep her own voice smooth and detached– "exactly what little details did you see fit to share with her, Francis?"

Tootsie raises her head from the crease of Mrs. Pasquini's slacks, as if she's picking up dangerous undercurrents. The little animal and Irene seem to be in complete emotional sync. Irene begins to nervously stroke Tootsie's back. Curiously, with each stroke, the little dog's tongue thrusts forward out of her mouth.

"Well." Francie seems oblivious to the pet and her owner's unease. "I just told her about Mignon being only twenty eight when she died, trying to have a baby sister for Pepper, and how many miscarriages she'd had before that, and, then, how hard it was on my daddy, only thirty years old himself and left with little Pepper, an eight-year-old son, to raise all alone. How vulnerable he was." Francie takes another draw on the cigarette.

Irene and Tootsie are now looking back and forth from Callahan to Francie like spectators at a tennis match.

Francie blows the smoke out, her mouth puckered in a purple O. "And I'd just gotten to the part about how my poor, lonesome daddy took Pepper out to some dude ranch in Wyoming that summer to recover, and they met your mama there. She was still a teenager, wasn't she, Callahan? The daughter of a real life buckaroo bronco rider, if I've got my story right. No mama of her own, only this cowboy to raise her up, and she's the one that led Daddy and Pepper on horseback trips to camp in the mountains. Am I still correct?" She wrinkles her nose like she finds telling the story mildly distasteful. "Starry skies around the campfire and such have their magic for some though I personally prefer a more sanitized environment." A stiff smile.

"She was eighteen," Callahan addresses Mrs. Pasquini. "My mother was an only child and motherless by then. Her father, my grandfather, was actually quite a well-known bronc rider in his day though by then he was the foreman on the Eaton Dude Ranch."

Francie interrupts her. "I've never quite gotten it straight, how it was your mama decided to come here to South Carolina that fall and never did make any effort at all to leave and go back where she belonged. And what about your high-falutin' English father and his responsibility for parenting you? What ever became of him?"

Francie's Southern drawl grows thicker as she becomes more vicious.

"Isn't he supposed to have been some titled big shot?" Francie turns away from Callahan then, her shoulders shrugging innocently as she tells Irene, "All I know is that by the time my mama, Ruby Roy, married my daddy and was able right away to give him the daughter he'd been longing for, a sweet little sister for Pepper"—she smiles coyly—"me, three years had passed, and Lila and Callahan had managed to appropriate a nice little hunk of real estate right in the middle of our island. And Lila, who only just died this spring"—her voice lowers in thick Southern incredulity—"*never* left."

Callahan tastes bitter fury. Pointedly, she lifts her wrist to look at her watch. She's already broken her resolution to be gone within ten minutes. "You know…" She pushes up out of the chair to stand. "I'd love to fill you in on all the details sometime, but right now, I've gotta run." She suspects her face is flushed red from anger and the heavy humidity of the day. Her tee shirt is stuck to her back.

Mrs. Pasquini looks genuinely disappointed as Callahan leans down to pat Tootsie goodbye. "Your house is just wonderful. I'd love a tour when it gets a little farther along."

The dog actually smiled again.

"Do, do come back anytime." Mrs. Pasquini stands and follows Callahan to the top of the stairs. "Are you sure you have to rush off so soon?"

"I am sure." Callahan descends the stairs, noting when she reaches the lower level that the boat is still gone from Ruby's pier.

Francie's raised shrill voice is still audible. "And I'd love to know why my father took Callahan's pregnant mother into our home and let Callahan be born there like one of his own, which I know she is not. Pepper has assured me that *I* was John's first daughter."

The bitch!

Callahan turns and walks back up to the top of the stairs, trembling as she struggles for composure, trickles of perspiration running between her breasts. "Francie," she says through clenched teeth.

Francie smiles uneasily.

"I," Callahan says, "am no more of an expert on the relationship between your father and my mother than you are. But since you're so intent upon giving Irene your take on all the glorious little details, let me try and be of some assistance." She makes eye contact with the wide-eyed little woman, who's now clutching her Maltese protectively to her breast.

"Francie's father," Callahan says, her voice steely, "befriended my mother when an English gentleman, Reginald Banks, who'd fathered me while a guest at the dude ranch, felt disinclined to accept his responsibility." She pauses to throw a slit-eyed smile in Francie's direction, then turns back to Mrs. Pasquini. "My own grandfather, the famous bronc rider we were just discussing, felt it as such a disgrace that he threw my mother out. It was John Dade who engaged an attorney of some international reputation and extracted a legitimate name for me and a sum of money from my wealthy, absent, polo-playing sire." She pauses for breath, then soldiers on. "Hence, I am Callahan Banks, in accordance with my father's demands. My mother was Lila Boone. The details of her relationship with Francie's father were the object of discussion among Charleston's socialites as long as I lived here and probably still are." Callahan pulls a tissue from her back pocket and mops perspiration off her face. "I do know this, Francie. My mother was too wounded by the experience to ever allow herself to fully trust a man again. She supported John's decision to marry your mother and did nothing to contribute to their break-up, contrary to what you like to imply." She takes another breath and turns apologetically to Mrs. Pasquini. "And that is all I have to say on the subject today or probably ever again."

Chapter Eight

This time Pepper will not surprise her. Callahan spots his empty red golf cart parked in front of her house the moment she pulls out of the woods.

He hasn't even given me time to return his call, and from the looks of it, he's gone in and made himself at home again. Maybe I do need a lock!

When she spots the yellow butterscotch candy wrapper in the ashtray on the first floor landing, though, Callahan grins. "Honey? Are you here?" She sprints up the second flight of stairs to where Honey's waiting at the top.

"Callahan! Oh my gosh, am I glad to see you." Honey extracts a piece of candy from her mouth with thumb and finger. "I hope, I hope, I hope. Have you, by any chance, seen little Harry Applegate? We're all praying he maybe bumped into you, and you took him around the island."

Who is Harry Applegate?

Then, Callahan remembers the brown-haired waif who captured the baby water moccasin, the one doomed to a short life without her cram course on island flora and fauna. "Hi, Honey, and huh uh, I haven't seen him. I just left Francie and Mrs. Pasquini. What's up?"

"Pepper said to find you as fast as I could." The tangled ringlets of Honey's sun-streaked blonde hair have clearly not been brushed, and without her make-up, she looks eyebrow-less. "I don't know the details.

I've only been here about ten minutes. Dr. Applegate came over to talk to Pepper early this morning, something about the right of way on their property. I was still in bed. The other two triplets went to Sunday school with their mom, but Harry talked his dad into letting him come along."

Callahan pats her arm. "Calm down. How bout a cup of coffee or maybe ice tea?"

"Oh, no, let me finish." Honey's lower lip quivers. "This is really serious. Dr. Applegate let Harry take their golf cart for a drive, made him promise to just drive up and down Pelican Flight Road. But you know how men are when they're talking business. They lost track of how long he'd been gone. Nobody's seen him or his golf cart in almost two hours." Honey's features draw in as she fights tears. "Oh, Callahan, I'd feel so awful if something like what happened to Vicky, and maybe JP, happened to that darling little boy."

"He should be easy to track on a golf cart." Callahan has a motherly impulse to hug Honey but settles for squeezing her hand. "Fill me in on anything else you know, and we'll go find him."

"I've already *told* you everything. Pepper and Dr. Applegate took our big cart out to the north end because it's faster, but there was no Harry at Ruby's place. Pepper called on his cell a minute ago to say he was headed back and to see if I'd found you yet. He did say a window in Ruby's shack was broken out."

Something contracts in Callahan's chest.

Somebody was *in there, and it couldn't have been Harry because he'd have let me in.*

Still gripping her candy, Honey continues. "Wallace was rebuilding a lawnmower motor up in the maintenance shed, and Pepper sent Vi to get him to check the south end and the dock. They thought maybe Harry was playing in one of the boats and lost track of time." Honey inserts the candy back into her mouth, rolls it to one cheek, and talks around it. "Wallace struck out though. So now, Pepper's called Cole. He's that worried, Callahan, worried enough to call the Sheriff."

Callahan throws a can of mosquito repellent, her cell phone, and a tube of sunscreen into her backpack, then adds two bottles of water and drapes the pack over one shoulder.

We may be out a while.

She crams a baseball cap on her head and motions Honey to follow her down the stairs. "Let's go find him." Callahan's completely confident she'll be able to track where Harry's gone. Her stomach flips uneasily. She's less confident that she'll find him safe and sound.

There's a beating of wings over the pond as they climb into her cart. As long as Callahan's watched those wood ducks from the deck, they still don't trust her down here at ground level.

I guess all creatures on the island are a little wary right now.

She backs her cart around the Dades' cart and heads down the drive with a mounting sense of urgency. This is clearly not a good day for a little boy to be alone somewhere on the island. "I can't believe they let him go out alone with all that's been going on."

Honey's head bobs agreement. "Men are so clueless sometimes."

Callahan pauses the golf cart at the end of her drive, where its tracks crisscross those of others' on the hard-sand surface of Pelican Flight. She gets out, squatting for a closer look. It's easy to identify the big knobby tire tracks of Pepper's heavier cart, first coming, then going back down the road. The weight of the two men in it makes its tracks deep and distinctive. Fortunately, the turn-off to Callahan's house is up the road from Twelve Oaks, Francie's, and the Pasquini's. So the only other new tracks besides Pepper's that she has to deal with are her own and–sure enough–a very smooth, slightly indented double track that would be left by a cart with a very light passenger.

Harry.

A bumpy incline on the road to the left shows the marks of the lighter cart spinning out.

The little guy didn't maintain enough speed to make it on his first try.

That spin out tells her something she was most hoping it wouldn't. *He was headed towards Lake Timicau and Ruby's shack.*

Callahan swallows, but the hard lump of fear in her throat will not be swallowed away.

"Callahan, can you tell anything from looking at all that dirt?" Honey's mouth puckers nervously around her candy. She seems anxious enough for the both of them.

Callahan stands and returns to the drivers seat, pointing the cart north to follow Harry's tracks. "He went north, and so far he hasn't come back. It's way easier to follow big golf cart tracks than small animal and bird tracks."

"But"–Honey frowns–"Pepper's already just been up there to look."

"Maybe Harry turned off. Let's see what his tire tracks have to tell us." Callahan has little trouble following them along the road. They often swerve erratically, crossing and recrossing her earlier tracks which tells her that Harry came up this road after she'd already come back down it. Probably, while she was at the Pasquinis. Occasionally, the light tracks are completely obliterated by deep ruts from Pepper's cart, but if she's patient, Callahan can soon spot the meandering smoother ones farther ahead on the road. Pepper may not have found little Harry up here, but, so far, she's sure it's the way he came.

Brilliant yellow-green swamp grass edging the southern edge of Lake Timicau comes into view in a clearing to their left. Callahan slows to examine the grass along the road. Harry could have been attracted by something on the lake and seduced from the road. A great blue heron, motionless as a yard sculpture, stands twenty feet away, poised to strike a fish.

Nope. The heron wouldn't be here if Harry's anywhere around.

She speeds on, reassured by the swerving tracks that form more noticeable large irregular "S"s as the sand grows deeper on the road. This driver was inexperienced and easily distracted by what he saw.

A crackle of paper means Honey's opening another butterscotch. Callahan smiles, amused. Honey slips the candy into her mouth, shoves the wrapper into the pocket of her shorts and shrugs apologetically. "Hey, it's my breakfast. You want one?"

"No thanks."

They enter the darkened part of the path into the Hundred Acre Wood, the shadows heightening Callahan's instincts. From the direction of the osprey nest, she hears a distant scream of bird-protest.

Something's disturbing those ospreys. That's the next place to look for tracks leaving the road.

When she reaches the clearing where the messy stick-built nest sits on its high platform, no little osprey heads are now visible. Cautioned by their shrieking parents, no doubt, the babies have crouched out of sight under the lip of the nest.

Callahan brakes and gets out. The noonday sun seers her back as she squats on the harder dry sand by the side of the road. Behind her, she hears the "sszzt" of Honey spraying mosquito repellent. It takes her a few minutes to spot the disturbed earth she's looking for and more time to find the slight depression beyond it in the grass to her right. The golf cart's faint tire marks lead away from the road into a dense growth of high shrubbery near the base of the osprey platform.

"Oh, my gosh," Honey whispers when Callahan gets back in the cart and turns off the road. "You've found him. Are you sure he came this way?"

"It looks like it." Callahan drives through thorny undergrowth, shrubs tearing at the sides of the cart, for no more than a hundred yards before spotting a shiny green reflection behind some myrtles. She speeds around them, eager to eyeball a healthy little boy with quizzical brown eyes, then exhales, disappointed. "Call Pepper and Cole, Honey. Tell them we've found the golf cart, but Harry's not in it."

Chapter Nine

"Harry, Harry Applegate, please answer if you can hear me. Harry?" Honey pauses, her voice grown hoarse from this futile exercise, but the only sound they hear is the plop of a mullet jumping below them in the bay.

The Applegate golf cart is parked near the osprey stand on the highest ground between Pelican Flight and Ruby's studio. From her vantage point, Callahan can see Ruby's empty front porch, the still-boatless dock, and gray mud flats rimming the water. To her right, a thick maritime forest edges a narrow beach where the bigger waves characteristic of this end of the island pound the shore.

Dense patches of cord grass and undergrowth fall away on both sides of the raised spit of land where they stand. Honey's continued to walk and call the boy for the last ten minutes while Callahan's stayed bent to the ground, looking for any clue that might tell her where he's gone. Except for spooking a cricket, though, she's found nothing. Finally, back aching and discouraged, she straightens. The child is so light and the cord grass so resilient, it's impossible. She uses her field glasses to scan the mud flats round Ruby's studio where hundreds of fiddler crabs teem over the mud, their normal behavior a sure sign that Harry's nowhere near the dock or the studio either.

Another bigger mullet flops noisily in the bay, and Callahan looks up, momentarily hopeful, then disappointed, by the circling rings on the water's surface.

Honey's finally stopped yelling and called Pepper again on her cell. A child anywhere at this end of the island would surely have heard them by now. Her voice is pleading. "Please hurry, Peps. We've had no luck finding him at all." She hangs up the phone, hooks it on her belt, and, flip-flops flapping, trots towards the end of the promontory, where Callahan stands. "So now what do we do?"

"We keep looking. He's somewhere near here, and he's got to have left clues. I just haven't found them yet." So far, except for a good sized oyster shell in the golf cart tray, Callahan's found no sign that Harry Applegate even left the golf cart. "What's taking Pepper so long?"

"He and Cole and Dr. Appplegate stopped at Francie's to check, but she wasn't there, and, of course, Harry wasn't either. They oughta be along any minute." Honey's eyes move from the bay and mud flats to the dark wall of forest on their right. "Callahan, you don't think Harry wandered into those woods, do you? I sure hope not. It's so spooky and snakey in there."

Not to mention, the cougars, though Harry's probably safe from them till dusk.

"I just can't tell, Honey. Why don't you wait for Pepper here, and I'll walk down by Timicau and see if by any chance Harry made it as far as those mud flats to get that oyster shell. At least, I can have a look at the whole shoreline before the tide comes in. We're missing a lot from this angle."

Callahan's head throbs, her eyes ache, from looking so hard to find nothing. Not a broken branch, the small depression of a footprint, nothing. With some difficulty, she makes her way through thorny bushes and spartina clumps down to the spongy ground that surrounds the bay. Sulfurous swamp smell becomes more intense.

Even Harry, light as he is, would sink into this boggy soil.

But there's no sign of him. No tracks at all until she reaches the very edge of the water below the outcropping where she and Honey had been standing. There, hidden by the overhang of the sand bluff, Callahan does spot deep sunken footsteps and a flattened grass trail along the edge of the bay towards Ruby's shed. She kneels, her knees sinking into the slimy ooze, mosquitoes swarming her head and arms. Pulling her hat bill down, she focuses on the tracks.

These prints are too big and deep, not the footprints of a little boy.

One set is familiar to her, though.

Mr. Hobnail Boots again.

There's a second set of footprints, much longer and wider, smooth-soled like a tennis shoe in the firmer soil at the grasses' edge.

Two adults went to Ruby's and both came back this way. And it happened sometime this morning because the tide hasn't come back in to wash them away.

The tracks returning from Ruby's are deeper than those walking towards it. *They were carrying something heavy when they came back. Harry? Is that why he can't answer us? They have Harry?*

She fingers the sandy mud of the crusts edging both sets of tracks. The mud in the returning tracks is softer than the crusts on those headed towards Ruby's, but not much softer.

They didn't stay very long. This can't be good.

Callahan makes herself take a deep breath, her concern for the child tightening her chest. She looks up at the sound of Honey sliding on her bottom down the bank above.

"I couldn't take it any longer, just waiting up there." Honey's voice betrays her anxiety. When she stands, her yellow shorts are snagged and coated in mud, one long tan leg bleeding from thorn scratches. Slapping at the horde of mosquitoes that abandon Callahan for her, she points at the tracks under the bank. "You've done it, Callahan. You've found his footprints, haven't you?"

"Well, there were two people here, but I'm afraid neither one of them was Harry. Probably both men and one of them a pretty big man from the length of his stride. And they appear to have left the shore right up there, see." She points several yards ahead where the footprints along the narrow beach veer left and disappear into the water.

Into that boat from Ruby's dock?

Struggling to keep her emotions in check, Callahan walks to examine them more closely.

Use your head. Time is of the essence here. You can fall apart when you get home.

"But wait, look there, Honey." Several feet beyond the tracks into the water there are new ones coming back out of it. Callahan trots up the beach to examine them. These new ones—again hobnail and smooth sole—march up the sand for only about fifteen feet before turning at right angles from the beach in the direction of a huge oak that bounds the maritime forest. "They began running here." She yells back to Honey. "The length between strides increases pretty dramatically."

Chasing Harry? Into the forest?

Sick at heart, she waits for Honey to catch up. Callahan's fears for the little boy's well being now seem more than justified to her. The day is officially a scorcher. Her knees are caked with drying mud. Her tee shirt clings to her chest with perspiration, and a few mosquitoes have even bitten her. She slaps at one. Still not a peep from Harry, the buzz of mosquitoes and the crash of waves the only sounds she hears, and then, the distant hum of a golf cart.

A golf cart? Reinforcements. Hallelujah!

From the direction of Pelican Flight comes a booming, unfamiliar, deep male voice. "Harry, Harry, It's Dad. Harry, Harry, where are you, son?"

Callahan and Honey clamor up the bank and sprint to Pepper's cart when it comes into the clearing. The adult ospreys, who'd settled back on their nest, shriek angry protests at these latest interlopers and fly away again.

And then, everything seems to happen at once. Before Callahan can report to the men what she's learned and her fears, a small, husky voice is answering Dr. Applegate from the direction of the forest. "Dad. Hey, Dad, it's me, Harry."

The child bursts out of the woods onto Pelican Flight, running after the golf cart. Harry's filthy dirty, his legs and arms covered with red bite welts, but he's alive, marvelously alive, and from the looks of it unharmed.

Callahan's head swims in relief. Dr. Applegate is at least six foot five with impossibly long legs. He leaps from Pepper's golf cart and lopes, giraffe-like, to scoop up his brown-haired, jug-eared little boy in an embrace so tender Callahan allows herself to forgive his careless parenting.

Cole, looking hilarious in khaki Bermudas and a red golf shirt with his pistol holster strapped around his waist, slaps Callahan on the back so heartily that she nearly topples. "Man, oh man, we could use a tracker like you in our department, honey. Maybe you oughta give up this teaching stuff and come home where you can do some *real* good."

Pepper seems to be stifling a smile when Callahan notices him, and, as usual, she finds him infuriating. In an obvious male-female once-over, his twinkly eyes move up her mud-caked legs to her equally muddy shorts, then pause and linger on her sweaty white—now almost see-through—tee shirt. When he sees her hair, jerked into an off-center ponytail under her hat, the corners of his mouth twitch in clear amusement. "Callahan, you're red as my alcoholic uncle. I've got a thermos of ice water here. Why don't you and Honey have a drink and cool off while we debrief little Harry, and then, we'll all go back and celebrate together."

She feels the sound of jungle drums in her ears, her body temperature rising with enough anger that she's surprised she doesn't spontaneously combust. Intentionally keeping her voice controlled and distant, she says, "No thanks, Pepper. I think I'll go home and cool off there."

Cole's eyebrows arch in surprise. Pepper, though, apparently unflappable, flashes a confident smile. "Well, I'll see you later then.

You do remember, don't you, Miss Banks, that you have a date for dinner tonight? After yesterday's mendacity, I'll not take no for an answer." He turns from her, apparently assured that the issue is resolved and addresses Harry. "What took you so long? If two such beauteous creatures were enduring the mid-day heat of a South Carolina summer in an effort to find me, you can bet I would've come a-running."

Chapter Ten

"Why?" Honey turns to Callahan, who's driving the golf cart. "Why would Harry come the minute Dr. Applegate calls him and completely ignore us while we're screaming our heads off? He's got to have heard us, Callahan."

"I don't know. I can't figure it either unless he was so scared of something that he only trusted his dad." The little golf cart enters the welcome coolness of The Hundred Acre Wood. Something's been eating at Callahan since the minute she heard Harry was lost.

I've put off facing it too long. What if we hadn't found him, and he was still out there tonight?

Now that Lila's dead, only Callahan knows about the cougars.

A little boy would be such easy prey.

She shudders, realizing she has no choice but to tell Pepper, dreading the prospect.

Maybe I ought to go with him tonight and get it over. I can't put it off any longer.

Her stomach knots. The beautiful, allegedly extinct cats have been a well-kept secret for over twenty years.

Pepper will probably kill them all for the security of his development. Well, I have to do it. I can't be responsible for what could happen if I don't.

"Callahan." Honey's sets her empty water bottle in the cup holder. "What are you so busy thinking about that you passed the turn-off to your own house?"

Surprised, Callahan brakes, turns the cart around and returns to her drive. "Sorry, probably some absent-minded professor thing."

When she pulls up beside Honey's golf cart in front of her house, she invites Honey in and is relieved when Honey declines in favor of a long, cool shower and a late breakfast at Twelve Oaks.

Honey leans across the cart seat to hug Callahan. "You were amazing out there today. I wish you'd consider moving back. We'd all love it if you lived on the island permanently."

Honey's never had to make choices based on what she can afford.

"Well, I wish I could, too." Callahan's hug back is equally warm. "I love every grain of sand on Timicau Island, but there are these little things called financial considerations…"

"Baloney." Honey climbs out of Callahan's cart into her own. She waves goodbye. "Pepper says you can afford to stay if you want to."

How dare he?

Callahan waits for the cart to disappear and, then, several minutes more to cool off in the house before dialing Twelve Oaks on her cell.

Vi must not be back yet since she always answers the phone. The answering machine clicks on, and Callahan deliberately leaves Varina, not Pepper, the message. "Hi, Vi. It's Callahan. Will you please tell Pepper that I'll meet him at the boat dock tonight at seven. Tell him it's not convenient for him to pick me up here."

He's not driving me back here in the dark after dinner. The man has "dangerous shoals" written all over him.

⌀

When she pulls up to the pier at seven sharp, Pepper's already there in the Boston Whaler, his back to her, the boat's green canvas tee top bobbing in gentle waves. She turns the cart key off and watches him open a wine bottle and pour wine into two stemmed glasses on the console beside the steering wheel. Three sea gulls hang above the boat like stringless kites. The muted percussion of ocean waves on the front of the island is barely audible in the humid air. It's several degrees cooler by the water, where the low-lying sun sparkles the surface of the bay with diamond-cut light.

What a perfect night for a boat ride. I don't get sea sick in water this calm. So why am I nervous?

She had a terrible time deciding what to wear tonight, unable to shake the sensation that Pepper's eyes are always on her.

Being around him makes me self-conscious as a teenager.

She settled on a loose-fitting white cotton blouse that didn't need tucking in, a touch of lace trimming its side-slitted bottom. Sleeveless and collarless, the blouse's neck dips into a small V, which frames three cultured pearls dangling from a leather thong necklace.

Demure, that's the look, a hands-off kind of girl.

She pulled on her most comfortable jeans first, then took them off because they were too hot. Then, tried a cooler short red cotton skirt, which she zipped, then unzipped, stepped out of and lobbed on the reject pile on the bed. She could imagine herself blushing red as the skirt when his sultry eyes wandered up her partially bare thighs.

Finally, she settled on an old standby, her favorite skirt to teach in, a gray, gored, light denim that brushes the top of her ankles. It's still uncomfortably warm, but she's well covered. Her one concession to the heat was strappy flat leather sandals.

At least, my toes are cool.

She'd washed her hair just before dressing, and it's still slightly damp, straight and flying untamed in the mild ocean breeze.

That plus no make-up ought to make me uninteresting enough to a man who's attracted to sophisticated, put-together women like Victoria Weatherly.

Pepper's so preoccupied with his preparations that he seems completely unaware of her presence there in the golf cart. He steps up on the dock, picks up a red and white cooler and places it on the boat's floor. *His* clothes are exactly what she'd expect. White duck pants, a crisply ironed cotton madras shirt in shades of blue and green, and some kind of leather moccasins without socks. And he's whistling! The tune's an aria from *Aida* though she can't name it. Surprisingly, he's hitting the high notes in perfect pitch.

Now, he's leaning over to take something out of the cooler that looks like a platter of food. As he peels the plastic wrap from its top, he walks around the console to an area in the bow where a white triangular leather platform stretches across the entire front of the boat. It's when he turns back that he sees her, stops whistling, and rubs one ear sheepishly.

"Hi." She gets out of the cart.

"Hi back." He picks up a wine glass and meets her half way up the pier.

"Inconvenient, huh?" A skeptical smile crosses his angular features. "Inconvenient for me to pick you up at home? And Vi tells me it's bad manners to call and argue about it." He hands her the wine glass before she can respond, his eyebrows raised in a look of anticipation. "Our first course this evening, Miss Banks, offered with the deliberate intention of lowering our levels of sobriety as quickly as possible. Whadda' you say? A fine New Zealand Sauvignon Blanc can make a good day perfect."

Callahan stifles a grin and takes a sip. "It's really grassy and wonderful."

"Good. I knew you'd like it. Shall we go then?" He takes her free hand, tucks it in the crook of his arm, and leads her to the boat with the pomp of a groomsman. "Seems to me, Miss Banks, that it's downright uncivilized for a Southern lady to deny her gentleman the privilege of picking her up at her home for a date."

Her gentleman?

He helps her step down into the Whaler. "If we let these little proprieties keep falling away, next thing you know, we'll be running around in loin cloths." His eyebrows are bushier than John's, but similarly shaped, and his blue eyes hold a teasing light she finds appealing in spite of herself.

"I'm not exactly your *date,* Pepper." She walks away from him there behind the steering console, towards the front of the boat, admiring it as she does. It's a special Whaler. She's been on enough Whalers to know. An old one, beautifully rehabbed with its teak wood accents polished to a high sheen. And, she noticed getting in that it has no name painted on its side.

Callahan sits down on the platform, her back to the bow, beside a platter of deviled eggs and cheese biscuits. There's room for the plate and Callahan and at least one more person to sit or stretch out. She's guessing these boat rides may be part of a well-rehearsed seduction routine.

How could he be interested in me when Victoria's been dead less than three days?

She decides to clear the air and set things straight first thing. "I wasn't going to come tonight, Pepper." She leans left to minimize the glare and make eye contact with him where he stands behind the console. "But I had to come because I have something important I've been putting off telling you."

His face falls.

"And, I've dreaded doing this and put it off way too long."

"Can we put it off just a little while longer then, whatever it is?" He reaches back, expertly flips lose the stern line that attaches the boat to the dock, and steers them out into the channel between the ocean and the Intracostal Waterway. The motor's so quiet that Callahan's surprised by their smooth and sudden movement away from the pier.

"I have a little something planned that doesn't need to be spoiled. We, umm, are not going straight to The Grill tonight, Callahan. Our reservations are at nine. I got myself a new anchor for my boat." He lifts his chin and peers over the windshield at her. "I thought it might be fun to spend a little time out here in the channel between Timicau and Oak Island and see what we can see. We for sure can count on the sun going down, which is a show in itself from this angle on the water. We'll have ourselves our own private cocktail party." He nods towards the food on the platter. "Vi did the fixings."

Callahan's about to protest this latest twist when she's startled by a loud sucking gasp directly behind her in the water. Something huge has surfaced to breathe, and she knows exactly what it is. She turns fast enough to see the shiny gray male dolphin–she knows it's a male because it's so big–breach the water in front of the boat. His overdeveloped dolphin forehead gives him the cerebral look of a college professor, and the upward curve of his mouth suggests he'd be a genial one. Pepper cuts the motor, and the great mammal rises nose-first out of the water to hang there, his small deep eyes connecting with hers in some tender interspecies recognition that sends trills of joy through her.

"Pepper, have you ever been so close to one?"

"Not in the wild."

The shuffles and whuffs of the sea mammal's breathing so fill the air that they demand full attention. For the next hour, the big male, who's followed the boat almost a quarter mile to Pepper's favorite anchorage between Timicau and Oak Islands, entertains them. Others in his pod join him there, frolicking in circles around the boat, clicking their mysterious communications.

When Pepper comes to the front of the boat to throw the shiny gray anchor splashing into the water, he sits down next to Callahan. "Well, you just keep surprising me." He shakes his head. "I know you're a biologist, but who told the dolphins? It's like they've come to study *you*."

She's engaged by the boyish quality of his smile. "If I didn't know better, I'd accuse you of staging this whole thing."

"They've never stuck around this long before, and I come out here every chance I get."

They laugh together, comfortably.

Just then, a female with a baby swimming so close it seems umbilically linked, grazes the side of the boat. Callahan leans far over the side as the sleek mammal arches her back to dive. In so doing, she allows Callahan to stroke the full length of satiny silver skin along her dorsal fin. That a wild animal mother would trust her enough to come this close thrills Callahan beyond measure. She's reminded of a favorite Thoreau quote she keeps on her office bulletin board. "I once had a sparrow alight upon my shoulder while I was hoeing the village garden, and I felt more distinguished by that circumstance than I should have been by any epaulet I could have worn."

Touching the mother dolphin is my sparrow circumstance.

The large male, then, tail-walks across the water in spectacular sea-creature choreography. Almost as if in competition, another and then another perform similar acrobatics, all within thirty feet of the boat. The cheese biscuits are swamped first, washed to the floor, and rendered inedible by a dolphin-created wave. More and bigger waves follow, drenching them both and destroying what's left of the eggs.

Christening us as pod members?

Except for oooing and ahhhing like fireworks spectators, neither Callahan nor Pepper has much to say to each other till, slowly, the flared match of the sun burns itself out on the horizon, its glorious red reflecting back at them on the water. Several times, Pepper leaves her to refill their wine glasses. Callahan knows she's sipped a lot of wine but is too taken in by the dolphins to really much care.

Then, as quickly as they came, the dolphins are gone, and the water grows dark and silent, as if nothing extraordinary lives beneath it. She turns to him. "Pepper, seriously, how could we be so lucky?" And then giggles, for only then does she take in the ravages of the waves on his appearance. His madras shirt is limp, the thick curls of his hair are stretched low across his forehead with the weight of water, and his white duck pants have become remarkably see-through. She averts her eyes to ignore the obvious bulge.

I must look every bit as soggy.

She reminds herself that she only came tonight to tell Pepper about the cougars, but every time she turns to speak to him, she breaks into new giggles. He looks little-boy embarrassed–he's covered his lap with a towel now–and she has an idea that it's a struggle for him not to laugh at her, as well.

Finally, she gives up on being business-like. The wine, the dolphins, the beauteous sunset over water, everything's making her head muzzy. He dries her face with the end of his towel, then wipes off his own. Instead of discussing cougars, she's hypnotized by his wonderful lemony smell.

I'm hopeless. It's the dolphins' fault, totally their fault.

Eventually, some sobriety and Callahan's determination prevail. She sits straight up in the boat, interlacing her fingers in her lap. "Pepper, I need to get this said, hard as it is. This has been so wonderful, but I really came tonight because I want you to know that there are cougars– you know big cats, lions, shy but potentially dangerous predators–at the north end of the island, and they've been there for over twenty years. Little Harry and Tom and Dick and teeny Mrs. Pasquini, and all the others you're going to sell the island away to could be in real danger. And I've been putting this off too long because, frankly, I'm most scared for the cougars. But when Harry got lost today, I realized it was wrong of me to keep it from you."

Pepper puts both hands on her shoulders and turns her to face him. "Miss Callahan," His lazy low voice holds no trace of anger or concern, only a tenderness which unsettles her further. He kisses the tip of her nose. "Thank you. I've been wondering when you'd fess up. I figured you above all others had to know. You and Lila. I kept hoping she'd trust me enough to talk to me about them, but it never happened."

He already knows? But how? He never goes down to that end of the island. She feels giddy, relieved of a heavy burden, but confused.

He smiles, a whimsical smile. "You see some pretty interesting things on Timicau when you sit off-shore in a flats boat fishing as many hours as I have. I've seen the cats off and on for years. Saw one once swimming in the inlet from Capers, headed this way. For years I kept them a secret, too, probably, for the same reason you and Lila did. Actually, Callahan, one of the many reasons I wanted *you* to have dinner with me tonight was to ask you to help me with something. What would you think if we got some experts like yourself to make up a committee that..."

His voice falters like he's searching for the right words. "Let me put it this way. Don't you think if everybody knew the score out here, there might be a way for the people and the animals to coexist sensibly? You and Lila and my family have done it now for three generations."

Callahan feels adrift on unfamiliar seas, the shadows of her fear and loathing for him swirling away into the darkening light. She can find no reason to distrust, let alone dislike, Pepper Dade at this moment though she's desperately trying to recapture that feeling to protect herself.

Pepper's voice is teasing now. "There's a lesson here. If you're worried about something, you ought'a stop fretting and come talk to ole Dr. Pepper." He smiles in a way that lets her know he's deliberately using the soda's name as a joke.

He doesn't telegraph what happens next. She doesn't even sense him make his move, so she's taken totally off guard. He's just laughing, and then he's kissing her. Her body, that body that's been so suffused with joy, so tense with fear, so relieved, and, then, disbelieving responds organically. It's as if each of her nerve endings has lined up with its synapse and is suddenly shot through with white-hot light. Never has a kiss affected her this way.

A far-away, rational Callahan screams, "resist him!" but the woman in his arms does not.

And then, he stops kissing her, stops far sooner than she wants him to. His breath is warm against the wet back of her neck. There's laughter in his voice. "I do admire a woman who's not afraid to get her hair wet."

Chapter Eleven

"I've been meaning to ask you." Pepper's looking out the side window of the restaurant, up the Waterway towards the Oak Island marina as the Aggie Gray passes by. "Is that your yellow Bug in our parking lot over there? The one with that ridiculous bumper sticker?"

Callahan doesn't answer him. Shivering and still chilled to the bone, she unfolds her arms from her chest and cups her hands over the votive candle in the center of the table, grateful for its warmth. The lights in the room are so dim that his face moves into shadow when she covers the small candle. Thank heavens, for modesty sake, her blouse dried quickly, but none of the rest of her has. She thoroughly regrets wearing the long denim skirt now. It's clammy and cold in this overly air conditioned room and won't dry for hours. Nor will her underwear or her wet hair, which is hopelessly tangled.

Pepper, on the other hand, looks completely normal again. His madras shirt's only slightly wrinkled from the dolphin splashes, and his soggy curls no longer droop low on his forehead.

You'd think nothing remarkable happened at all.

He completely dried out in the ten-minute open-throttle boat ride to the restaurant. You got to the Morgan Creek Grill on time in the summer, or you didn't eat. Normally, Callahan would love being here at The Grill with its fabulous seafood and shabby chic décor. The stuffed marlin over the bar is the biggest one she's ever seen. Tonight, though, tonight is different.

I still can't believe I let him kiss me.

She feels even more disheveled on the inside than the out.

A perky college-girl waitress, obviously hustling a big tip, has already taken their dinner orders and delivered Callahan's hot tea, Pepper's vodka martini, crusty rolls and butter. From where Callahan sits on the opposite side of the table for two, she can't see the parking lot. Her window looks down on a floodlit pier where Pepper's nameless Whaler bobs and strains at its ropes in the wake of the passing ferry.

"Callahan." His voice breaks her reverie. "Are you ignoring me?"

She laughs. "Sorry, I've got a bad habit of getting lost in my own thoughts. Yes, Mr. Dade, it is my VW over there." She lets her hands leave the candle's warmth to finger comb her hair, then gives up. It'll hang straight once it's dry.

Why should I care how I look anyway?

Pepper reaches under the table and produces a red backpack he brought with him from the boat. He unzips it and takes out a navy man-size fleece jacket. With a grin that says, "I don't miss a trick," he hands it to her. She slips it over her shoulders, rewarding him with a grateful smile for the instant flood of warmth it provides.

He acts like nothing happened between us on the boat at all.

"So, exactly what *does* your bumper sticker mean?"

He's interrupted by the petite blonde waitress—ponytail swinging, lashes fluttering—who deposits two Caesar salads in front of them. Pepper vaguely nods thanks as she swishes away. "Where was I? Oh, yes, JP called me over to take a look at your bumper sticker the other morning." Pepper shakes his head in mock bafflement, the corners of his eyes crinkling in good-humor. "I told him I didn't understand it either."

Picking up on his tone, Callahan narrows her eyes to slits. "You'd better not be insulting my bumper sticker because I'm crazy about it. Do you know I've had people honk at me on the highway, lean out their windows, and beg to know where I got it?" She bought it at a trendy little book store on Wall Street in Asheville, and it still makes her smile every time she sees it:

"Don't meddle in the affairs of dragons for you are crunchy and good with catsup".

"It's one of those things," she tells Pepper in a tone of feigned condescension, "that if you don't get it, there's no use trying to explain." She's glad for the natural lead-in to JP, though. "So, Pepper, about JP. Are you actually worried about him, or do you think he'll turn up for work tomorrow, first of the week, Monday and all?"

Pepper replaces his backpack under the table, scoops butter from a miniature porcelain tub, and puts it on his butter plate.

"Seriously, do you really think something could have happened to him?" JP sounds big, strong, and self-sufficient enough to Callahan to more than take care of himself.

Pepper butters a piece of his roll, takes a bite, and picks up his martini glass, swilling its lemon twist in a circle. His eyes follow the lemon like he's divining from tealeaves.

He's sorting out how much to tell me.

"You know." The teasing tone in his voice has gone somber. "I don't quite know what to make of it. I do know a little more about the situation than you, and I don't think Cole would mind my telling you this much." He sets the glass down. "Robbie Pasquini, Irene's husband, was up there on their third floor the day Victoria died, and he's not what you'd call the most loyal of husbands, if you catch my drift." Pepper's eyebrows narrow in concentration. He picks up his fork and begins cutting his salad. "Robbie has... umm, how shall we put it? A bit of a wandering eye, not exactly a zipper problem at his age, I don't think, just that potential. Irene's the one with the money, so he's allegedly curbed his natural instincts since he married her last year." Pepper smiles weakly. He takes a bite of his salad and seems preoccupied as he chews.

He likes the way he just tactfully danced around the truth. I wonder if he approves or disapproves of Robbie.

Callahan remembers Robert Pasquini from the ferry. The small-boned, debonair, sallow-faced, seventy-something man might have been handsome once, a Latin lover type.

But now?

She has a hard time picturing him as a playboy.

But someone—who was it, Annie Applegate or Cole?—alluded to the fact that Victoria and Robbie Pasquini worked out together at the same health spa. Is that significant?

"Well." Pepper finally gets his salad swallowed. "It seems that Robbie saw somebody down there in Francie's cabana Thursday around two o'clock. Noticed her because she filled out her bright blue bikini so satisfactorily. Or so he reports. The angle from up there into the cabana is just right for viewing, so Robbie had hopes of getting a better look at my immodest sister, topless again. Seems he's surprised Francie out on the beach a time or two but still hasn't gotten his fill of ogling her. This time, though, when he looked through Irene's new high powered binoculars, he hit pay dirt."

Pepper stops talking and—*of all times*—goes back to chewing more lettuce.

Callahan takes a bite of her own salad, feeling suspended in time as she waits to hear the rest of what Pepper has to say. The chatter of other diners and the clink of flatware against china become background music. She has the illusion that she and Pepper are as isolated at this small table in this darkened room as if they were back on her Timicau Island porch.

Finally, he sets his fork down on his salad plate, takes another sip of his martini, uses the napkin in his lap to wipe his mouth and picks up right where he left off. "Got more than he bargained for, old Robbie did. What he saw down there was not Francie but my own faithless ex-girlfriend Victoria and his *own* foreman JP doing a good bit more than lunching together."

Pepper's mouth tightens in a hard angry line, though his voice betrays nothing unusual. "In fact, Robbie found what JP and Victoria were doing so absorbing that he stayed to watch and missed the two thirty ferry to the mainland, where Irene was waiting to pick him up. He told Cole he spent the better part of that hour enjoying live porn up close and personal." Pepper shakes his head disgustedly and raises both hands in an open-palms gesture that says I have no use for any of them.

"Where was Francie during all this, Pepper? Did she catch them?" Callahan's thinking that if Francie had, Cole could have a possible murder suspect on his hands. You didn't cross Francis Dade lightly.

"No, she was off-island, getting her hair frizzed."

Pepper must have thought the same thing.

"I guess JP knew she was going to be gone and took advantage of that circumstance to do a little extra curricular banging with Victoria. They're sure Francie was gone because she signed the ferry log at one thirty when she left Timicau." Pepper pauses. "And the Captain and mate both confirm that. Francie didn't come back to the island till dinner time."

The waitress arrives with Callahan's seafood platter and a steaming plate of fried shrimp for Pepper. She whisks their empty salad plates away. "Enjoy your dinner," she says to Pepper in a sultry drawl.

"Do they know what time Victoria died, how long after Robbie saw her with JP, I mean?" Just as Callahan asks the question, the waitress is back, eyebrows raised in perky interest as she refills their water glasses.

Pepper ignores the blonde. "Cole estimates time of death as sometime between three and five pm, mostly because of the people who did and didn't see her after I left at nine that morning. The doc who did the post couldn't tell a thing from Vicky's body temperatures because she'd been in the ocean too long."

"Pepper"—Callahan waits till the hovering waitress finally does leave—"if JP had something to do with Victoria's death, maybe he's gone missing because he doesn't want to be questioned about it. But"—she's already second-guessing her own theory—"why would he want to kill her if the two of them were lovers?"

Pepper shrugs. "Who knows? JP. Francie. Robbie. Ruby, Juby. Even our dear departed Victoria. Each of them with morals sorry as an alley cat. It's the thing I find most puzzling about our little hometown, Callahan. I'm capable of ignoring the transgressions of people like JP because he wasn't brought up to know any better. But when people like Francie and Victoria—debutantes, members of the true upper crust in Charleston—behave like white trash, it's more than I can stomach." He sets his glass down hard on the table. "Because they do know better!" His mouth hardens into that line again. "The way I see it, people like that deserve whatever it is they frigging finally get. They bring it on themselves."

No wonder he's not more upset over Victoria's death.

Then, Callahan has a chilling thought.

You, Pepper Dade, would have as much reason to hate Victoria with her sleazy morals as Francie would. What do you think it is that she "deserved to frigging finally get?"

Chapter Twelve

MONDAY, JULY 6TH

Monday, nine thirty a.m., Callahan carries her coffee cup to the sun-spattered porch, her eyes instinctively seeking a cleared trail in the paisley-patterned duckweed that covers the pond's surface. She spots the path, a distinctive cleared area in the middle of fuzzy green where Albert has passed, but the alligator must be in the rushes or under water now. Three tiny Merganser ducks sit motionless on the pond, like decorator tacks on a bulletin board.

Mergansers this time of year? They should have long ago flown north for the summer.

Their disproportionately large, wedge-shaped black and white heads always strike her as impossibly top-heavy. When they fly, they appear doomed to topple headfirst back to earth, but, of course, they never do. She smiles, this complexity of creatures a source of endless pleasure and fascination. She'll enjoy them even if they are out of season.

She sighs, a bit discouraged about how little she's been able to accomplish in the four days she's been home. Callahan's still acutely aware that there are decisions to be made.

Hopefully, JP will show up back at the Pasquini house this morning, and I'll be free to focus on my own problems and stop worrying about whether there's a murderer prowling the island.

First thing this morning, she called Richard Levinthal, Lila's accountant, for an appointment. With his help, she planned to analyze the numbers and decide whether she can afford to keep Lila's house as a rental or will need to sell it. Either way, it's time to begin cleaning things out. But Richard Levinthal had left on a two-week vacation this morning!

She lowers herself into the rocker nearest the kitchen door, shoulders sagging as she places her coffee cup beside field glasses on top of the stepladder end table.

How could I know he'd change his plans and leave a week early? When I called last week from Asheville, his secretary said he'd be here till mid-July. Shit.

Callahan can't remember a twenty four-hour period in her life when her emotions have been more volatile. She's felt confident, confused, insecure, giddy, angry, tender, terrified, lustful, and now, pretty well spent. Last night, before they'd even had dinner, she'd already experienced wild euphoria with the dolphins and, then, the angst of a newly kissed adolescent. By the time dinner was served and she'd heard Pepper's descriptions of Robert Pasquini's voyeur views, she'd felt herself go stiff with suspicion, and, yes, even fear of Pepper.

Surely, if Francie had a motive to kill Victoria for cheating with JP, Pepper had a stronger one. Cole was sure Francie was not on the island Thursday afternoon, but Pepper could easily have come back in his Whaler, beached it in front of Francie's gazebo, and come upon Victoria there with JP. Once Robbie Pasquini left, no one would know Pepper had even been back to the island. We only have his word for it that they even broke up Thursday. No one else's.

All Callahan wanted by dinner's end last night was to get as far from Pepper Dade as possible. A large cloud bank had moved in while they were eating, covering the moon and stars and so darkening the night sky that Pepper was forced to navigate the inky Intracostal Waterway, its oversized shadows and hidden reefs, with one small beam from his spotlight and years of developed instinct.

For Callahan, the ride back to Timicau was interminable. She sat shivering in the bow of the boat, miserable in the presence of this man she was beginning to fear all over again. Pepper, seemingly oblivious to her plight, whistled a medley of *Porgy and Bess* tunes to himself as he steered the boat through a series of dark, narrow, oyster-bed-lined channels that all looked alike to her.

"Fish gotta swim, birds gotta fly."

She knew the words to the tune and even found his choice of a love song annoying.

When the dock finally emerged from the fog, low-lit, a floating ghostly specter, Callahan felt immense relief. Still whistling, Pepper slowed the boat, steered it to the dock, and threw the bowline over a pier cleat. A big coon foraging in a trash can there raised up on its hind legs, hissing. "Hello, big boy." Pepper laughed out loud, jumped to the dock, and tied off the boat. The coon scurried resentfully away with that awkward three-point coon-shuffle that reminded her of a stiff old man on a cane.

She stepped out of the boat on to the pier, unzipped Pepper's fleece, and handed it to him. "Thanks again." Before she could leave, he grasped her arm and held her there.

"I'm really ready to go, Pepper." Both her sense of fear and attraction were so heightened by the closeness to him that blood pounded in her ears.

He didn't loose the grip. The small lights along the edge of the dock gave off too little light for her to read his expression, but his voice held hurt. "I wasn't expecting anything of you, Callahan. It's just that there's something I meant to ask on the way back tonight, and I've had to concentrate too hard getting us here to do it."

Her thin white blouse provided no warmth in the clammy chill of the pier. She forcefully folded her arms across herself, making him release his grasp. She didn't move away from him but was ready to. "What's so important that you have to ask it right now when I'm freezing? Let's talk another time."

He cocked his head sideways, his body language registering disappointment.

He probably thought I'd sleep with him. Gone too many days without a woman.

Even as she thought it, she disliked her own cynicism.

"Callahan." His breath warmed her cheek as he spoke. She stepped away, turned, and headed for her golf cart with Pepper close on her heels. She found the cart, got in it, and turned its lights on, a source of reassurance somehow. But before she could leave, he went ahead and asked her what he wanted to, anyway. "I hope you'll stay on the island forever, honey. I mean that truly. But if you ever want to sell Lila's little house, I hope you'll give me first refusal. I'll pay whatever you want for it."

This morning, ten hours later, Callahan still feels sickened by that memory. She takes a drink of her strong coffee, leans back and rocks violently, discharging fury. It was the studied ease with which he tried to get her to sell her house that chafes the most.

That son of a bitch. He took me out to dinner, wooed me with wine and dolphins, all to soften me up for the pitch.

Something spooks the Mergansers just then. They lift noisily off the pond, their heads flashing black and white in the morning's weak yellow light. Whatever startled them is across the pond and off to Callahan's right.

She scans the far side with her binoculars.

A gator, a deer, probably a coon? No. It's something bigger crouched in the myrtles.

She adjusts the focus on her glasses, and when the object comes into focus, her elbows jerk so violently she knocks the coffee cup clattering off the stepladder to the floor. She steadies the binoculars and looks again. Perfectly framed in the lens, on the far side of the pond, is the scarred face of her childhood nightmares, a face she hasn't seen in at least ten years but has never forgotten. He's here on *her* property, in Albert's territory, where no sane man would go during alligator nesting season.

His dirty-green canvas hat is pulled crookedly across the right side of his face, exposing a scar that runs ear to mouth, bisecting his left cheek. His skin is as sallow as she remembers it, and he's grown a thin, straight moustache that does nothing but accentuate the dissatisfied angles and planes of his face. Evidently, he didn't hear the coffee cup fall and break.

Or doesn't care.

Juby T. Roy's eyes, black and cruel as a Doberman's, are narrowed in concentration, a shock of dirty gray-brown hair stuck to one side of his forehead. The stealthy movement of his reedy body inching forward in the rushes is barely perceptible though the mergansers detected him. She shivers.

It's like watching a snake, a snake nicknamed Bulova.

He's in dangerous territory, but he has not come undefended. He's aiming a very long-barreled gun towards the place in the rushes on the far side of her pond where Albert's trail ends.

Callahan stands and screams as loud as her lungs will allow, ignoring even her field glasses when they slide from her lap and thump to the floor. "Don't you dare shoot my alligator!"

Chapter Thirteen

And then, there's only silence. Silence and the trembling of Callahan's body as she stares at the spot where she saw Juby. There's no report from a gun. No dead bird, no wounded alligator. Just unnerving silence.

Did he hear me? He has to have heard me.

And no movement. No movement in the bushes. No Albert slithering back to the safety of the pond, no alarm-flight from the thirty or so night herons who roost there in the myrtles every day within thirty feet of where Juby was crouched.

He's that creepy. Even the night herons don't know he's there. They'd surely have flown by now if they did.

It takes several seconds for Callahan to develop the resolve to reach a trembling hand for her field glasses and actually scan the pond's far bank again.

What if he's aiming that rifle at me this time?

The man never did a thing to Callahan when she was a child except inhabit her nightmares. Inhabit her nightmares and invade her solitary world. He'd appear from nowhere, like a spirit on a moor, when she was most alone on the north end of the island, startling and always spooking her.

Of course, he had no right to be there. She knew it, and he did as well, his ironic smile as he tipped his dirty felt hat to her, his tacit acknowledgement. Then, without speaking, he'd step back into the underbrush and disappear. He never showed himself or let her come upon him unless she was completely alone and vulnerable. And yet, he'd done her no harm.

She long ago concluded that he hunted on the island lots more than anyone suspected. And though, to everyone else, he was completely elusive, she'd developed a warning instinct for Juby's primitive vibration, the same protective inner buzz that unfailingly alerted her when an animal predator was nearby. He was the only human who'd ever triggered that instinct in her.

Her skin would prickle as she jogged through a dense wood, trailing a mother bobcat, her sense of security melt unexpectedly just as she'd shinnied to the top of a tree to count the creamy white eggs in a Great Horned Owl's nest. And she'd know that Juby Roy was within feet, maybe inches, of her, camouflaged in a tangled thicket or crouched behind a massive fallen oak limb by the game trail. Even when she sensed he was near, she couldn't bring herself to look for him. The prospect of spotting that gaunt, unshaven, empty-eyed face terrified her more than being startled if he chose to appear.

Long before she learned in grad school that it's the flight of the prey that triggers the predator's pursuit instinct, she'd intuitively resisted her own panicky need to flee from him. When she sensed him lurking nearby, with force of will, she made herself walk slowly away.

Gradually, she'd even grown to accept his presence in her wilderness, convincing herself that though he did seem to stalk her, he wouldn't hurt her. She and Juby were not predator or prey. They were, both of them, solitary forest creatures circling and measuring one another with the wary instincts of all things wild.

She purposefully never told Lila about Juby for fear that she might curtail her freedom. The summer Callahan turned eleven, she read *To Kill a Mockingbird,* identified with Scout, and declared Juby T. her own personal Boo Radley, spooky eyes and all.

The impression held until one hot July day in 1984, when Callahan's indomitable mother came face to face with Juby in a Charleston courtroom. When Lila came home that night, she declared him the spookiest man she'd ever seen. "They say he's as good fighting with a straight razor as most men are with a knife, but somebody must have been better at least once because he has a scar clear across one side of his face."

Like Zorro, Callahan had always thought.

Lila had gone to court with John to testify against Ruby in the custody hearing for Francie and Honey, ages ten and one. Instead of sitting in the front of the courtroom, on the cushioned and backed bench beside his half-sister, Juby T. had positioned himself on a hard, backless bench to the left of Lila and John, where he sat the whole day, his slit-eyed gaze narrowed at them, mouth drawn into a deprecating sneer. Ruby fought for–and lost–both of her daughters that day. With Lila's help, John had proved Ruby to be the unfit and careless mother she really was.

Patting the sofa that night, Lila beckoned Callahan to sit next to her, and drew her twelve-year-old daughter protectively into the crook of her arm. "The way he looked at me today, Callie, made my skin crawl. He hates me now, honey. I hear he sneaks onto the island sometime. If you ever see him–you'll know him by the scar–run! It's not beyond him to harm you to get even with me."

Callahan got goose bumps all over, but still didn't tell Lila what she knew and discounted her mother's advice on the spot.

I shouldn't run from him. It's the wrong thing to run.

And now, he's back, and he seems to have come and gone, just like he always does.

Callahan can find no trace of Juby as she scans the banks of the pond with her binoculars. No taut-faced, blank-eyed stare from the myrtles. Nothing but the undergrowth's palette of a thousand greens and a tranquil pond.

She trains the glasses on the original spot where she saw him again and continues listening. A yellow slider turtle on a log in front of the bushes slips noiselessly back into the water. One night heron squawks—sometimes a sign of alarm—but doesn't squawk again, and nothing else moves.

She takes a deep breath, inhaling her own relief. She knows what to expect now. Whatever Juby was about to shoot will live. Once again, he's morphed back into the swamp as if he were never there.

But, of course, he was, and there's a reason.

She's never seen him anywhere around her house before today.

So what can it mean? Is he here to watch me? He could be circling around behind the myrtles or skulking towards my door at the bottom of the steps this very minute.

The adult Callahan can no longer implicitly trust the child's belief in the man's quirky decency.

Hurting me could still be a way to get even after all these years. Ruby's family is like that.

John had warned her. "They're capable of holding a grudge forever, Callahan, and waiting decades to even the score."

Did Juby even the score with John by killing Pepper's girl friend? And maybe Francie's boy friend as well? Would he sacrifice me next because of Mother's testimony? Stop this. There's nothing to be gained by scaring yourself to death.

Callahan shakes her head to clear the fear-goblins but decides to play it safe and get off the porch. Taking her time as she's always done with the man, she pauses, stoops, shakily scoops up the broken coffee-stained pieces of the cherry red cup she knocked several feet across the floor.

With that discipline honed in childhood, she purposefully turns her back on the pond and walks the ten or so steps into the kitchen. She'll not give in to her panic nor let him see she's afraid if he's out there watching.

But how can I protect myself if he comes up here after me?

She has no way to lock the barn door at the bottom of her stairs, so he could easily walk up to the porch.

Did I pull the door closed when I came in last night?

She can't remember. She's hoping she did because she'd at least hear a warning roll as it slid open across its track. She tries visualizing herself coming home last night, but all she sees is a Callahan so furious with Pepper that she gave attention to nothing else. She decides to lock every one of the French doors that separates the living quarters on the second floor from the porch.

There's comfort in doing something physical. She pulls Lila's longest, thinnest butcher knife from the storage block and carries it with her as she begins latching the doors one by one. They were designed to weather hurricane force winds, a latch connecting door to frame on both top and bottom, and a lock on the swinging door of each pair once it is battened down. If she does it properly, the locks will hold.

Though the doors, she observes ruefully, *are mostly made of glass. Breakable glass.*

Still, it's all she can do, so she sets about doing it efficiently, testing each door with her weight once she's anchored it to the frame and thrown the lock. He'd have to break glass to get in, and she'd have the advantage of foreknowledge and some chance to defend herself. She picks up the knife from the floor by her foot and carries it to the next door, working her way around the porch.

Four doors done, two to go.

Her senses are on red alert, her eyes combing the pond's banks for irregularity in bushes or water, her ears straining for subtle bird complaints, a rustle in the bushes, or—*God forbid*—a step on the stairs.

It's almost too quiet.

When the doors are secured, she takes a shallow breath, but won't relax till the windows are done. The upper floor has seven windows, *t*hree banked over the kitchen sink close to where the top of the stairs reach the upper porch, three across the front of the house and one extra large one in the bathroom on the same side.

She starts with the kitchen windows. A tiny, bright green lizard scurries up the side of the sink as she reaches for the middle one. She scoops the little reptile up. His heart, palpitating against his ribs into the palm of her hands, feels as terrified as her own. She cracks the bottom of the right window and slips him out into the realm of the porch where he belongs, wishing—with a whimsical smile—that she could rescue herself so easily. Then, she secures that window and the other two, each time double-checking that the locks are completely engaged.

There.

Those three are done, and the three bigger windows that line the east side of the living room are usually kept locked. Consciously tightening her grip on the knife, she spins again to scan the pond—nothing has changed—and walks into the living room.

She was right. The three windows there are well secured. She pulls each lock again to be sure. Which leaves only the large window in the half bath that opens out on the front deck and...

Oh shit

It is usually left open. A full-sized man could have already slipped through it and be waiting for her now behind the closed door to her left.

I should have locked the bathroom window the minute I got the doors done.

Her lizard-fearful heart racing, she walks towards the closed bathroom door and pauses, trying to think logically.

I do have to go in there. It's the only way to secure the whole top floor. Should I call Cole or Pepper or someone else before I do? I have this knife, but no gun, no other way to defend myself. Where's my cell phone? Oh shit again.

She'd thrown it on her bed in frustration this morning when she learned that Lila's accountant had left early on his vacation. The phone's a full floor below her now, and she's not about to trot down outside stairs and risk running into Juby.

So she must muster the courage to go in that bathroom and lock that last window. She tries futilely to draw in a full breath, reaches for the bathroom door handle and turns it.

If fear made Callahan breathless, the deliciously empty space that greets her on the other side of the door should restore her breath, but it doesn't. Not yet. Because the window is gaping, completely open. She rushes in, jerks it down, terror pounding in her ears, and throws the final lock. Then, and only then, does she collapse weak-kneed on the closed top of the toilet seat.

Now what?

For a few minutes, she sits and just stares at the stark white walls of the tiny room, its aging white lavatory sink to her right, its familiar rust-stained stopper dangling from a chain. She's wearing shorts, so she's vaguely aware of the sticky vinyl of the toilet seat cover against her upper legs as she struggles to regain equilibrium. Most people place mirrors over lavatory sinks, but not Lila. No mirrors. Over the sink to Callahan's right is a picture of a Moroccan tree of life with vivid red, blue and green birds and polka-dotted forest creatures. It's been there for as long as she can remember.

Ragged thoughts of Juby T. Roy, images mercifully long forgotten, suddenly race unbidden back into her consciousness. Crazed carousel thoughts, each chasing the other faster than she can push it away until, like the carousel switch has been thrown, she makes a sudden and intuitive connection.

It was Juby inside Ruby's studio yesterday. I ignored my body's warning. I even forgot my own rules and ran.

She remembers her clumsy trek through the pluff mud back to the golf cart and her frantic departure.

Did he come here today because I ran from him yesterday?

Callahan's hands begin to shake uncontrollably. She's got to do something to get her mind off all of this.

Lila's towels–she's staring right at them–could be her something. She brightens at the thought. Wildly colorful towels, probably fifty of them in varying ages and states of deterioration, are neatly stacked in the linen closet to her left. Her mother would never throw a towel away. "You need some for the beach, and some for the house, and some for washing down the golf cart, and scrubbing the deck chairs. Not to mention towels for the outside shower and the inside tub. I have a use for every towel I own."

Callahan knows she'll have to clean them out eventually, regardless of whether she sells or rents the house.

So what's wrong with right now?

Purposefully seeking distraction, she stands, pulls down the window blind so Juby can't creep up on the porch, peek in, and surprise her. She reaches for the overhead light and screws in the bulb. The pull cord's been broken forever. Light floods the newly darkened room. One by one, she pulls a stack of towels from a shelf, lowers it to the floor and sits down beside it, the tile cool to her bare feet and legs.

The fluffy bounty elicits welcome memories. Callahan finds comfort in the towels' textures, colors and the feelings they evoke. She fondles a threadbare, faded green one with dancing elephant ballerinas in pink tutus, her childhood favorite, before resolutely putting it on the throwaway pile. Every other towel that's frayed, ragged, or worn is destined to join the dancing elephants. Then, she'll pick two or three sentimental favorites to keep for housework when she's all done.

There are several towels thick and respectable enough to save. She spends the next ten minutes purging two of the three piles in a sorting frenzy that belies the importance of the task. Gradually, her fears dissipate into the simple rewarding feeling of accomplishing something. Callahan's so absorbed that she fails to notice the corner of a small pine box protruding beneath a heavy navy beach towel at the bottom of the last pile. When she finally picks up that last towel for inspection, she sees the box, sits back on her heels, and stares in surprise. It's rough-hewn, about the size of two cigar boxes, end to end, and obviously made by a child or an unskilled craftsman. It's so distinctively asymmetrical that she's quite sure she's never laid eyes on it before. With trembling hands, she picks it up.

A small metal lock secures the box's lid to its bottom, but both the lock and the box's hinges are so thoroughly oxidized that when she puts pressure on the clasp, the top comes off in her hands. A sense of giddy anticipation floods her.

The items on the top are childlike treasures, the kinds of things The Littlest Angel would present before the Heavenly Throne of God: a perfect sea turtle egg, an arrowhead, a collapsed cat's cradle, two shark's teeth, and a flawless pink moon shell. She removes them one by one, reverently placing each on the lip of the lavatory as she longs to know their significance to her mother.

Beneath the childish objects are three stacks of envelopes. When she picks up the first packet, it's letters tied together with pink satin ribbon, she exposes the back side of a small hand mirror, the first and only mirror she's ever seen in Lila's house. It's a lovely little oval shape, soft silver and hammered in a way that makes it seem distinctly Mexican.

Will this box finally give up the secrets of Mother's past she guarded so protectively from me right up till the end?

Callahan carefully transfers the other two packets of envelopes—both bound together with red string— to the vanity top, and reaches for the contraband object, the mirror's metal cool to her hands as she turns it over. Half of the glass surface on the mirror is shattered, so that only one side of her own face, ruddy cheeks and a puzzled dark eye, stare back in a distorted reflection.

A mirror? A mirror in this house where Lila banned them? Why this one?

Shaking her head in disbelief, she sets the forbidden object down and counts the envelopes in the packet she holds—one, two, three, four, five, noticing that each of the five identical khaki-colored envelopes has a formally embossed return address in dark brown lettering: Twelve

Oaks Plantation. Timicau Island, South Carolina. The envelopes are of a fine quality once-stiff velum, but soft now with age. With care, she unties the ribbon and turns the top one over to see her mother's name on the address: Miss Lila Boone, Saddlestring, Wyoming. It's postmarked August 17, 1970.

Six months before I was born.

Callahan shivers in real anticipation now, all fears of Juby receding into the fervor of her curiosity. Here, most assuredly, is a relic of Lila's secret past and a chance for her to learn more. With eager fingers, Callahan pulls the top letter out of its envelope and unfolds it. Before it's even completely opened, she recognizes John Dade's business-like handwriting in light brown ink. "My Dear Little Lila..."

Callahan's reading's interrupted by a low rumble, the sound of the barn door under her house being opened. Alarmed, she leaps to her feet and frantically looks for the knife, which she finds under the short stack of good towels on the floor. Someone big is already on the stairs now, climbing at a fast pace, the heavy thud of footsteps on the stairs growing closer.

Chapter Fourteen

Before she can think how else to defend herself, someone's reached the top of the stairs and is yelling her name. "Callahan, are you up here?" Her body goes limp in relief though his familiar voice holds an uncharacteristic tone of urgency. He's already jerking a door handle when, still clutching the butcher knife, she walks out into the living room. "Hurry, Callahan. I really need to talk to you."

She slips the knife under a potted fern on an end table and does hurry to open the door, the thudding of her heart receding to a mild arrhythmia because, mercifully, it's *not* Juby, but Pepper Dade standing there, sane and solid as a bridge support.

"Thank God, *you're* here," he says when she opens the door.

Thank God you are.

Callahan's so relieved she has to stifle an urge to hug him. "C'mon in." She's surprised at his appearance. He's unshaven, the blonde stubble on his face appealing in a scruffy terrier way. He's wearing a washed-out pair of jeans that are frayed at the seams and a shapeless gray tee shirt. He's not wearing his glasses so his eyes, a pensive blue-gray today, are more prominent in his face. Even his naturally relaxed body appears taunt. "What's up, Pepper?"

"Francie and Honey are shopping." He raises both hands in a gesture of frustration. "Shopping on the one day of the year when I need them! And Wallace and Vi are in town at a funeral." His face is pink from the exertion of running up the stairs, and his chest is still heaving. "I feel like Rocky twelve rounds into an Apollo fight. As if enough hasn't already happened, I've got another crisis." He turns away from her, back towards the stairs. "You coming, Harry?"

Harry Applegate, red-faced and wide-eyed, appears at the top of her steps, pauses and openly gawks at the view. "Man, would you take a look at that gator."

Following his gaze, Callahan's glad to see that Albert and several smaller alligators have reappeared on the pond. Pepper goes to Harry, drapes a friendly arm around his shoulders, and steers him purposefully towards Callahan.

"We call the big one Albert," Callahan tells the little boy. She points to the next largest gator, lying in Albert's shadow on the pond's sandy bank. "That's Tipper. She's huge for a female. We named her that the year Al Gore ran for President…"

"Hate to be the one to interrupt fascinating local color," Pepper says, "but right now I've got a crisis of gargantuan proportions on my hands." He nods towards the back of the boy, who's now headed to the far edge of the porch and a better vantage point on the gators, the heels of his tennis shoes blinking with imbedded lights Callahan covets. "Harry and his mama found Robbie Pasquini in a bad way about fifteen minutes ago." The sides of Pepper's mouth twitch like he's fighting for control. "Flat on his back, Callahan, at the bottom of the steps of their house. It looks like he fell the full two flights and had been there a while. He's hurt bad. After I got 911, I called Cole because I truly don't know whether this is foul play or not. Harry's mama, Annie, is a nurse so she'll ride with Robbie on the helicopter and stay with him till we find Irene."

The whop, whop, whop of an approaching whirlybird is now audible over the inland waterway. It's headed towards the south end of the island, where Pepper had a landing pad built only weeks before. "They'll

Medevac him right out, but nobody's here to take care of Harry while I go across to pick up Cole."

"So"–Callahan interrupts Pepper this time–"Robbie's still alive, then?"

"He's real bloody." Harry's raspy voice issues this report without his turning around or taking his eyes off the alligators. "And his teeth are sticking out of his chin."

Pepper raises an eyebrow at the graphic description, nods a serious yes to her question, and follows it with a tentative shrug of his shoulders that says, "I don't know how much longer he'll be alive." He turns towards the stairs. "I'll get back as soon as I can, but it may take us a while. Thanks, Callahan."

Pepper's already disappeared into the stairwell before Callahan fully realizes she's been co-opted into babysitting. She hears the slap of his leather moccasins receding down the stairs, the sound of her door rolling shut, the squeal of the back-up signal on his golf cart, and he's gone.

So it wasn't Sir Galahad coming to rescue me from Juby. Instead of being liberated, I now have the additional responsibility of taking care of this sweaty, jug-eared little boy when I don't know how to protect myself from Juby, let alone Harry.

Resigned, but not pleased, she sighs and walks to Harry, who seems so mesmerized by this proximity to the gators that he's frozen in space. Once she reaches him, she just stands there beside him, completely at a loss about what to do with a nine-year old boy.

You have to feed and water them a lot.

She knows that much from observing her friends' and neighbors' male children.

He smells like something washed up from the sea and left on the sand too long.

At least, she can go downstairs and get her cell phone. Since she heard Pepper open the door when he came and close it when he left, she knows that Juby hasn't had a chance to sneak into her house. So far.

"Are you Pepper's girl friend or something?" Harry's random inquiry takes her by surprise.

"Pepper's girl friend?" She cocks her head to look at him suspiciously. "What would make you think a thing like that?"

"I was just wondering." He lifts his shoulders with the smile of an innocent. "You guys act like it, is all."

"Well, no. I'm not." She can't think how else to defend herself from the charge, so she picks up her field glasses from the table and places the strap over Harry's head. "Here, you can get even closer with these. I've got to run downstairs and get something, and I'll be right back. Then, we'll have something cool to drink and get better acquainted. I understand you know a lot about nature."

"I do," Harry's big-toothed smile disarms her. "I'm pretty sure I'm right about you and Pepper, too. My mom's always telling my dad what good instincts I have."

He's still standing with the glasses trained on Albert when she comes back up the stairs, mission accomplished. She drops the little cell phone in the front pocket of her denim shorts, determined not to be separated from it again. There's a flash of white beyond the deck and the distinctive shriek of an osprey. "Look, Harry!"

He lowers the glasses in time to see the large white-breasted bird fly by within feet of the porch. "Wow! That's the closest I ever got to an osprey, even closer than yesterday. Did you know that they never get divorced after they get mated?"

"You're absolutely right about that. They're very faithful birds, much like Canada geese." Callahan and Harry both stand silent watching the bird till it soars into the distance, a circling speck over the impoundment. "It's called monogamy, when you have only one mate."

"I know." Harry's forehead lowers like she's insulted his intelligence. "But a lot of people, like my brother Tom, who's so dumb he calls cottage cheese, college cheese, don't understand scientific terms."

"Speaking of your brothers, where are they?"

Harry's left the edge of the porch, climbed into one of the green rockers, and is rocking vigorously. Both of his knees are skinned and covered in Batman Band-Aids, and his scrawny bare legs extending out of baggy green camping shorts are covered with red welts from mosquito bites. "They're at a swim meet," Harry reports, rocking so far back in the chair that it tips precariously. He compensates with no sign of alarm, throwing his weight forward to rebalance the chair, and keeps talking. "They're good at running and swimming and stuff like that. I'm good at spiders and snakes. Did you know that an adult water moccasin eats ten rats a month? People think snakes are bad, but we'd have a rodent-infested world if we didn't have snakes around."

As he talks on, Callahan's eyes, like tongue to toothache, return again and again to that spot in the myrtles where she saw Juby.

"Aren't those banana spiders?" Harry points to several large webs hanging from the rafters beyond the screens along the front of the house.

"They are." She pulls her attention back. "And they're fascinating."

"Arachnids," Harry says, casually scratching a mosquito bite on his wrist till it starts to bleed. He puts his mouth to the wound and sucks it clean.

"Arachnids, they are." Callahan's about to be impressed by this freckle-faced little naturalist.

"So tell me more about em." Harry leaves the rocker to insert himself into a basket-like chair that hangs from a rope on the ceiling.

The child's in perpetual motion.

Using the tip of his toe on the floor as a lever he twists the chair in a circle, winding it up. Then, he picks up the foot, and the chair flies into a frenetic, dizzying spin.

I hope those old ropes are up to the challenge.

The ropes hold, the chair slows, and Harry looks as if nothing has even happened. He sucks the blood off his wrist again and leans around the chair's side to make eye contact with Callahan. "When are we gonna talk about those banana spiders?"

"Well." She points to the spider nearest Harry. With its muti-colored, many-jointed legs open, it's bigger than a fifty-cent piece and distinctive because of its bright yellow lower abdomen. "They are also called golden silk spiders. A lot of people don't like spiders, but they have a job to do just like snakes. I leave all of their webs up here because they catch mosquitoes and flies. Their webs can be as big as five feet across, so that's a pretty big fishing net, if what you're fishing for is bugs. This one's an orb weaver. It builds a spiral web and spends its whole day out there, hanging upside down in it. You're looking at the female. She's lots bigger than the male. See those two littler spiders over there to her left? They're males, fixing to fight for her favors. Spiders fall in love just like ospreys do."

"Do they bite?" He's moved to try out another rocker and is scratching a welt on his ear.

"Ospreys?"

"No, banana spiders." Another scowl on Harry's face.

This child's so intense that he doesn't like being misunderstood.

"Well, you know, most all spiders bite, but very few are poisonous, and these spiders aren't aggressive. You'd have to hold them or squeeze them to..." Her eyes go to the pond. Albert has slid back into the water, and Tipper quickly follows.

"Whatcha looking at?"

And he's super observant.

He gets out of the chair and walks over to her, his moldy smell coming along with him.

Maybe those tennis shoes with lights can't be dried so they gradually mildew.

"My tarantula's a boy," he tells her conversationally. "You can tell because he has hairs on his legs." The child throws out the fact, but his eyes are riveted on the disturbed water where the alligators have just disappeared.

He's picking up on my alarm.

She decides to be honest with him.

He's the kind of kid that will run into Juby sometime, anyway.

"There's a man," she says softly, "that's been hanging around here today, and he's a little scary."

Harry pats her arm with a moist, chubby hand. "Does he look like Scarface?"

Callahan's astounded.

Is the child a mind reader?

"Why, yes, but how did you know?"

"Because," Harry says, his intense, raisin-brown eyes widening with authority, "that's the very same guy I had to hide from yesterday when you kept trying to get me to come out and I wouldn't."

Chapter Fifteen

Three peanut butter sandwiches, five glasses of lemonade, three Reese's peanut butter cups, two apples and four bags of popcorn later, Callahan finally hears the squeal of golf cart brakes below her house. And she's almost sorry to hear them.

She checks her watch. Pepper left Harry here around eleven this morning. It's six o'clock now, so in seven hours she's fallen hopelessly in love with a brash nine year old scientist whose stomach is bottomless.

Between lemonade refills and trips to the microwave for more popcorn, it's taken her most of the day to extract the complete details of yesterday's adventures from Harry. There's been no further sign of Juby today, but he's definitely the man who chased Harry yesterday. After hearing Harry's story, Callahan has little doubt.

Seduced from the road by the snowy underbelly of a large osprey, Harry had followed the bird to its nest on the raised platform, where Callahan and Honey later found the cart. In search of a higher vantage point for viewing the osprey chicks in the nest, Harry left the cart and climbed the tallest sand dune buffering the beach, where he crouched to hide from the screeching osprey adults. It wasn't until a few minutes later, when he began to unfold himself for a peek down into the nest, that he noticed two men behind and below him. They were lowering something long, white, and clearly heavy into a boat at Ruby's dock.

The scar-face man knocked his own hat into the water and begun yelling at, "a black guy big as Shaquille O'Neal," who fished the hat out of the water with the end of an oar. Then, they untied the boat from the pier and, with their load, headed up the creek and out into the ocean. The female osprey spotted Harry again and began screaming. Juby must have noticed because he looked up, saw Harry, turned the boat around, and sped towards the dune where Harry had been hiding. The boat roared onto the sand, and Juby jumped out, running up the dune after him. "He was saying lots of cuss words, including taking the Lord's name in vain, which even my dad's not supposed to do. He was real mad about something, Callahan."

Harry had stopped telling his story long enough to rock back and forth in the chair and take another fistful of popcorn. "I couldn't think of anything bad I did really, well anything they'd know about, but that guy had a mean voice, so I decided it was time to act like a genie and disappear." Nodding agreement with himself, Harry removed a popcorn kernel from his mouth, then put it back in and cracked it between his teeth. "That big guy, after he tied up the boat, I could hear him coming, too. So, I headed into the trees where I already knew some good places to hide and watch deer." Harry's mouth curved into an affable smile as if, upon review, he was even more pleased with himself. "I could hear sticks cracking and crashing behind me. My first hiding place I got to was a big rotten log. They weren't that far back, so I crawled into it like this." He got up from the chair, walked solemnly around behind it, and lowered himself between the back rockers and chair seat, curling into a surprisingly compact ball. "Then, I pulled a bunch of pine straw in around me for camouflage"–he mimed that action with his eyes squeezed tightly closed–"and they ran right by my log." Grinning, he emerged from under the rocker and stood, his eyes straying to the last uneaten Reese's Peanut Butter Cup on the table.

Callahan handed it to him. "That must have been so scary. Wasn't it buggy in the log? And hard to lie still?"

"You bet." Harry nodded soberly, sat down in the rocker and began unwrapping the candy. He pointed to the wound on his wrist. "This one's the itchiest. I could hear Scarface and Shaq shaking the ground, running all over the place, shouting, and about a hundred female mosquitoes all started biting me at once. I couldn't move or slap em or anything." He paused for a big bite of candy and cocked his head inquiringly at Callahan, who was sipping her lemonade. "Did you know that only female mosquitoes bite? They need blood to make muzzie for their eggs. Males just suck on plants."

"Yes, Harry, I did know that." Smiling at his precocity, Callahan still felt horror at the thought of the vulnerable child stuffed into a log. "No snakes in there, I hope. What happened next?"

I know this is going to end alright, and I'm still terrified for him.

"No snakes." His teeth were completely coated in peanut butter and chocolate, but his smile was magnificent. "They kept running around, yelling and shouting swear words. Sometimes, Tommie and Dick and I practice being super heroes. So that's what I did." His round brown eyes locked into hers. "I turned my body into stone so it couldn't move." His chest inflated. "The Shaq guy fell down once pretty near me." Harry's eyes brightened and widened. "That time he said 'shit' and something I couldn't understand about his mother. But"–Harry threw both arms over his head joyfully–"they had no hope of catching a super hero turned to stone."

He bestowed another charming buck-toothed smile on Callahan. "I did hear you and Honey yelling, but I figured they were such evil villains that they had captured you and forced you to yell to get me to come out. I made a plan to stay stone till dark, but then, my Dad came."

"Harry, you were amazing." Unasked, Callahan refilled both their lemonade glasses and took the empty candy wrapper. "You made several very brave decisions. I'm curious"–she loved getting into the head of this clever child–"what would you have done if Shaq or Scarface had found you inside that log?"

Harry's nose looked like someone had rolled it out of play dough and stuck it on his face. He wrinkled it confidently. "Oh, I had that figured out, too. My mom says one of the best things I'm good at is making noise." He took three straight gulps of the lemonade, dried his mouth on the red and yellow striped fabric of his tee shirt's upper arm. He was wearing the tee shirt both backward and inside out but seemed oblivious to the shirt label positioned directly under his chin. "If those guys found me, I was gonna open my super hero mouth and just holler bloody murder!" Harry demonstrated that for her, too, issuing forth a shriek so startlingly loud and piercing that it spooked some of the night herons on the far side of the pond.

"Well, now, that's quite a holler." Callahan had turned away so he wouldn't see her bemusement.

Still absorbed in memories of the day, she notices now, for the first time, a bank of gray storm clouds gathering on the horizon. "Looks like we're in for a little afternoon shower, Dr. Applegate."

A great streak of lightening splits the sky over the mainland, and there's the sound of the door rolling open at the bottom of the steps.

"Thousand one, thousand two, thousand three, thousand four, thousand five." A rumble of loud thunder booms over the impound-ment. "One mile," Harry announces, his eyes slitting above the choco-late remnants of his smile. "If you get to five, Callahan, before you hear the thunder, you are exactly one mile away from the lightening."

"And you," says an exuberant Annie Applegate, who has huffed up the last steps to the deck, "are five seconds away from coming home with me and releasing Dr. Banks here from a day of unexpected servitude."

"Oh, Annie, it was really such a pleasure. How's Robbie?"

Annie's upper cheeks pinch towards her eyes, her mouth into an uneasy grimace. "Too soon to say," she says. "He's just out of surgery–a ruptured spleen, a punctured lung, and at least one fractured vertebra–but he's alive."

"Mama! Mama!" Harry's tugging at his mother's white shirttail insistently. "Guess what? She's not Dr. Banks. She's Callahan, and I'm

Dr. Applegate. And we're going to teach each other nature classes. Next time, it's gonna be on the yellow-billed cuckoo. Did you know all thrushes and robins–they're in the same family– add something white to their nests? Look at that alligator, the big one. The way he's all stretched out on top of the water. He's showing the other alligators he's dominant."

⌒⌐

Looking rumpled and exhausted, Pepper arrives at the top of the stairs about thirty minutes after the Applegates have left. He opens his arms to her, and it seems the natural thing for Callahan to go into them. He kisses the top of her head. "Thank you." She feels the resonance of his deep voice and the lowering of his chest in a long sigh. He speaks into the hair on top of her head. "You are the only good and perfect thing that has happened to me this whole day. I got really flummoxed when I had time to put two and two together. Then, I've been sick with worry about you all day. Callahan, why were all your doors shut and locked when I came up here this morning? I tried calling you about twenty times, but, of course, you didn't answer your phone."

Well, at least I had it in my pocket. I just didn't think to turn it on.

He smells of old leather and wilted starch, a lemon-tinged weariness. Compassion for him softens her heart. She pulls away. "It's a long story, but the bottom line is that there's no way to lock the door down at the foot of my stairs. I was about to pour some wine. You want a glass?"

"Do I ever!"

They collapse in side-by side rockers, sipping a cool wine. "Cole thinks it's likely that Robbie was pushed." Pepper's voice holds a discouragement that's new. "He says anyone who wanted to do Robbie harm could have just hidden behind that stack of lumber on their second floor, waited till he got close enough to the edge, and run hard at his back to shove him over." Pepper circles his shoulders like he could roll away the tensions of the day. "Cole did a lot of measuring, and believe it or not, we even used some geometry to figure out the angles. He says with the trajectory of Robbie's fall, he either had to run and jump, which makes no sense at all, or he was pushed." Pepper takes another drink and leans back into the rocker.

He's picked that creaky one again. It may break yet.

"We got Irene to the hospital, and, of course, she feels useless as titties on a boar hog right now. There's absolutely nothing she can do but wait. He's still unconscious, so only time will tell."

As the early evening sun tints the impoundment pink, Callahan lets herself chat companionably with Pepper about her day from Juby through Harry, omitting only the finding of Lila's letters, something she finds too personal and unsettling to share.

Which seems days ago now. Is it really still Monday?

Lightning streaks the distant western sky, the sweet smell of far off rain freshening the air. The wine's cool and soothing. She surprises herself, as they rock in the lowering light, by spilling out Juby stories, from her childhood terrors to his appearance here this morning, as well as the primal warning she felt yesterday at Ruby's shed. When she tells Pepper she locked the shed door from the outside before leaving yesterday, his brows pull together.

"God a'mighty, Callahan. First, what in the hell made you decide to take yourself all alone out there with all that's going on? And, second, it may be that you just saved your skin when you locked that door of Ruby's shack because somebody had already broken the window and gotten out by the time Whart Applegate and I went out there to look for Harry yesterday afternoon."

"Yes, I know. I've thought about that. What could they have been hiding in there, Pepper? Something heavy, big and white? Harry says it covered the whole bottom of the boat. Do you think they'd really have hurt Harry if he hadn't had the sense to run and hide?" Even as she talks, she's distracted, titillated really, by the physical presence of the man rocking next to her.

It must be pheromones, this constant pull towards him. I wonder if he feels it, too.

Pepper's in shadow now, the wine in his glass almost gone, the creak of his rocker less frequent. "I don't know if they would have hurt him, Callahan, but I do know I'm glad we didn't have to find out. There's something evil and non-salubrious going on on our little island right now, and I intend to find out what it is. I want you to do something for me." His voice goes husky. "I know I'm drastically changing the subject, but I want you to come home with me tonight."

"Home with you?" Confused, she stiffens.

"Don't get your britches in a bundle." He's sensing her pique. "I'm not inviting you to my boudoir though can't say as I'd refuse, should you wander in." He leans towards her. "We have between us this alchemy of female and male, as good as any I, myself, have experienced in forty two years of living." He kisses his hand and touches it to her lips. "We should not let such a rare thing go to waste indefinitely."

Experiencing a flood of desire, she pulls away from the touch of his hand.

"Tonight, though, I just want to protect you. I wouldn't sleep a wink." His smiles ruefully and self-corrects. "Well, tired as I am, I might sleep, but it would be a troubled sleep if you were out here alone and vulnerable." Pepper stands slowly, with the fatigue of a traveler. "Go pack your things, honey. From what I know of you, you'll travel light. I'll call Vi on my cell and tell her you're coming for dinner and make sure there are clean sheets in the guest room. Today, I've got more than I can say grace over, but tomorrow morning, we'll get Wallace over here and work out a way to lock that door at the bottom of your stairs."

Chapter Sixteen

LATER MONDAY NIGHT

I am actually grateful to be here.

Callahan climbs out of the peach-colored bathtub in the Twelve Oaks guest suite and rubs her body dry with a warmed towel that looks brand new.

No Lila towels here.

She slips a fine-cotton white nightie over her head, turns out the bathroom lights, and walks across the deep plush of the bedroom carpet to the nearest of the two single beds.

Dinner tonight was the usual mouth-watering Vi fare. Though she seemed put out with Pepper and atypically sharp-tongued, Vi's mood affected her cooking not at all. Fresh grouper in lemon sauce, wild rice, collard greens, fruit salad, and homemade cloverleaf rolls. All served at a candlelit dining table, plus civilized dinner table conversations with Honey and Pepper, mostly about Harry, his remarkable mind and daring escape. The key lime pie was the perfect finale.

And now—*oh bliss*—Callahan lowers herself onto ironed sheets and fluffy down pillows for one night of safe harbor sleep.

I bet I sleep like a bear cub.

She turns on a bedside lamp, plumps two pillows against the chintz-covered headboard and takes her latest edition of *SC Wildlife* from the side table.

A light tap on the bedroom door. It opens and Honey comes in. "Mind if I hang out for a few minutes?" She's wearing polished cotton turquoise pajamas, her blonde hair hanging to her shoulders in ringlets.

She's such a natural beauty with those sympathetic brown eyes.

"I'm really glad you're here safe and sound with us, Callahan. Nobody should be alone on this island tonight." Honey walks to the other bed, sits down on its edge across from her. "What do you make of all that's been happening?"

"You probably know more about it than I do." Callahan closes the magazine and sets it back on the table. "I'm pretty much just an observer."

Honey pushes two peach-fringed decorative pillows behind her own back and props herself against the headboard of the other twin bed, her bare feet on the velveteen duvet comforter. "Well, the latest is that before Robbie Pasquini fell this morning, he left Cole a message asking him to call back because he remembered something he thought might be significant."

Honey sneezes suddenly, produces a tissue from her PJ pocket and mops her nose. "Of course, there's no way to find out what that is now, unless he'd already told Irene." She sneezes again and then again, four more times in a row, her eyes becoming reddened and puffy. "This is so annoying. I never know what's going to trigger my allergies. Between Francie and me, one of us will always find something to kachoo about." She blows her nose and lobs the tissue into a nearby wastebasket. "Barron, my Persian cat–his full name was Barron Von Bellyrub, don't you just love that?–he was the worst, and I loved him so. Francie says the reason Pepper doesn't have allergies is they come from our mother's side, but, of course, I've had no contact with Ruby so I wouldn't know."

She produces a bottle of pearl-colored fingernail polish from her pajama top pocket, unscrews the top, sets it on the bedside table, dips the brush and begins painting the nails on her left hand.

Callahan can't help but notice the quiver of Honey's full lower lip. "You and I are both sort of half-orphans aren't we, Honey? Though I can see it would be much harder to be cut off from your mother than your father."

I can't imagine growing up without Lila.

"Has Ruby not even made an effort to see you since John died?"

Honey's lips tighten. She shakes her head no, dips the brush back into the polish bottle but doesn't draw it immediately back out. "I've pretty much given up on ever knowing her, Callahan." Her brown eyes are luminous with unshed tears. "She and Francie get together a lot, but according to Francie, Ruby never even asks about me." The hurt look that crosses Honey's face disappears as fast as it comes. She straightens her back, reaches for the nail polish, and begins painting the nails on her right hand. "You know, I hate to say this, but I've even begun to wonder if Ruby and Francie could have anything to do with what's been going on out here."

"Ruby and Francie? Why?" Callahan's never heard Honey criticize anyone before, let alone someone in her family.

Honey's lips are still drawn into a thin tight line. Her large eyes go narrow. "Well, for starters, Francie was hateful after Daddy died." Her usually lazy drawl holds a sting of resentment. "She insisted on having her new house and her full one third in cash as soon as soon as the estate settled, so Pepper had no choice but to develop the island to come up with the money. See, even though Daddy's estate was large, a good deal of it was tied up in real property, not liquid assets." She finishes her nails and delivers several drying breath puffs to each hand, then smiles a rare sarcastic smile. "Pepper suspects that Ruby fomented Francie's discontent, that Ruby just couldn't wait to get her hands on Francie's money. He was going to fight Francie, but after he talked to our lawyers, he concluded we'd save a lot of cash as well as good will—even though we'd eventually win—if we just went ahead and paid her off."

Honey shifts on her bed and cocks her head sideways at Callahan. "So there's no logical reason for Francie to make trouble, except you know Francie. She only seems happy when things are in a stew." Honey shrugs. "She's got her cash and her new house, and nothing more to gain. Actually," Honey sighs, "I guess I don't *really* believe my sister's capable of killing somebody, but she sure can be a bitch. It's been so great, having her out of this house..." Honey stops mid-sentence. "I've no business telling you this. Only people with bad breeding talk about their families to outsiders. I guess, somehow, Callahan, I just can't consider you an outsider."

"Well, thanks for that. It's okay. You're not telling me anything I don't already know about Francie."

But, of course, she is.

Seemingly through with the topic of Francie now, Honey has become preoccupied with tightening down the top on the nail polish bottle, so Callahan's surprised when she speaks again. "It puzzles me, though, how different Francie is from Peps and me, you know, values and all. You feel more like a Dade, Callahan, than Francie does."

God forbid!

Then, Honey really is finished. She readjusts the pillows behind her own back, and her face softens back to its normal contours. "Let's talk about something besides Francie. I've been curious to know if you have any memories of what it was like when you lived at Twelve Oaks as a little girl. You know, the way it was when Pepper was the only other child here, and Daddy was trying to recover from Mignon's death. I actually wish Mignon had been my mother, too. It's easier to have a dead mother than a live one who ignores you."

Callahan can't think how to deal with this subject tactfully, so she decides to dodge the mother issue. "No memories," she says. "None at all. Just the same things you've probably already been told. Lila came to Twelve Oaks shortly before I was born, and we lived here only till she built the house on Boone Pond. I was too young to remember how long I was here or even why. And right up to the end, Lila refused to tell me any more than that my father was a Brit and was dead." Callahan's eyelids are growing heavy.

It's been a long and demanding day.

She allows herself the luxury of slipping into the fine cotton sheets under the peach-colored duvet and yawns.

Honey notices. "I'm so sorry. I bet you're beat, and here I am still yakking away and keeping you from going to sleep." She stands, snaps off the bedside lamp on her side, walks to the door, and smiles sheepishly. "You get a good night's sleep. We still will have plenty to talk about in the morning."

Callahan's sure she'll fall instantly asleep, but her mind's a racehorse galloping a circular track of endless possibilities.

Did someone really push Robbie Pasquini off his house today? Is JP dead out there somewhere, not just off on a drunk? And what really killed Victoria?

So much has happened in the last five days, and she's so sleepy that she finds it difficult to organize the facts.

And why am I letting myself get drawn into it? It's this darned scientific mind of mine that insists upon analyzing things even when I don't want it to.

Willing or not, she finds herself piecing together the details of the past five days and trying to make sense of them.

I came back to Timicau Island on Thursday, the day Victoria mysteriously died. Friday, after Victoria was found, we all had that session with Cole at Twelve Oaks. On Saturday, the Fourth of July, JP officially came up missing. Then, on Sunday, there were the two men at Ruby's studio, loading a large white object into a boat and threatening little Harry Applegate. It's hard to believe today's only Monday. And now, poor Mr. Pasquini has taken this horrible fall. I can't help but believe that Juby Roy's somehow tied into it all.

Okay, get logical. Who could have a reason to harm four such disparate people as Victoria, JP, Harry, and Mr. Pasquini?

Juby? Getting even for what John did to Ruby, fighting intruders invading the island, something twisted like that? He just seems more of a loner, a solitary but not a violent man. Yet I do *feel creepy when he's around.*

And JP? If he killed Victoria, what possible motive could he have had? Pepper doesn't like JP. I know that from his tone of voice when he talks about him. Robbie Pasquini saw JP having sex on the beach with Victoria the day she died while JP was allegedly still Francie's lover. So if JP did something to harm Victoria that Robbie accidentally saw, it's possible JP first ran away and, then, came back to keep Robbie from implicating him. Which could explain everything but Harry. Maybe Harry was just in the wrong place at the wrong time.

Who else? Well, the other logical suspects would have to be Pepper, Francie and even Honey. Interesting that Honey implied Francie wanted Pepper to build her a new house while only three days ago Francie'd complained to me that Pepper forced her to leave Twelve Oaks. It's clear there's little love left between the two sisters or Francie and Pepper. So was Honey ill-informed, Pepper keeping secrets, or Francie just being her usual malcontented self?

Callahan makes a mental note to ask Pepper about this next time she has a chance. It will also reassure her about him if Honey's right that he's only selling lots on the island because Francie's forced him to.

Really, though, none of John's children has anything to gain from Victoria's death, do they? Maybe Francie, if she found out JP was cheating on her, but Francie and Honey were off the island the day Victoria died. So even if they had means and motive, they had no opportunity. Because of his boat, Pepper could have been on the island each time there was a disappearance, giving him both opportunity and means, but what could his motive be? He broke up with Victoria the day she died. Or did he? We only have his word about that. Still, Honey knows him a lot better than I do, and she obviously trusts him. Honey has good instincts.

What about other people on the island, less obvious ones? Wallace or Vi who was uncharacteristically peevish tonight, or the Pasquinis or Applegates?

They all had opportunity, but Callahan can come up with no real-istic motives. She yawns again, her eyes now truly too heavy for real concentration. She wills herself to stop thinking, slides down deeper under the duvet as her body warms and relaxes into sleep. She's deliciously leaving consciousness when a frightening thought jerks her fully awake.

If Irene Pasquini knows what Robbie was calling Cole about, she could be the next one in real danger.

Chapter Seventeen

TUESDAY, JULY 7

She sleeps the sleep of an exhausted child and is awakened the next morning by an insistent knock on the bedroom door. It's eight am, and sunlight filtering through sheer window curtains fills the room with a gauzy haze.

"May I come in?"

Pepper.

"Hang on." Groggy, Callahan sits up in bed, props herself against the headboard, and finger combs her hair. "Okay, come in."

Nadine bounds ahead of Pepper, who's carrying a large tray. "Good morning. Hope I'm not waking you too early, but I've got Wallace rigging a lock for that door at the bottom of your stairs, and I wanted to get your okay before he gets too far into the project."

Pepper looks like he's been up for hours. He's clean shaven, ruddy cheeked, and wearing a washed out pair of ironed jeans and a blue checked cotton shirt that does that thing with his eyes again. "How about some breakfast?"

Callahan squints at him. "Good morning, yourself. Wow, this *is* service, breakfast in bed." She still feels rumpled and heavy with sleep.

He leans forward to set the footed tray on her lap, and his lips brush her forehead.

Was that a kiss?

He smells soap-scrubbed. Besides a yellow rose in a silver bud vase, the tray holds a poached egg in a small cup, two croissants, a pat of butter, a small dish of strawberry jam, a napkin in a monogrammed silver napkin ring, a cup of coffee and a tiny cream pitcher with matching sugar bowl. He produces *The Charleston Post & Courier* from his back pocket with a flourish and lays it on the bed beside her.

She sips the coffee first. It's strong and hot, and the cream is thick. *Yum.*

She takes a bite of the perfectly poached egg and smiles gratefully up at him, but he doesn't return her smile. "Pepper, is something wrong?"

He shuffles a foot on the carpet and shakes his head. "We've had us a bit more bad news this morning, Callahan." He scratches the top of his left ear. "They found JP Mellincamp's body washed up on the south end of Oak Island late yesterday. Over ten miles from here, but then the current runs that way." He points at the headline on the newspaper. "MISSING TIMICAU CARPENTER'S DROWNING, SECOND IN LESS THAN A WEEK."

"In addition to being a damn shame, this will not do my business any good."

Before she can ask for details, his cell phone rings. Annoyance clouds his features. He pulls the phone from his shirt pocket and checks the caller's number. "Damn. It's Irene Pasquini, returning my call. Hang on, Callahan. This shouldn't take long."

But it does. By the time he's settled himself on the edge of the other bed and punched the speaker button, Callahan's buttered her croissant.

"Irene," Pepper says, "thanks for getting back to me. How's Robbie doing? Better I hope."

JP dead?

Callahan bites into the croissant, the shock of the terrible news starting to hit her, and takes a steadying drink of coffee.

Two people from the island dead now, and Robbie Pasquini might be the third. Was Harry meant to be number four?

"Irene, I want you to know"–Pepper stands and begins pacing the room–"that I have put Wallace temporarily in charge of your crew this morning because we've gotten some bad news about JP..."

Callahan involuntarily shutters, resisting a strong impulse to bolt from this bedroom, this house, and all its bad news. She takes one more bite of the croissant and eyes the egg, but she's lost her appetite. Moving the breakfast tray across the bed, she slides from under the covers, gives nearby Nadine's velvet ear a squeeze, and heads for the bathroom, her overnight bag, clean clothes, and any excuse she can think of to head home fast.

She hears Pepper's cell phone ring again while she's still in the bathroom dressing. When she comes out, her canvas overnight bag slung over her shoulder, he points to the phone and mouths the word "Cole."

"How quickly," Pepper is saying, "will you be able to get the autopsy results on JP?"

Callahan takes pen and paper from the desktop and scribbles a message she hands to Pepper. "Tell Cole to protect Irene Pasquini. If Irene knows what Robbie was planning to tell him, she could be the next person in real danger."

Pepper nods after he reads it. "Good point." He mouths the words. "I'll tell him."

She doesn't wait for Pepper to get off the phone, just throws him what she hopes appears to be a friendly wave, and heads across the room. In the bathroom, she remembered Lila's letters, is astounded she's virtually forgotten about them in the demands and confusion of the past twenty-four hours. With Wallace or some other carpenter working on her door lock, she's got to get home fast before anyone uses that bathroom and sees them.

This time, Pepper places a hand over the telephone receiver. "What's your hurry?"

"I gotta go." She opens the door.

"Never mind. I'll be over in a few minutes, anyway. I want to see what Wallace has rigged up over there."

Rigged up is the operative word, Callahan thinks as she drives her golf cart between the stately oaks lining the path from Twelve Oaks. Wallace might be able to lock the barn door at the bottom of her stairs, but the open outside wall of the staircase is secured by only three rows of stretched, twisted metal cables and a wooden handrail.

A tin snip is all it would take to bypass any lock he'll put on the door at the bottom.

Still, Callahan's relieved to be out of the big house and away from the Dades. It's already hot and humid at only nine o'clock. The day's going to be a scorcher.

"Well, good morning, if it isn't Miss Callie." Wallace's bald pate is shiny and his gray workman's shirt wet with sweat when she brakes to a stop in front of her house. He slaps a mosquito on his cheek and smiles his endearing gap-toothed smile. "This is one impossible job Mister Pepper's asked me to do here. I've got it fixed so's you can at least slip a lock through it when you leave." He demonstrates with a large metal combination lock. "So nobody's going to be able to open up your door and go in while you're gone. And I've put you a place to move the lock inside the same way. But..." Wallace chews on the edge of his lip, his thick white moustache twitching uneasily. "See here." He points to the cables behind the door that run up the open side of the ascending stairs. "Less'n we bring some lumber in and build you a wall all the way to the top of them stairs, most anybody who wants to could snip a cable, crawl under it and walk right on up." He extends himself to his full height, well over six feet, stretching his back out as he does. His brows furrow.

"Why don't you just come on back and stay at Twelve Oaks till all this trouble gets past us?"

His kind, low voice is another of his appealing qualities. Not for the first time, Callahan thinks how blessed the Dades have been to have the service of two such fine people as Vi and Wallace all these years.

"I can't keep you one hundert percent safe over here, Miss Callahan, and since I nearly brung you into this world, it troubles me extra hard."

She smiles warmly at him as she walks to the bottom of the steps to admire his handiwork. "I can't leave my home, Wallace. What you've done here will give me great peace of mind. I'll check the cables every time I've been gone and be able to know there's no one upstairs. I don't really think I'm the one in danger, anyway. I'm not a Dade, and I haven't been involved in what's going on out here at all. How about a glass of sweet tea?" She hasn't forgotten his weakness.

His smile is rueful as he begins collecting tools. "Can't today. Would you give me a rainy day check? They wants me over to the Pasquini house next. I got to run that building crew there till they find somebody to take JP's place. Ain't this all just one big crying shame?"

Callahan nods agreement and gives him a hug of thanks. He turns to leave, then comes back and points at the lock where he's hooked its arm through the hasp on the doorframe. "I forgot to tell you. I set the combination for your birthday." He smiles. "That's one day I won't never forget. February twenty-one. You surprised us all coming so early. Did you know Varina and me was with your mama all that day? And you had one brave mama."

She does know—he's always loved telling her the story— and also that even though she weighed barely five pounds, she was healthy from the start. "I've always been so grateful for what you and Vi did for us."

What Callahan never has been able to understand is why Lila chose to deliver her premature daughter on a South Carolina island with strangers when her husband was thousands of miles across the ocean in

London and her only other living relative, her father, another thousand away in Saddlestring, Wyoming. So maybe she's about to find out.

The broken mirror and the letters are still in the box in the bathroom where she left them, apparently undisturbed. She picks up the box and carries it to the kitchen, where she pours herself a glass of that ice tea she offered Wallace, minus any sugar.

Callahan carries her glass and the box to a small stepladder on the porch beside the long front porch swing and removes the three stacks of letters from the box, leaving the broken mirror. With her pulse racing, she lays them on the faded green seat of the swing's cushion.

Here goes.

She has an idea she may not like all of what she's about to learn.

But knowing the truth has to be better than not knowing.

Recognizing John's even, masculine handwriting on the envelope at the top of the first stack, she selects his letters and begins to read. The earliest is postmarked August 17, 1970.

> Dear Prettiest Girl in the World, (Pepper's still calling you that and told me yesterday that he wants me to broach the idea of our getting married again. He says I shouldn't take no for an answer. ("She's more fun than any mother I know and prettier, too.")
>
> I have to tell you, Lila, that I can't disagree with him though it's hard for me to picture how my little dark-eyed cowgirl, braids, boots and fiery spirit, could find any pleasure living with a man fifteen years her senior on a steamy island in South Carolina. Plus there'd be the adjustment to Charleston and– I'm told– the snootiest society in the US of A.

I pointed all that out to him, but in his ten-year-old wisdom, he sees none of these things as insurmountable obstacles. Like Pepper, Lila, I miss you too much. We talk often about the night you took us camping in High Meadows. Do you remember the look in Pepper's eyes when the coyotes began serenading us from the perimeter? Yes our world has lost much dazzle in the two weeks since we left you in Wyoming.

When Mignon died last winter, I'd resigned myself to a loveless life of raising and caring for my beloved little boy. Then–what a miracle–we met you. When I learned that only two months earlier you'd fallen in love with Reggie Banks, it seemed too cruel a twist of fate. I find myself resenting that lucky bastard even as I second-guess him. If he's so crazy about you, why did he leave right after the polo matches and go home to England? Is he in regular touch?

Could his luster be dimming with distance? It's wretched of me to say this, but I hope so!

Please consider making room in your heart for a small boy and a lonely man who miss and adore you more than we can say.

Love, John

Callahan doesn't need her fingers to do the math. As Wallace has so lovingly reminded her, she was born on February twenty-first, a full month premature, six months after this letter was written. Her father was in England, and John was urging Lila to come to South Carolina and marry him like he had no idea that Lila was already married and at least two months pregnant.

Callahan reaches for John's next letter in the stack of six, this one postmarked a month later, September twenty-fifth. It's a short letter, a single paragraph that isn't dated and has no salutation, John's precise script covering only the upper half of the thick vellum stationery page.

> Lila, is there any way this baby could be mine? I can't forget those two nights when Pepper left us to go on the pack trip, how willingly you came to my cabin, how perfect that little time we had together turned out to be. You tried to deny it, said you'd made a mistake, and that you'd promised to marry Reggie when he came back for his fall polo matches. But your body said otherwise. If this is my child, I will marry you in a heartbeat, Charleston gossips or no. It would be an answered prayer. I love you dearly.
>
> John.

Mother wasn't married to Reggie in September when John wrote? Unless John was somehow in the dark.

Callahan's fingers tremble as she takes another sip of her tea, replaces the glass and—with a wobbly sense of unease—unfolds the third letter, dated and postmarked October 1, 1970.

> My dear little girl, What a hard time of it you are having. I had no idea that you'd clung to a belief in the promises of this callous man through all the secretive days of your early pregnancy. And now he's utterly

abandoned you? No word from Reggie at all? How I wish I could be there to hold and protect you now that Curly has thrown you out. The fates can be cruel, Lila, and men like your father sometimes crueler.

He seemed so solid, a good man, and I know he adores you. How could he treat you like this? Pepper and I rode to town with him the day we left the ranch, and Pepper was so full of cowboy questions for him that I had no chance to engage him in adult conversation. Still, I have a hard time believing that Curly wouldn't stand by you when Reggie has abandoned you so completely.

Where will you go? What will you do? I have no way to phone you since I don't know where you are. I'm just grateful for this post office box. Please call me collect, Lila. You can always come here, and I'll help you track down the son of bitch and see that he does right by you and your little baby.

Thank you for not trying to deceive me into believing that this could be my child. Still, I wish it were, and I love you regardless. You have a place here if you need to come. I'll stay home Sunday nights until you reach me by phone. Please call and let's talk.

Love, John

Blinking back salty tears, Callahan flips that envelope over. She hadn't noticed the change of address. It is no longer Lila Boone, Bar T Ranch, Saddlestring, Wyoming but PO Box 337, Sheridan, Wyoming. Her mother was kicked out by her own father? Yet Lila never had an unkind thing to say about Curly Boone.

So is everything she told me a lie? Can Curly still be living? Was Reggie really *crushed to death under a falling polo pony when I was two?*

Callahan's throat is closing, her breath coming in short unsteady wheezes.

Maybe I need to take this in just a little at a time. Why did Lila save these letters? Did she just forget about them, or did she want me to eventually know the truth even though she couldn't face telling me? I think I like her story about the dolphins delivering me on the sand bar better.

"Callahan, my God!" Pepper's sounds angry as he stomps to the top of her stairs, clutching the metal combination lock in his right hand. "How can I keep you safe, honey, when you won't even lock the door after Wallace spends the whole morning fixing it for you?"

Chapter Eighteen

Pepper stops short, the anger on his face dissolving into concern when he spots her on the porch swing. "Callahan, what's wrong? Are you hurt? Has Juby been back?"

She shakes her head no, tears of bewilderment flooding her cheeks. *Juby seems inconsequential at the moment.*

Pepper runs the length of the porch. She sees him take in the open box on the floor, the yellowed letters in her lap. "My God." He reaches for the top letter. "That's Daddy's handwriting. Where did you find these?"

Fighting for composure, she tells him between sobs how she discovered the primitive box that now sits on the floor beneath the swing. "From what I've been reading, most everything Lila ever told me was a lie, our whole life just one big rotten fabrication. Why would she hide the truth about my father and her father and who knows what else from me?" Callahan strangles on her own tears.

Pepper moves the box aside with the toe of his Docksider and pushes the other two stacks of letters across the swing to clear a seat for himself beside her. When he sits down, he opens his arms, and she lets herself fall into them, the stiff, starch-scented front of his shirt chaffing against her forehead. "I'm not sure Reggie Banks was ever even married to Lila, Pepper, assuming he even *was* my father. Or whether he's dead or alive." She can barely breathe, she's crying so hard.

He kisses the top of her head, the swing swaying crookedly under its unbalanced load. "Someone should have told you the truth a long time ago, but Daddy and I could never convince your stubborn mama of that fact." His voice goes low with concern. "There's a good bit that Lila was determined to keep from you. I'm not one to kick dirt off a shallow grave, and, in a way, it's not all bad. Your mama loved you so much, Callahan, that she made up a better history than she could give you, herself."

Pepper's arms around her and the rise and fall of his chest as he speaks are comforting, somehow. She has no impulse to talk or move. A fly beyond the screen buzzes a distant hum. Pepper's encircling presence and, crazily, the buzz of that fly are threads to cling to.

She'd like to stay here permanently, contained by the solid musculature of the man. The front of his shirt is now soaked with her tears.

How long has he held me?

She has no idea. The swing has stopped moving. The buzzing fly's gone quiet.

Probably trapped in a banana spider web.

Pepper's making no attempt to talk her back to reality. Finally, slowly, Callahan pulls away from him and sits up.

He turns sideways in the swing to face her. Still doesn't speak, but his head is cocked as he watches her, concern narrowing his eyes.

"I'm not up for too many more revelations today, Pepper, but I guess I'd best listen to what you know since I don't think I could feel any worse than I already do."

He looks away from her, out across the porch, where a fly is, indeed, struggling in a banana spider's web. "What's the hurry? You've already gotten a shit load of unwelcome news. Why don't you just give this much a little time to sink in?" He pulls a folded blue handkerchief from his jean pocket, wipes her cheeks and hands it to her.

She blows her nose. "No, go ahead, talk. I've got to have Lila's whole story if I'm ever to figure out how I fit into it."

"Well, okay, but there's a good bit more." He stands, rubs his ear twice, shoves his hands in his jean's pockets, takes them immediately back out, and walks to the end of the porch. Then, back. "Where to begin?" He pauses in front of her on the swing, frowning, his eyes fixed on the house behind her like answers might be written there on the wall. "I've known what happened since I was a kid. Daddy and Vi and Wallace and I, all at different times, begged Lila to tell you. But she'd sworn us to secrecy and would never release us from our promises. Even now, I'm trying to convince myself that her leaving these letters for you is her way of finally saying it's okay." He extends an index finger and swipes new tears from Callahan's cheeks.

She almost smiles at the tenderness of his gesture, pointing at the tears still streaming down her cheeks. "I'm sorry. I just can't stop crying."

He eases himself down beside her again, runs his hands through his hair, front to back, squinches up his face, and rounds an arm behind her. "Well, your world as you know it has just pretty well tilted off its axis. So let's take it one bruise at a time."

Callahan finds the solid touch of his arm grounding.

He shakes his head sadly. "Lila just never could bring herself to expose you to the meanness and sordid nature of it all."

Pepper's pleading Mother's case.

"She wanted you to grow up a happy, secure little girl. And the way you've turned out, Callahan, she may just be vindicated."

He hasn't just lost his entire history like I have.

She's growing impatient with his meandering justifications.

"Well"—he takes a deep breath—"this is like doing a back flip. Once we start, there's no telling where we'll land." Pepper scowls. "Let's begin with your father, that peckerwood Reggie Banks. The man could steal the shortening from a ginger cake and never break the crust." Pepper's voice holds clear distaste. "Unfortunately, he *was* your biological father, and, no, he never did make it to the altar with Lila though he baited a trap to seduce her with that promise. And all starry-eyed, innocent, young and in love, she fell into it." Pepper pulls Callahan closer. She can feel the steady thudding of his heart. "In the end, though, I can promise you it was all for the best that you weren't involved with him or his people. They marry their cousins over there, you know. I think it makes them mean."

"So you knew Reggie?"

"I just met him once, after a polo game that first week Daddy and I went to Wyoming, but he was leaving the next day to go back to the UK. I do remember that I took a strong dislike to him, something I rarely did as a kid. He was aristocratic looking, like English royalty. You favor him in that way, but right off Daddy pegged him as a pompous, self-centered, manipulative bastard. And, as usual, Daddy was right."

"What about Lila's father, my grandfather?" Callahan can hear the hesitancy and hurt in her own voice. "Curly? Did you know him? Did he really kick her out when he found out she was pregnant?" Her head is swimming. "Is he dead?"

"Oh, man." Pepper cups her chin in his hand, raises her face to his, and kisses her lightly on the tip of her nose. "Oh, man," he says it again. "I'd rather fall on a grenade for you than have to do this. It's probably somewhere in all those letters, anyway." He smudges more tears from under her eyes with a roughened thumb. "What if I tell you how I saw it all play out, and then you can get the rest of the nitty gritty from the letters?"

He points to the return address on the top letter in the red-string tied stack nearest him: Hopping and Banks, Barristers at Law. London, England. "Naturally, having a Brit for a father, you had English grandparents, may still have for all I know. They were highbrows, your grandfather a barrister, well-connected. And they had no interest whatsoever in welcoming an illegitimate part-Hispanic granddaughter into their midst.

Part Hispanic?

"They were of the boys will be boys mentality, and my daddy played a brilliant part, if you ask me, in extracting a goodly sum of money for Lila if she promised to just make you disappear. In fact"–Pepper's lips turn down like he's sucked a lemon–"I heard tell that you weren't the only illegitimate child ole Reggie fathered. And, yes, he did finally do the world a favor and die when you were still a toddler. That's one relative you *can* cross off your list. Under a polo pony as described, and the horse deserves a medal for its magnificent clumsiness."

Part Hispanic?

Callahan can scarcely take in the rest of what Pepper's saying. She's making the connection to her mother's gypsy *dark* good looks. "Part-Hispanic?"

"One quarter to be exact. I know this is a lot to absorb. Lila's mother, your grandma, was Mexican, some kind of a high class beauty, fiery and impetuous like your mama and rich and spoiled to round out the picture. Your granddaddy worked as a wrangler on her parents' cattle ranch in the Yucatan when he was seventeen or eighteen. Evidently, there wasn't a bronco born Curly couldn't ride, and that swept Conchita, or whatever her name was, off her feet. She ran away to the States with him, and her family disowned her. Temporarily. Disowned her, till she saw the error of her ways, tucked her tail between her legs and hightailed it back home. Problem is, she forgot to take her little girl along with her." Pepper points at the silver-rimmed mirror in the open box on the floor. "That mirror belonged to your grandmother. It's the only thing Lila had left of her mother's. She was two when Conchita left. That mirror's another story in itself. The way I see it, your mama had about as much chance as a treed coon on a night with a full moon. You had cold-hearted aristocratic forbearers on both sides."

"She didn't die either? Lila's mother, my grandmother?" Callahan can replace only one distorted memory at a time.

"Ah, shit. I do hate hurting you. No, she did not. For all I know, she may still be alive. And Curly, too, though they'd all be old as Methuselah.

My daddy sent your mama a ticket to fly here when he found out she was pregnant and alone, working in a laundry in Sheridan, Wyoming. She got on that plane to Charleston and never looked back. Never went home again and never trusted another human being either, thanks to her papa and her mama and that asshole Reggie Banks. Which was a tragic thing because my daddy would have married Lila on any terms."

The very sinews of Callahan's body are collapsing into themselves. The world beyond the swing darkens and spins dizzily out of focus. Limp as linen in August, she slumps against the solid frame of Pepper Dade, the little girl she thought she was lost to her forever.

Chapter Nineteen

Pepper doesn't leave her side the rest of Tuesday, nor go home that night. He calls Vi, and she delivers his dop kit, clean clothes, and a bottle of sedatives.

By six-thirty, he's produced a tomato and cheese omelet that Callahan would find edible on any other day. He insists she take at least a few bites—a ploy Lila used to get her to eat as a child—before leading her in a zombie-like state downstairs. In her room, he raises her chin with an open palm and studies her face. "You're white as a fish belly."

Even in her haze, she's aware of a current from his hand.

How is it possible to feel totally numb except for a bizarre attraction to a man you don't even trust?

He produces a small green bottle out of his shirt pocket, uncaps it, pours out two little white pills, and hands her a glass of water from the bedside table.

Should I be afraid to take these, afraid of him?

"Here, swallow, and then, get ready for bed. Unless they've lost potency, they'll work fast. Henry Ravenel, Daddy's doctor, prescribed them for Honey when Daddy died, and it was the only way she made it through." He pulls back the bed covers. "I'm going to hang out in your mama's room tonight. Tomorrow morning's Victoria's memorial service, so I'll have to leave for a bit, but I'll come right back."

Too muddled to sort through her qualms about him, Callahan swallows the pills.

If I'm about to be poisoned, I'm not even sure I care.

Her eyelids grow heavy before she even gets her teeth brushed. She recaps the toothpaste, sleepwalks to her bed, and at once falls into a drugged sleep. She's only vaguely aware of Pepper straightening her covers or standing over her during the night. He doesn't use the excuse of her grief to suggest she might need company in her bed but sleeps alone in Lila's bedroom.

The next morning, though, smiling and amiable, he's quick to point out his exercised virtue. "This is the second time I've slept under the same roof with you, Callie Banks, and still you remain unmolested. It is not in my nature to exercise this much self control." He's sitting on the edge of her bed, having already proffered a wake-up cup of hot tea with cream. "I tried to be quiet, climbed the ladder up to roof to read yesterday's *Wall Street Journal*, and sat on that little open deck your mama added, but an egret flew over and pooped all over it. Which put an unappetizing end to my morning edification." He's already dressed for the memorial service in a blue-and-white seersucker suit, bright yellow button-down collar shirt, and hunter green tie with embroidered red alligators.

Disoriented, both from the sleeping pills and the cacophony of his colors, Callahan sits up and shakes her head in a cobweb-clearing maneuver that works not at all. "What *time* is it? Sorry about your paper."

"Nine o'clock."

"Nine o'clock?" She takes the red pottery cup from him. "No kidding? It's already nine o'clock? I've never taken a sleeping pill before. It feels like somebody stuffed my head with rotten sea weed."

"Well, at least you slept. I actually *don't* sleep well alone in strange houses."

Is it the alone or the strange house he's complaining about?

She can't remember seeing him in a coat and tie before though surely she must have at the funerals. He gives the impression of a grown-up choirboy, scrubbed and forced into unwelcome garb, his hair, in need of a trim, curling above his collar in a way that makes him look deceptively innocent.

Nothing he has on matches anything else, but somehow he carries it off.

He sticks his finger into the knot of his tie, tugs it loose, and unbuttons the top button of his shirt.

"Except for your head full of rotten seaweed, aren't you better than last night?"

Callahan gives him a weak smile. "Maybe." She takes a sip and holds the hot liquid in the front of her mouth, blowing across it till it's cool enough to swallow.

"Any chance you'd want to reward Dr. Pepper for his forbearance before he has to leave you?"

Pepper's mood's so light it should be contagious, but she can muster no enthusiasm for banter. Thankfully, the hot tea is clearing her head a bit. "Not this morning, Sir Galahad, though I am truly grateful for all you've done." She means this, even as she wonders why he's appointed himself her caretaker. "I hope Vicky's funeral won't be too hard on you."

It really is strange he's not a little more subdued.

She waits till it's ten o'clock and he's headed for the steps to leave before she calls out to him. "Pepper, please don't come back. I'm used to coping on my own. I'll do what I always do when my world goes topsy-turvy. I'll take a big towel, a book and a bottle of water up to north beach away from the noise of the carpenters. The ocean and sand will do the rest. I'll be fine. It's the best place in the world to regain perspective." She gives him the cheeriest smile she can muster. "Thank you for helping me make it through last night. I'll be alright now."

He doesn't leave, just stands there looking dubious. It's at least eighty degrees outside already, the atmosphere heavy and humid. "I'm just not sure you should be alone all day." He's wearing penny loafers and no socks with the seersucker suit. His face glistens with perspiration. "But I'll give some thought to what you say you want. Vi says I think I know what's best for everybody else, but I don't always." He cocks his head and scratches his ear. "No, I can tell already, I'm going to need to come back by and check on you later. Least, it'll make me feel better."

Twenty minutes after he's gone, Callahan's face down on the warm sand at north beach, heat radiating through her beach towel into the bare skin of her solar plexus, good tonic. The tide's going out, and, as usual, there's the slight cooling of the ocean breeze. "This feels so good." She surprises herself by saying it out loud.

Regardless of what's going on in my life, my worst disappointments shrink into proportion on this beach. I'm healthy. I'm fine. Lila would be angry at me for letting myself get so upset. She's probably already in negotiations with St. Peter about her next incarnation and lobbying him to get her back to Timicau Island as fast as possible.

Callahan smiles inwardly at the image.

Nothing major has really changed, just my understanding of how I got here.

She promises herself she'll finish reading the letters and sort out their meaning, but only later when her psyche gives her the go-ahead.

I may even have some living relatives I can track down.

Exhaling a long slow breath, she closes her eyes and relaxes, deep and then deeper into the healing rhythm of surf swishing sand.

So if she isn't asleep, she's close to it when Harry Applegate, his cheeks brilliant pink under a turquoise baseball hat, skids to a stop spewing sand across her back. His sides are heaving from what appears to be a wide open run down the beach, his round pink belly bulging over the top of yellow tank shorts, "Callahan, boy, oh boy, oh boy, am I ever glad to see you. You're the very best person I needed to find."

She sits up groggily, swiping sand off of her black bikini and her beach towel. "Well, if it isn't Dr. Applegate. What's up, Harry?"

"We've got some rescuing to do." He points up the beach in the direction of Ruby's shack.

Where he shouldn't be alone.

"There's a school of jellyfish stranded up there, and they're all going to die if we don't get them back in the water quick."

She stands to squint a hundred yards up the shore where large dark blobs dot the surface from the wrack line down to the lapping water. "Oh, brother, Harry, it's just about impossible to rescue a stranded jellyfish."

His face falls.

"But," she says, "we can still go up and have a look. C'mon." Callahan identifies the species before they reach them. "They're moon jellyfish," she tells the worried little boy, "the most common ones to wash up here on our beaches. We get a good many between April and November. And there were a lot in this smack. A smack is the collective term for jellyfish like a herd of cattle, a smack of jellyfish." She points to the twenty or thirty stranded bodies and the short tentacles beneath each gelatinous body. "You know not to touch them, don't you? They can still sting."

"Yeah, I know that." His voice is raspy. Standing about a foot from her and less than a foot from the nearest jellyfish, he strikes a bit of a pompous pose. "But I'm not really afraid of jellyfish." He pulls the hat bill low over his eyes, places both hands on the bulges of his chubby waist, fists balled tightly. "Now, if this was a man-of-war, a Portuguese man-of-war, *that* would worry me." A seagull screams overhead, and, startled, Harry jumps.

Rough, tough cream puff.

Callahan gets such a kick out of this child. "Moon jellyfish can get pretty big, Harry, up to eighteen inches across, and their stings really do hurt. Technically, a Portuguese man-of-war isn't even a jellyfish." She squats and points at the umbrella-shaped, translucent, gelatinous blob nearest her foot. "See those four purple horseshoe-shaped things inside?

That's its reproductive system. And those four frilly oral arms hanging underneath its body surround the mouth and push food towards it. That's also where the developing larvae, their babies, hang out."

"Good," he says in a business-like tone. "Good information."

Realizing he's way too worried about their plight to absorb much of what she's telling him about the jellyfish, she stands back up,

"Look!" His face brightens. "Look there, Callahan." He points at one jellyfish closer to the lapping waves and runs to it. "This one's still alive for sure. Its insides are moving. It'd be real easy to get some sticks and just slide him back in the ocean."

She joins him there in the shallow water, to have a look. "There *are still* pulsations in this one." Callahan's always loved being able to see the inner workings of a live creature like this.

Wish I could understand my own workings as easily.

She sighs, searching for a way to tell Harry that the disappointment is worse when you try and fail in a rescue attempt than if you learn to accept the inevitable. "It's no good, Harry. I've done it a hundred times, and it never works. They're too fragile. Don't get too near those tentacles." He's bent over and extended an exploratory index finger to the top of the live one's bulging body.

"Problem is, they're ninety-five percent water." She continues watching him warily, warm surf lapping over her toes and ankles "Muscle fibers thread through the fluid inside to hold them together, and they collapse if they're bruised. About the only way to move one is in a bucket of water, but these guys are too far-gone to make it worth trying."

"Well, double darn and screw it." Harry's clearly crestfallen. "I just don't like not doing anything to try to help."

Stifling a smile, Callahan pats his freckled shoulder. "I don't either, but it's truly kinder. I've never gotten even one that's been dragged along the beach on an outgoing tide to survive. Did you know they don't have brains?" Something catches her peripheral vision, a movement back behind the dunes to her left. She turns her head but sees nothing.

"If they don't have brains, does that mean they can't feel pain?"

"Well, that's my take on it." Her heart's begun pounding, her instinctual protective impulses triggered.

Why?

"It always makes me feel a little better to think about it that way. I don't think they suffer much."

"But how can jellyfishes do stuff without brains?"

By piquing his interest, she realizes, she's been able to distract him from his concern. She sees the movement again out of the corner of her eye. Her eyes sweep the dunes.

Looking for what?

"Whatcha doing, Callahan?" This time, Harry turns to follow her gaze, so they both spot the golf cart headed towards them on the dunes at the same time.

"I thought I saw something back there a minute ago. I guess it was just that cart. What was your question, Harry? Oh, I know, how can they work without a brain?" She keeps an eye on the approaching vehicle. "Jellyfish are invertebrates, you know, like sea anemones. Not only do they have no brain, they have no heart, eyes, ears or even bones. They just drift around in big groups and sting and eat and reproduce. They're even hard to keep in a tank as pets. If the currents aren't perfectly balanced, they'll hang up over a pump or bump the side of the aquarium, and that'll kill them. They are just magnificently designed to live in the ocean, and when they get out of it, they're pretty well doomed."

"Yoo hoo, Callahan." Callahan recognizes Francie's gold golf cart and shrill voice before she's pulled to a stop on the top of the dune. She waves extravagantly, her blonde hair tied back with a brilliant red scarf. "Could you come up here a minute, sweetie? I have something very important to ask you."

The "something important" turns out to be that Francie's having a luncheon at her house tomorrow at noon. "We're going to console poor Irene and give Honey a proper send-off to school. Now that we're becoming a little community here on Timicau, we need to act like it." This party, Francie puzzlingly insists, will not be complete without Callahan, who can think of no believable excuse on the spur of the moment to avoid going.

So reluctantly Callahan accepts, and Francie, smiling gaily, backs the golf cart up and turns it around. "See you tomorrow, then." A flutter of a pink-nailed hand as she drives off towards her own house.

The dune upon which Callahan stands is the first in a series that roll back towards higher ground on the island. Tiny quartz crystals captured there in the sand catch the mid-day sun and glisten like diamonds. The dune itself, sparkling white and ironed smooth by high spring tides, is pristine, disturbed only by her own footprints, and to the left the golf cart tracks. Callahan turns back towards the ocean where Harry's now flipped a jellyfish over with a large piece of driftwood.

He'll get himself stung yet.

When she steps down from the dune to walk back to him, a disturbed area in the sand low and to her left catches her eye. It's a footprint, one in a series of deep, fresh footprints that lead from the damp sand behind the dune at a crooked angle through the sea oats back towards the center of the island.

These are hardly her own footsteps and certainly not Francie's. Callahan moves closer for a look, and when she squats, recognition makes her shiver even in the noonday heat.

The distinctive hobnail boots again. Juby? Whoever was here, ran away, probably when Francie drove out on the dune in her cart.

She takes some time to study what the footsteps have to tell her. Whoever's wearing the boots weighs over a hundred and fifty pounds, is under six feet tall, and was kneeling behind the dune only minutes ago.

Clearly, hiding to watch Harry and me down on the beach with the jellyfish.

Chapter Twenty

Today, Francie's a cowgirl. Greeting Honey and Callahan as they pull up in their golf carts, she stands in front of the double front doors of her gleaming white wanna-be plantation house, wearing a brown jersey cowgirl skirt with a fringed bottom and leather Concho accents. "Hi, y'all." She turns in an admire-me circle, arms overhead, hands shimmying.

A little outfit like that probably came off a designer rack on the top floor of Saks with a four-figure price tag. Not to mention the matching fringed vest and aqua silk blouse, clingy and western cut with tiny pearl buttons.

Waving excitedly, Francie flashes a large turquoise and silver ring on her right thumb—her unusually large right thumb, Callahan notices. The piece de re'sistance, though, is bright red cowboy boots. Callahan estimates that Francie wears at least a size nine shoe so you can't miss those boots. She's tall, really, deceptively tall, five-eight or nine.

Maybe it's because she's so curvaceous that you don't notice her height.

"Whadya think? Bet Garth would lick his delicious ole' whiskery chops if he saw me today." Francie points to her blonde hair which has been teased into a beehive that adds several more inches of hair height. "The higher the hair, the closer to heaven I always say." Her smile is radiant as she opens her arms to Honey, who's gotten out of her golf cart to walk up the steps.

A bit stiff-armed and wary, that sisterly hug. Honey and I are obviously under-dressed. This is a real luncheon.

Like Honey, Callahan has on sandals, a thin cotton shirt and light cotton pants. Irene pulls in behind Callahan's cart just then, and the cowgirl disentangles from her sister to rush to her newest guest. "Oh, Irene," she says, dripping Southern drawl on the petite little woman in a beige linen pantsuit. "I am sooo flattered you'd pull yourself away from Robbie and come today. Like I told Callahan yesterday, we're about to be neighbors on this little island, so it's only right that we support you when you're going through such a trial." Francie whirls in a circle towards Callahan, her skirt flying out like a square dancer's. "You *are* going to stay here for good and become one of us now, aren't you, Callahan?"

Caught off guard, Callahan's confused by Francie's uncharacteristic interest in her. "I don't know, but I rather doubt it. I'll probably just be here for a few more weeks."

Francie takes Irene by the hand and leads her across the paved driveway to Callahan in her golf cart. "If my amorous brother has anything to say about it, you'll stay. I'm sure you all have noticed"–she looks brightly at the two other women–"that he's made a rather dramatic recovery from Vicky's death. All I hear these days is Pepper worrying about poor little ole Callahan. It's enough to give you a sick headache. Well, now..." Twirling one of the Conchos that hang from a leather strap on her skirt, Francie turns towards her house. "These boots may be pretty, but they are hot as Hades to wear. I did so want to seat us in my garden or maybe the pergola, but I told Vi–she's helping me today, Vi is–we'd best err on the side of comfort, so we're eating in the dining room. I think my cats are going to be excited to meet all of you. I have Persians, you know, seven of them. I gave them the Italian names for the seven dwarfs because I couldn't find any Persians to help me with

Persian dwarf names. Each kitten, when I got her, I insisted had to be the runt of the litter. So there's Felicia and Stupida and Medica and Timida and...you don't need to know them all, but the way Grumpy came out is my favorite. She's called Scorbutica, though I've shortened it just to Butica." Francie giggles. "I hope they'll come out and social-ize. Callahan will tell you cats are quite territorial, so it's taken them a while to adjust to living in a new house."

When Callahan gets a gander at the entry hall and the view from there into the living room, her worst expectations are confirmed. Everything about the house is a testimonial to garish taste and too much money. The massive, modern, crystal chandelier that hangs two stories in the entry hall is bright enough to blind you when it's lit, as it is today, and Francie's taste for hideous colors is jarring. Turquoise runs rampant. The turquoise silk fabric on the living room sofa is as bright as Harry Applegate's baseball hat, and beige draperies in that room are paired with turquoise sheers that filter turquoise-tinted light into the room.

Rather like living in an aquarium.

A matching pair of wingback chairs in the living room is uphol-stered in a modern yellow, black and orange diamond print on a tur-quoise background. The carpet, like nothing else in the room, is stark white.

It's a lot to take in all at once as Francie, radiating excitement, tours them through the house, cross-examining one, then another of them, on so many subjects that Callahan's head begins to spin. "And here's where we're lunching." Francie sweeps ahead into the dining room with its mus-tard yellow walls and mud brown accents—chair seats, crown molding and tablecloth. "Here's my little sunshine room. I didn't even use a decorator, I was so determined to put my *own* mark on this house." She pauses to catch her breath. "Tell me now, Irene, how is our dear Robbie doing?"

Irene manages to get herself seated in a straight-backed brown chair, a mustard yellow salad plate on a brown tablecloth before her.

"You know, I felt so guilty leaving him to come here today, but his doctor encouraged me to take a few hours off. And, Robbie's definitely better. They've kept him in a drug-induced coma until the swelling in his head subsides. They're decreasing some of his sedation today, and we're hoping he'll gradually come back to consciousness. The neurologist says the next twenty-four hours are critical, but he's cautiously optimistic."

"Wonderful news!" Francie claps her hands in childlike pleasure. "I shall come sit with you all day tomorrow. You should not have to endure the suspense by yourself." She sweeps an arm skyward, the fringe along the full length of her aqua shirtsleeves waving gaily.

This is quite the fringy-est outfit I've ever seen.

Callahan has to bite her lip to keep from laughing. The centerpiece, though not fringy, is also hard to ignore. It's an expanse of candles and jeweled fake fruit in tones of–no surprises here–mustard and brown.

You'd have to really shop hard to find brown plums and mustard-colored grapes.

The table is over-long for the proportions of the room. Callahan counts the fourteen chairs silently. The gaudy faux fruit runs all the way down the center of the table to where the four of them sit, clustered at the table's end, near a swinging door into the kitchen.

Their salad plates hold tossed salads garnished with nut-covered goat cheese balls, so they begin to eat at once. Vi, in her efficient and understated manner, slips in and out to distribute mimosas, remove dishes, and replace them with the next course. When Callahan smiles and tells Vi hi, Vi answers with a knowing wink.

She really is a candidate for sainthood.

Over cold cucumber soup, Francie announces, "I guess you've all gotten the update about JP." Irene nods yes, but Honey and Callahan say they have not. "Well, it looks like he probably had an accident on his wind surfer, hit his head or something and drowned. That's a relief, isn't it, that he wasn't murdered? Maybe we've all just gotten a little too paranoid for our own good out here. I can't wait to tell that to those annoying reporters so they'll leave me alone."

She's not exactly acting the grieving lover, but then why would I expect her to be?

"How'd you find that out, Francie?" It's Honey asking the question, as she skims the soupspoon away from herself before sipping it.

Shoveling her soup directly from bowl towards mouth, Francie says, "Cole called me. Says they'd found water in JP's lungs. You know they didn't find any water in Vicky's."

"Cole called me as well." It's Irene, speaking pleasantly, but firmly, as she finishes her soup. "I understood what he had to say a little differently. He said they're still reserving judgment because, while there was some water in JP's lungs, there wasn't as much there or in his stomach as they'd expect to find in someone who drowned." Irene hands Vi her empty soup bowl with a smile and takes her marinated chicken breast. "And they didn't find the kinds of abrasions or cuts they'd expect if JP had knocked himself out on the boom or fallen."

The cowgirl, Callahan notices, has begun drumming blood red fingernails on the brown tablecloth. "Well, still, I feel better it was a probable drowning. I hated the thought of anyone doing something to make JP suffer." Francie examines the long curved nails of her right hand, frowns, then dips her napkin in her water glass and scrubs something off her index finger. She shakes her head melodramatically, her voice going syrupy. "I will miss JP. He *was* the very best hung man I've ever seen."

The luncheon guests go strangely quiet at this revelation.

What do you say after something that tasteless?

They finally do make it to dessert, Vi's thick, rich lemon squares, and Callahan decides to take a stab at gaining the floor. "Honey, Francie said this was also a send-off for you, that you're leaving for Salem soon. Isn't it kind of early to be going back to college?"

"It is, Callahan." Honey sets her mimosa glass back on the table. "But I'm going to the second term of summer school. I leave Sunday. Pepper says he'd feel better if I'm off the island until they sort out what's going on. I decided it was a good idea to take just Spanish this session and get my language requirement out of the way. I've never been any good at foreign languages."

"Well, I think it's pure hogwash." Francie slams her water glass down. "It's enough to make me peevish. Pepper's so worried about Honey that he's moving her off the island, but he doesn't give enough of a rat's ass about me to take notice that I'm here all alone, too."

It is a bit curious since he's rigged a lock for me and tried to get me to stay at Twelve Oaks.

"There's nothing going on here but an unfortunate convergence of circumstances." Francie does, indeed, sound very peevish. "I've just asked Mother to my new house." She lowers her voice in an aside to Irene. "Mother's not been welcome at Twelve Oaks since the divorce, you see, and I realized the other day that since I now have my own house, there's no reason she can't visit me here anytime she wants to." Francie's eyelids flutter. "Mother will just be crushed when she hears you've left, Honey, and she won't get to see you." She throws both hands in the air, fringe swaying. "What is the point of living on this beautiful island if you don't stay here long enough to..."

Callahan again is taken by Francie's large right thumb.

What did Lila say about big thumbs when she was teaching me palm reading? Big thumbs are significant.

Francie drones on through the rest of dessert, making more proclamations and assailing them with one inane question after another. "Okay everybody, listen up. I'm doing a survey of your favorite foods. I already know that Honey's is butterscotch ice cream, and Irene's is risotto. But I haven't asked Callahan. What about you, Callahan?"

Feeling a bit foolish, Callahan confesses that a PB & J is probably about as good as it gets for her. Finally, mercifully, as if on cue, each guest seems to have had enough and presents an excuse to leave. Honey has packing to do. Callahan has "paper work." Only an antsy Irene, who must return to her husband's sickbed, has a reason to leave that's probably valid.

"The cats!" Francie moans as she walks them to the door. "The cats haven't even come downstairs. You really will have to come back again soon and meet Butica. She's a calico, and so beautiful."

Callahan slumps in relief when she drives her golf cart around the turn, and Francie's house disappears from view. She's had the unnerving impression throughout the whole meal that something was going on which she was completely missing, but maybe Honey wasn't. Honey had waited in the driveway–Callahan's sure it was purposeful–till Irene and Francie were saying their goodbyes before placing a hand on Callahan's arm to draw her close. Her brown eyes were soft with concern, her voice quiet and conspiratorial. "Callahan, much as I love my brother, I really care about you, too. Be careful with Pepper. He's broken a lot of hearts, and I really don't want yours to be the next one."

So Honey, ten years my junior, has turned into my protector, and Francie has undergone a personality implant?

Callahan's losing her natural equilibrium.

Today's Francie isn't even distantly related to the one I know. She's never cared about Honey before or about sharing their mother with her. Clearly, Irene Pasquini is not a woman the old Francie would have even wanted to associate with. Nor would Francie care about Robbie or our favorite foods or any of those other frivolous topics which seemed to completely absorb her today. As for Francie's alleged interest in community building, I've lost enough red scarves, doll clothes, rare seashells, and boyfriends to run, not walk, from any friendship circle that includes Francis Dade.

Another thing. Why is Francie making such a big deal about Pepper being interested in me? Which he obviously isn't because, though he said he'd be back in touch with me after Victoria's funeral, I haven't heard a word from him since he left yesterday morning. True, I discouraged him from coming back, but he made such a point of saying he was coming that I expected him, and—admit it to yourself, Callahan—was disappointed when he didn't. The whole lot of them just perplex me to the point of exasperation.

Callahan pulls into her own driveway, half expecting Pepper to be there waiting, but he isn't. She feels a recurrence of the vague unease she's felt ever since he left yesterday. When she spots Wallace's lock still tightly clamped to her door where she left it, she's flooded with gratitude. Her house, at least, is secure.

Still, she has the unnerving impression that she may be like a lab frog dumbly languishing in a pot of cool water over a low flame, while someone—she doesn't know who—patiently waits for the water to heat up and begin to boil.

Chapter Twenty-One

Because Callahan remembered to snap Wallace's lock closed before leaving for Francie's, all she has to do now is check the cables on the side of the house to be sure the house is secure and dial in her birth date.

There's something a little reassuring about this.

She snaps the lock open, rolls back the door and climbs the stairs, still unable to shed a feeling of foreboding. Her mood lifts, though, when she reaches the top deck and spots two wood storks, lounging in the live oak beyond the screen.

You almost never get this close to them. They're usually way out in the impoundment.

Almost as big as great egrets, which can be five feet tall, wood storks, in her experience, are temperamentally very different. Instead of flying away in squawking protest, egret-like, the wood stork in the tree closest to her momentarily stops preening his wings, turns a bald, narrow head to stare imperiously down a startlingly large beak at her, and resumes preening his flight feathers.

Curious, not frightened.

He ignores her completely as she walks closer, within three feet of the oak, on her way to her kitchen door. The anxieties of the day lighten a bit.

It's hard to be miserable when there are wood storks to spy on.

Indulging herself in the rare opportunity, she soon settles in a front porch rocker and spends the next two hours bird watching.

I doubt if I'll have many more opportunities like this.

It's fascinating how distinctively different the markings on the two birds are. The one highest in the oak is the younger. His feathers are still mostly gray, in route to becoming white like the other bird's, though a distinctive black trim the length of an extended wing is clearly visible. The wind kicks up a bit. White downy feathers on his pate—they will disappear at maturity—catch the gusts and stand out at awkward angles, making the bird appear more cartoon character than real.

The temperature's cooler than the sweltering of this morning, a front moving towards them from the west. Back on the mainland, a flash of lightning scribbles light across the sky. Gathering clouds filter the sun in splashes of light and intensity, heightening colors around the pond in that way light before a storm can do. The duckweed that frosted the entire pond's surface this morning is now blown into compact islands of brilliant green, the water the peaty brown of an old Victorian sofa. Yellow sunlight through the banks of gathering clouds tints the few bits of duckweed left free-floating, a striking chartreuse. The far bank of the pond is lined with vibrant, purple flowers, the color of a favorite sweater Callahan once owned. Surprisingly, the flowers are unfamiliar to her though she notes the depth and vibrancy of their color so she can look them up later. Out beyond the porch, all is a kaleidoscope of shadow and hue, an ever-changing tableau, watercolor-washed before her eyes. How desperately—Callahan swallows a lump that rises in her throat—she wishes she did not have to give it up.

Something moves between the overhanging cattails on the far side of the pond. Callahan stiffens, then smiles.

Albert.

He, too, is a creature of the shadows today. Only his head, the gnarled gray of an ancient rampart, floats innocuously on the water's surface till he begins swimming lazily across the pond towards her. The distinctive movement of his powerful tail, almost imperceptible below the water's surface, shapes the duckweed into loopy green "S"s. Seconds later, the wind picks up and, in a matter of minutes, scatters the duckweed's geometry into an intricate paisley covering the entire face of the pond.

Dante.

Callahan's reminded of her favorite Dante quote: "Nature is the art of God." How artfully and easily the gator has splatter-painted the water. Leaning back in the rocker, she feels tension drain from her.

I'm so blessed to have this world beyond my porch to intrigue and nurture me. But for how much longer?

As Albert nears her side of the pond, she stands to creep close to the edge for a better look. She's so focused on the gator that she kicks over her own purse, spilling everything in it on the floor beside the rocker. When she returns its contents, the illuminated message on her cell phone catches her eye, informing her that she has fifteen unanswered messages.

It never occurs to me to check the darn thing for messages when I'm on the island. Fifteen? Now, that's some kind of a world record for a lazy Charleston week in the middle of the summer.

Curious, she scrolls through the numbers. The first seven are actually predictable, from friends and colleagues in Asheville over the past few days. The last eight, all in the past twenty-four hours, are all from the same Charleston number.

Pepper.

She enters her code and listens to his messages. The gist of them all is the same: something very important came up with Cole, and he had to stay on the mainland last night. Why didn't she leave her cell phone on? Was she alright? Would she please call him? Why was she not answering her cell phone? He wanted her to reconsider coming to stay at Twelve Oaks with them till this thing sorted itself out. Why didn't she answer the goddamn cell phone? Callahan senses more anger and urgency in each successive message.

"It is really important," he says, "that you keep your door locked. You do have your door locked, don't you?"

I did this morning, but I'm not sure I locked it behind me when I came home from Francie's. I probably ought to check. Boy, talk about ambivalent feelings. If I'm honest with myself, I guess I'm glad he was trying to reach me, but, he's probably just gotten tied up with another woman on the mainland and is making excuses. His own sister just got through warning me about him today. It's pointless to expect anything but heartache from a man like Pepper Dade. Still, he does sound genuinely concerned. How many times did he call? Eight? Well of one thing, I am very sure. I will not stay at Twelve Oaks.

A blue heron, squawking indignantly, flies up from below the deck and away across the impoundment. Albert is now nowhere to be seen.

Either he just lost an early dinner or he's crawled out onto the bank under the deck and spooked the bird.

Albert's being down there is no deterrent to Callahan's checking her lock. It's hard to believe, she supposes, her lack of fear of the old gator, but the few times that he's ever come up on the bank near her house, he's always slipped quietly back into the water when she appeared.

I find him more predictable than Pepper. All Pepper's demands just scramble my brain. Sometimes, I wish my life were as simple as those jellyfish's. It frustrating to have no clarity about your own feelings, not even be sure how to protect yourself. And from whom?

Seeking reassurance, Callahan reminds herself that her ability to sense a threat, infallible since childhood, has always served her well, and this is no time to ignore it.

So I will go downstairs and check the padlock.

When she gets to the bottom of the stairs, there's no sign of Albert, but it's a good thing she came down because she hadn't relocked the padlock. She does it now. By the time she walks back to the upper deck, she's concluded that she probably owes Pepper a call, so she pushes his last number and lets her phone dial him.

"Callahan!" His voice holds palpable relief. "Thank God. I was in Charleston last night and all day today. I just got back to Twelve Oaks and was about to come over there and storm the Bastille till Honey reported that she'd seen you at Francie's. Don't you ever check your cell phone?"

"Not much."

"Well, how am I supposed to reach you when I need to?"

Callahan's throat tightens. "Is there some reason I'm not aware of that you *should* be able to reach me whenever you want to?"

Big sigh on the far end. "You're probably right, but Cole's developed some pretty worrisome theories. I can't discuss them yet, but you have no idea how concerned I've been about you."

Why me?

"Won't you let me come get you right now? We'll have dinner, and you can stay here till Cole's had a little more time to sort this through. Besides, I have some actual business information you need to have."

Callahan's shoulders sag.

I don't appreciate all this pressure to do what he wants when he wants me to do it. What kind of business, anyway?

The last thing she wants is to pass one more complex and confusing minute in the presence of a Dade today. She has her own life to reclaim. "Pepper, no. Thank you, but no. I've got a house full of things to go through here. Surely, whatever you have to tell me can wait."

"Callahan. It can't." His voice lowers with authority.

And fear?

"I simply will not take no for an answer. Either you come here, or I'm coming there."

I could just lock him out, but he'd probably get Wallace to let him in.

At that moment, the deck beneath her feet begins to vibrate with a ferocious sound, something akin to a cross between a boat motor and a lion's roar.

Albert!

Callahan can't see him, but she can picture what he's doing and why. Feet on the shore, head thrown back, body floating behind him so the water can carry the sound across the impoundment, the biggest bull alligator on the island is calling for a mate below her house. The sound is deafening coming off of the water at such close range.

"What in the hell is that?"

"It's Albert. He's courting."

Or is he cautioning me?

"Well, can you get him to quiet down long enough for us to settle this? I can't hear a word you're saying."

"I wasn't talking, actually. Give me a minute, and I'll go inside." Callahan makes a snap decision as she walks from porch to house that if she has to see Pepper, she'll take herself to Twelve Oaks and leave when she's ready to.

"Okay," she reluctantly tells Pepper. "I'll come as soon as possible." Albert begins another round of come-hither roars. "It's four right now. I'll be there by five, and you do *not* need to come get me."

Somewhere, across the impoundment, Callahan hears a female gator roar her response to Albert even though the living room doors are all tightly closed.

Chapter Twenty-Two

Just as Callahan raises her hand to ring the bell, Honey throws open the massive front door at Twelve Oaks and rushes out carrying a monogrammed paisley duffle. "Callahan! I'm so glad you've come. At least I can tell you goodbye." Honey's breathless. "Pepper insists I leave early for school. He doesn't want me on the island another night." She bestows a one-armed hug on Callahan. "Wallace and Vi are waiting round back for me, so I've gotta run." Her lovely eyes soften in a look of concern. "Pepper's waiting for you in his office. His office door is on the far side of the library."

It seems like it's been months, not days, since Callahan last stood at this library door with Cole and went weak-kneed with memories of John.

If they made a perfume called "Old Books," I'd spray myself.

She inhales deeply. A single lamp on the library table to her left throws a circle of light across the cream carpet. Muted classical music, *Mozart,* and a soft yellow glow issue from Pepper's half-open office door on the far side of the room.

It all appears so elegant and normal, but something's very wrong here, or Pepper wouldn't be sending Honey away.

Her pulse quickens when she steps into the library. She has a curious self-protective impulse to cower.

I'm a small red fox in a deep wood.

"Callahan?" Pepper appears at his office door, backlit by buttery light "Come in here. I want to get my arms around you and make sure you're still in one piece."

The walk across the library is probably twenty feet, but it might as well be a mile through a swamp, the way her feet resist movement. "Pepper, this is all a bit unnerving. Why are you sending Honey off-island tonight, and what business is so important that I had to drop everything and come over here?"

He crosses the distance between them and draws her into a bear hug. "I don't blame you for being confused. I am, too." He kisses the top of her ear. "I sent Honey off for the same reason I'm asking you to stay at Twelve Oaks tonight. If Cole's theory is right, you both could be in danger. As for the business, let's go in my office, and we'll talk about that in there."

She lets him hold her longer than a moment, grateful for his utter solidity, but is still tense and bewildered. "What about Francie? Are you sending her away, too?"

He sighs, drops his arms heavily, and nods. "I'm looking for her, but so far I haven't been able to track her down. She may be in Charleston with Ruby. I left a message on her cell." He takes Callahan's hand and leads her to his office. "Let's talk about what I can talk about, your business." He closes the door behind them.

"So does that mean we're the only people left on the island tonight? Are Vi and Wallace coming back?"

Pepper frowns. "Aren't you the little question box?" He motions her to the worn leather sofa. "I'm sorry to say, I'm not answer man tonight. I can't find Francie, and I have no clue when Wallace and Vi will come back, if they do. And, I can't–I won't–tell you what Cole's learned that gave me a hellacious, sleepless night last night. Or who I'm trying to protect you from. It's too grim a prospect to share unless I'm damn sure he's right."

Something under the corner table in the room thumps, and Callahan jerks uneasily.

A crinkle of amusement creases Pepper's eyes. "Ah, Nadine. Come here, girl." He pats his leg. "Miss Banks is feeling a bit skittish, I think. Maybe you can reassure her."

Well he's right about that. I really don't like being alone in this house with him one bit.

Though she's feeling both pissy and patronized, Callahan's mouth involuntarily draws into a grin when the bony frame of the hound dog unfolds from a beanbag bed under the table and ambles her way. "Well, hi there, girl." She rubs the velvety ears, scratches the sweet spot at the top of Nadine's tail, and collects slathered dog kisses from hand to elbow.

Standing quietly above them, arms folded across his chest, Pepper's scowl softens. "Well, I think I'll declare this the best moment of my day though there has been no real competition. Nadine and I turn into oysters when we're around you, Callahan, both of us getting too attached."

Even though Callahan's delighted to see the dog, she still feels miserably uneasy with her master.

The mood of his office, with its classical music, familiar smells of cherry pipe tobacco, old leather and spent ashes in the small fireplace, is seductive. She's aware of the rich greens and browns of three duck prints, the polished brass of antique andirons, and the lit lamp on the desk, a one-of-a-kind made from a large brass bullet casing circa some long ago war. She's determined to keep the mood light. "I really think this is my favorite room at Twelve Oaks, Pepper. I've always loved it."

He sends her a crooked grin. "Best I can tell, Callahan, you have a long list of things you love. Let's see, you love Harry Applegate and Tootsie and Albert the Gator and those big cats on the back of the island and turtles and snakes and all birds of all species. Nadine and I were hoping that, with extra good behavior, we might eventually work our way onto your list."

"Well, Nadine's already there." She gives him a teasingly deprecating look. "And it's not that I'm not a discriminating person. It's just that there's an awful lot to appreciate out here. It's a rare place, and if you'd stop giving me so many orders, you'd probably improve your odds of making it, too." She smiles down at the dog's woeful face and is rewarded with floor thumps from an enthusiastic tail.

"Name one thing." He runs a hand over his curly hair. "One thing besides Francie, whom nobody could love, you *don't* like. And,"–his teeth flash white–"I'm exempt today because you're put out with me."

His humor really is seductive. The small red fox emerges from under a rock.

"Well, let's see. I don't like NASCAR races on TV, though I seldom watch TV, but it puzzles me how anyone can sit there hour after hour watching cars zoom around in a circle." Nadine repositions her back towards Pepper for more scratching. "And I don't like praline buttermilk pretzels. Somebody gave Lila some last Christmas, and they were ghastly. Oh, and, of course, I don't like bad wine." She feels herself warming to the exercise. "Or jellyfish stranded on beaches or men who think they have a right to control my life without even answering my questions. How's that for a start?"

"It's pretty good except for the way you slipped me in there at the end. Still, I do like a woman who knows her mind." He nods his head, then cocks it sideways. "You need to develop a more open mind about me, Callahan. Is there no room in your world for a sweet-tempered old bachelor?"

He's unrelenting.

"Sweet tempered? Well, maybe, but, Pepper, your girl friend died mysteriously only last week. How could I possibly give you an honest answer to a question like that? Truthfully, I hardly know you, except for what a big tease you were when I was little. Which, as I think back on it, would make me call Cole the sweet-tempered one." She smiles genially.

Pepper's eyes twinkle. "But, darlin, I've seen and acknowledged the error of my ways. A man needs to have reason for hope." Another engaging smile, and he walks to his desk, opens a drawer, and takes out a leather-bound ledger book. He carries it back to the sofa and sits down beside her. The old sofa cushions give under his weight and slide her uncomfortably close to him. His breath smells like peppermint.

Worn gold lettering on the front of the fat ledger book catches Callahan's eye. "Lila Boone Financial Records."

"First order of business," he's saying. "Ever wonder why your last name is Banks when your mama's was Boone?"

"Until Tuesday, I thought I knew. Lila always said that my father insisted I take his name when they married, but she would change her name for no man." She turns to Pepper's too-close face. "Not true, right?"

"Right." He taps his index finger on the tip of her nose, a gesture she finds annoying. "You are Callahan Banks because when my daddy finalized the financial settlement for your support from the Banks family, they insisted you take their name as part of the deal. A strange request, given the circumstances, but the amount of money they were giving was substantial enough that Daddy talked Lila into agreeing."

"Why are you telling me this now, Pepper?"

"Well, I assumed you'd learn it all from Lila's accountant. Then, Honey told me that at Francie's today you said you might only be here another week or two, just long enough to clean up the house and get it ready to rent or sell. I gave his office a call and found out he's on vacation, so I decided it was important you find out in a timely way what I've known since Daddy died, and I took over Lila's books."

A streak of lightning flashes outside the office window, followed in five seconds by a boom of thunder.

About a mile away, Callahan calculates, *since Harry reminded me that sound travels a mile in five seconds.*

That storm has taken all day getting here, but it's very close now.

"You see," Pepper's saying, "I helped your mama with her investments after Daddy died. Here." He sets the book in her lap. "This really is yours to keep, has been all along." He opens the book to the last ledger page where rows of neat blue ink figures are entered in even columns, month by month, under the title "Year 2004."

Callahan's eyes go to the latest figures for July.

This can't be right.

She squints, the light so low in the room that she's sure she must be mistaken, because she's looking at a seven-figure balance.

"Thanks to your mother's frugality and my Daddy's brilliant investment advice," Pepper boasts, "particularly during the booms and the busts of the nineties, that eighty thousand pounds he extracted from the Banks family back in"–here Pepper turns to the first page of the ledger book and points to its initial entry in 1972–"has doubled and doubled and redoubled. You, Miss Banks, are very well fixed." He smiles expansively, opening his hands, palms up. "There's no reason for you to sell your house. It's all paid for, and no need for you to even work unless you want to." His eyebrows raise in a look of feigned innocence. "Now, haven't I at least worked my way somewhere in the vicinity of Nadine on your list?" He leans towards her and gathers her into his arms. "How about showing old Dr. Pepper how grateful you are?"

Stunned, relieved, almost unable to absorb what she's heard, Callahan Banks has a moment of complete spontaneity. "I agree with you. You're right." She accommodates that obnoxious nose touching, self-proclaimed, sweet-tempered bachelor by giving him her best full-fledged, more-than-gratitude kiss and follows it with another.

No one in Pepper's office, except the suddenly neglected Nadine, who rushes back to her bed and hides, trembling under the table, notices that the sky outside the window is cracking and booming in a violent thunderstorm.

Chapter Twenty-Three

I held him off another night. Better said, I held myself off.

Relieved, alone in her own bed, away from Pepper and Twelve Oaks, Callahan sighs. The strength of her physical response to him in his office tonight—tonight being the second time, for she also remembers his kiss in the boat—was as dizzying and unexpected as her car hitting a patch of ice.

And as potentially disastrous.

She took herself off of birth control pills two months ago after ending a ten month relationship with Greg Justice, a handsome, gung ho veterinarian Lila always found slightly boring.

And Mother was right. Greg's a good buddy, but I've never had chemistry with a man, like I do with Pepper.

They remain good friends, she and Greg, and her body's enjoying this chance to reestablish its own rhythms, though she doubts she's ovulated yet. It's probably because she's a biologist that she senses her fertile times so clearly, the dull ache of Mitteschmertz in her side, signaling ovulation, followed by an almost uncomfortable fullness that says there's a readying occurring.

Her next thought startles her so much that she sits up in bed.

Maybe it doesn't matter any more. With the money. What if I did have a child? I could afford to raise her just like Lila did me. Right here. Or maybe not a girl. Maybe my own little Dr. Applegate. And get a dog, too.

Her toes curl in pleasure as she plays with the possibilities. She had waited until Pepper, who insisted upon following her home, left before opening the worn leather cover of the old ledger book, then stood staring at the seven numbers on the final line for long minutes as she tried to wrap her mind around the idea that she was financially secure.

And Lila was, too. Why did she never tell me? She'd not like my sending Pepper home tonight.

"Real magnetism between a man and a woman is rare in my experience." Lila had said it more than once. "Don't ignore it if it comes your way, Callahan, because you can't know if it will ever come again." Callahan had suspected Lila was talking about Reggie Banks. Was her own father the only man for whom Lila had ever felt such an attraction?

It could be why she'd never marry John. So why did *I make Pepper go?*

Pondering, Callahan's only a little surprised when she unearths the truth.

It's not because I'm afraid of Pepper or even because I'm annoyed at him for not sharing what he knows. It's because I'm afraid for Callahan Banks. Because the physical pull is too strong between us, and it would be very stupid to succumb to it. And because I may be fertile, and because he's a Dade and, as Honey reminded me, a known womanizer. He had to go so I could protect myself.

Actually, getting him to leave her here tonight had taken some doing. She'd gotten him as far as the top of the stairs on the upper porch before he planted himself there under the light. The wild rainstorm had come and gone, and the high-pitched love songs of serenading tree frogs filled the dark air beyond the screen. For at least ten minutes, Pepper had seemed to be casting about for things to discuss, his roughened hand sandpapering her cheek as he stroked her hair. "Did you know that Wallace's little brother named his first son Oraldist?"

"Oraldist? I've never heard the name. Why Oraldist?"

Pepper cocked his head. "Say it a couple of time, Callahan, out loud."

So she did. "Oraldist, Oraldist…" The second time, she cackled. "Our oldest, right? Now, I'd call that an original name."

"Wallace gets a big kick out of it, but strange name or not, Oraldist has done okay for himself. He's a senior at Clemson this year, a chem major." Pepper shook his head, bemused, then frowned. "Callahan, let me stay. I'd feel a hell of a lot better if you did. I'll even suffer another night in Lila's room."

"Pepper, I'll be fine."

"I hate the thought of you here unprotected and all Louisiana lonesome."

"Louisiana lonesome?"

His lips crawled into a sheepish smile. "I read somewhere you get Louisiana lonesome when you're all bayou self."

She stifled a chuckle. "That's really bad."

He kissed the tip of her nose. She allowed herself to lean into him, his scent momentarily weakening her resolve.

There a lot more to the influence of pheromones on people than we even realize. I'm sure of it.

"What do you mean that's bad?" His voice, falsely aggrieved. "Anybody ever tell you you've got a sassy mouth?" The laughter on his face quickly faded to an expression of concern that had shadowed his countenance off and on all night. "Seriously, Callahan, I'm even packing a little pistol now." He pointed to the inside pocket of his yellow windbreaker. "And I don't even like guns. Please come back to Twelve Oaks, leave the island, or let me stay."

He's probably deliberately exaggerating so I will let him stay.

She wished she wanted him to leave more. Steeling herself, she crossed her arms and stepped back. "Pepper, it's hard for me to believe anything too serious is going on when you won't even tell me what it is. There's no reason I can't be perfectly safe here once I lock myself in."

He looked thoroughly miserable. "I'm not sure yet who you should be afraid of. For now, just take my word and don't trust anybody but me." He rubbed one eye, stared at the floor and scratched his ear twice before meeting her gaze.

She noticed the wide angle of generosity between his thumb and index finger, Lila's hand-reading lore in her head making her inclined to believe she could trust him.

"I can't tell you," he said earnestly, "because Cole doesn't have hard evidence. But he's working on it. We should know soon. I've got an obligation to protect the reputation of his suspects until he's firmly convinced of their guilt."

She felt some stiffening in her spine, her resolve returned, unfolded her arms and pointed towards the steps. "Go on, I'll be just fine."

"Come back to Twelve Oaks."

"No."

"Please." He leaned forward and tried to kiss her.

She turned away. "Please, go. I'm beat."

"What you are is stubborn, and I won't sleep worth a damn for worrying about you. I'll call you first thing in the morning."

But he did leave, which convinced her that he probably *was* exaggerating to get her to let him stay. She wished she were gladder he was gone, though. She ached with what she diagnosed as a purely physical longing for him.

Trying to shake it off, she decided to be sure her whole house was well locked so that anyone who cut the cables and made it on to her stairs still would be unable to get inside either level of the house, itself. She began with the bathroom on the top floor, checking locks on the window there and the others on the kitchen and backside of the house. When she'd closed and locked each of the French doors that rimmed the front deck, she headed down to the two bedrooms off the second floor deck. There, again, she checked windows and doors before climbing into bed with Lila's financial record book.

Now, as she takes the time to thumb through year after year, page after page of John's tidy handwriting, Callahan's gradually beginning to process the implications of her wonderful news.

I could leave Asheville, if I wanted to, and move home.

She pictures the two eager young adjunct instructors in the Biology Department scrambling to apply for her job.

I could call Andrew Turner.

The head of the Biology Department at The College of Charleston, an old flame from grad school days, has been trying to recruit her to teach animal behavior there for years.

Tell him I'm interested in beginning work next January, take a semester off, and settle into my new reality. This house is mine free and clear. No renters, no real estate agents! Lila lived frugally all of her life, yet she financed private high school and college and some of grad school for me. I should have paid more attention to that. I was her only extravagance. Well, me and her wine. Thank you, Lila, for this last and most amazing gift.

She settles back lazily on her pillows, sets the ledger on the bedside table, and turns out the lamp. But with her eyes closed, the Pepper images return again to assail her. The slant of his smile when he's teasing, the depth of the blue in his eyes when he's worried, and always the damn attraction of his scent.

I should be capable of loving the news he's brought me without lusting after the messenger.

Callahan sits up in bed again, throws her feet over the edge, and heads for the bathroom, determined to exorcize Pepper Dade from her consciousness and fully enjoy this most amazing of nights. The cool rough tile's familiar to her bare feet, which know their way even in the pitch dark. A thousand times, she's walked this route, no five thousand.

Pitch dark?

Something's different. Her senses are on alert before she recognizes why. The tiny light on her electric toothbrush, her orienting beacon on the vanity, in the bathroom, is out.

Suspecting a burned out bulb, Callahan never-the-less feels for the cord to the charger when she reaches it in the bathroom and finds it unplugged.

Puzzling. Maybe Wallace used this bathroom when he was fixing my door lock yesterday.

She's able to finger the plugholes and reconnect the charger in the dark. Voila–the tiny light shines merrily again. She dismisses the incident until minutes later when she reaches for the toilet paper roll. There's an unfamiliar fold on the end of the first piece of paper.

This time, Callahan flips the wall switch. Eyes blinking in the sudden brightness, she examines the paper. Instead of hanging loosely, it's been neatly creased into a "V." She's seen this kind of touch in hotel bathrooms after the maids have cleaned the room. Her heart hammers with fear.

Somehow, someone got in my house today while I was gone, even though the door was locked. And they must want me to know it.

Chapter Twenty-Four

Callahan actually considers calling Pepper to come back, but, feeling foolish after the firm, self-sufficient stand she's just taken, she quickly abandons the idea. Grabbing a can of wasp spray, the only weapon in the house she can conjure up to use in her own defense, she heads for the bottom of the stairs to examine both the lock and the wires.

The wires are tight and in position along the outside of the stair case, and the lock firmly closed, both inside and outside hasps anchored solidly into the wall. So she heads back upstairs, body taut, index finger positioned on the spray can trigger, to inspect three closets and an attic crawl space, the only spots in the house she can imagine someone being able to hide undetected.

All clear.

Reassured, but not reassured, she falls exhausted back into bed.

Someone unplugged my toothbrush and folded that paper to scare me off the island. But how did they get in and out of this house if the wires are intact and the lock still secure? Wallace is the only one who knows the combination, but Wallace has no reason to want to frighten me.

She shivers.

And if they got in once, what's to keep them from doing it again? Maybe I ought to buy a little pistol like Pepper's, but I'd probably end up shooting myself!

In the middle of the night, still only half asleep, she hears the crack of a rifle far across the impoundment. Then, nothing more. Swallowing a lump of fear in her throat, she remembers a chilling Barry Lopez study about predator and prey. The predator, the biologist said, carries on a conversation with its victim as it tries to discern if it's ready to die. Threatening with stares, body movement, scents, the hunter stalks and studies the prey, its body language, its scent, its gait, and then waits.

And maybe trifles with its safe-places, to scare it out of hiding, forcing it to flee and then . . .

∽

Her cell phone's vibrations startle Callahan awake the next morning. Groggy, she reaches to answer it.

"Callahan?" It's Irene Pasquini's cheerful, scratchy voice. "I'm calling with wonderful news and a brash request. My Robbie is back. He's very weak, but, oh my, he is himself again, and I am so grateful! Nursie, here, insists that I take a break. Chief Hunnicut is coming this afternoon, and they're not allowing any visitors. So, I can leave when Bobby goes down for x-rays at eleven-thirty. I was wondering if you'd meet Tootsie and me at The Morgan Creek Grill for a little girly lunch."

"Why, of course, Irene. Thank you." Puzzled about why Irene would call her, Callahan reaches for the alarm clock and is amazed she's slept till ten o'clock. "What grand news about Robbie. I'd be happy to meet you. Let's see. I promised to give Pepper a call, but I have just enough time to leave him a message, jump in the shower, and make it to the dock for the eleven-thirty ferry." She hangs up, resets her cell phone from vibrate to ring, and notices Pepper's already called her three times.

I must have slept through all those vibrations. Think I'll wait and call him from the ferry. I don't have time to defend myself right now.

Outside of the Morgan Creek Grill, on the deck overlooking the waterway, under a red and white striped umbrella, Irene and Callahan sip ice tea and diet Coke as they finish delicious tuna salads, Irene's treat.

Tootsie's curled in Irene's denim-clad lap, sound asleep. Callahan was amused when she arrived at The Grill to note that both she and Irene were in blue denim today: Callahan, in her favorite gored skirt with sleeveless white blouse, and Irene in a stylish pant suit, a fine white cotton blouse, a perky red scarf knotted at the neck. She's chatted merrily throughout the meal, bombarding Callahan with impressions and questions. Nothing but a friendly lunch seems to be going on.

Maybe she just needs companionship or wants to know me better. I hate it that I'm questioning everybody's motives now.

"I did know," Irene is saying, "what Robbie wanted to tell Chief Hunnicut, but I didn't know, couldn't tell him, much in the way of details when he came to interview me. Of course, Robbie couldn't either, so the Chief is hoping to talk to Robbie later today, if he feels up to it. Chief Hunnicut thinks what Robbie saw may be the break he needs, so he's requested I keep it confidential for now." Irene sets her Coke glass down and leans across the table to whisper conspiratorially. "Otherwise, I'd love to share it with you." She pauses to spoon a piece of ice out of her glass. "Pepper was a God-send yesterday." She chatters on as she holds the ice out to Tootsie, who awakens and begins licking it. "So we're crossing our fingers that Robbie will remember more since he's getting better."

Pepper was with the Pasquinis yesterday, and she thinks I knew that.

Tootsie, whose silver white hair shade perfectly matches her owner's, is a dog version of Irene, busy and focused all the time. Irene excavates for another ice cube, holds it for Tootsie and shifts conversational gears to ask Callahan a series of logistical questions: Where does she get her "wonderful hair cut," does she have a local internist, what market has the freshest fish, and, most important of all, does she have an opinion about which veterinary practice would be best for Tootsie's care?

Callahan easily provides Irene with fish and haircut names, but her vet and internist knowledge is outdated since she's lived away from Charleston for fourteen years. A few more trivialities pass between them. Callahan compliments Tootsie's manners, Irene beams, and they part.

It's almost two pm when Callahan steps on the dock and ambles towards the ferry. She totally enjoyed her time with Irene but still remains mystified about why she was asked. She's so absorbed in replaying their conversation, looking for some clue, that the source of a war whoop emanating from the *Aggie Gray* doesn't register till she reaches its gangplank.

"Callahan!" Harry Applegate squeals in delight when she steps on to the ferry and sits down. He's pretzeled between his two brothers in a wrestling match but struggles to break loose and runs up to her, wet socks flapping around his ankles. "You always come around at the best times." He tugs the bill of his turquoise baseball hat down on his head, pooching out his ears, and lowers his voice significantly. "We have another big problem."

Tom and Dick–Callahan has no idea which redhead is which–run past her, screaming. The second one steps on her left foot, but seems oblivious he's done it. Her look of reproof barely grazes the back of his green t-shirt as he disappears out the side door, following his brother as they thunder upstairs to the top deck.

Their screeches, mercifully muted once they leave, are fairly authentic Apache war woops, Callahan thinks. She returns her attention to young Dr. Applegate, the tip of whose sunburned nose is peeled down to a raw, reddened sore. Sun exposure has also darkened and exaggerated the freckles covering his nose and cheeks. "What's up, Harry?"

"We've got us a really sick seagull down there." Harry's brown eyes widen in concern as he points out the boat window towards the end of the dock. "His nose is running, and he keeps sneezing. How can you catch a seagull to doctor it for a cold?"

Laughing, she invites him to join her, patting the white leather seat where she sits. "This time," she says as he bobs up in a backwards motion that lands him squarely on the bench beside her, "it's better news than the jellyfish. Your seagull doesn't have a cold. He's just sneezing excess salt out of his body."

His brow furrows. "Whadda ya mean?"

Cellular Biologist seeking origins of DNA. This child may save the world.

"Well," she says. "It's a special adaptation. Gulls and a lot of other seabirds drink saltwater. They have to, to get the fluids they need when there's no fresh water available. But their kidneys aren't very efficient, so they've worked out a different way to eliminate the excess salt from their bodies."

As usual, Harry seems completely absorbed in what she's saying, his mouth falling open in rapt concentration.

"Seagulls," she continues, "have specialized glands called nasal glands over their eyes, with ducts that lead to their nostrils. When they get too much salt in their bodies, they produce nasal fluid to drain it out. So sometimes, their noses run, and sometimes, they simply sneeze it out. Your seagull is definitely too salty, but he's not sick."

"Whew!" Harry lets out a heavy breath. "That *is* good news." One of his brothers appears at the window of the ferry door and motions him to come on. "Uh, oh," Harry says "I gotta go. We're seeing who can spot the most dolphins, and I'm four up. Thanks, Callahan."

As Harry bolts through the side entrance, his mother enters the door from the dock with a diminutive elderly couple in tow. "Callahan!" Annie Applegate smiles warmly. "I'm so glad you're here. I'd like you to meet Dr. and Mrs. Peacock. They're looking at the lot next to ours, and I thought they might enjoy seeing how we're progressing."

Another buyer?

Callahan stiffens. These two frail people have just assumed enemy-intruder status.

"Polly and Porter—aren't those just the cutest names you've ever heard?—meet Callahan Banks," Annie says. "She's the Biology Professor that Harry was telling you about on the ride here today."

The two Peacocks' smiles are so tentative Callahan wonders if they sense her disgruntled mood.

How many people do I have to get used to sharing Timicau Island with?

They are pale-skinned and seventy-ish and seem to have lived together so long they've become clones. They're the same height, have the same kind of gray-brown thinning hair parted on the same sides, wear round, wire-rimmed spectacles, and even the same shy hopeful smiles.

Inwardly chastising herself for being inhospitable, Callahan stands and contorts her mouth into a smile as she extends a hand to Polly Peacock. "Well, it's an interesting island," she says, turning to shake Porter's hand next. "A few people like it, but most find it a bit too inconvenient."

This isn't good. It's not my job to drive people away, but it's the best I can muster at the moment.

"We have talked ourselves to death about the inconvenience of those golf carts." Polly's voice is so small it would be lost in a stiff wind. "But Porter"–here she gazes adoringly at the tiny man beside her–"is an ornithologist, and the birds on the island are just too enticing for him."

An ornithologist named Peacock?

Callahan's reminded of a former Botany Professor whose first name was Fern.

Porter smiles ingratiatingly at Callahan, shrugs his shoulders, and follows his wife and Annie to the benched seats on the other side of the boat.

It's not like me to instantly dislike people, let alone fellow bird lovers.

Feeling guilty now, Callahan tries making eye contact in order to deliver a more welcoming smile to the newcomers. So it takes her a minute to notice the warning chill that passes over her.

Startled, sensing danger, she turns towards the open door of the ferry, where a fifty-something woman is leaning against the doorframe, her right hand on a cocked hip. She's rather noisily chewing gum and blatantly staring Callahan up and down with eyes lined and lashes heavily mascara-ed black.

Callahan's skin crawls under the gaze.

Who is this woman?

The woman stops smacking her gum, and her thickly coated purple-red lips twist into a smirk. She looks like Lily Munster, badly aged, with long, dull, dyed-black hair falling straight from a window's peak to bare, over-tanned shoulders above a tight black jersey tee. "You're Lila's girl, aren't you?" The gravely voice proclaims a lifetime of smoking. "I remember that hank of hair. You never did know how to fix up, did you, darlin? I kept telling Lila a good strong perm would do wonders for you, but she'd have no part of it."

An icy calm overtakes Callahan, the reaction she has in the woods when she must think clearly to protect herself. She's beginning to connect the Francie-slant of those darkly lined eyes. The woman's wearing cork-heeled, black wedged-sandals, their laces twining up her leg under a purple and red rayon skirt that just brushes the top of her ankles.

Callahan hasn't seen this woman in over twenty years, but the sway of her hips as she sashays territorially on board the boat and the toss of her head are Francie-esque to the max. Once, she had been a beautiful woman.

"Hello, Ruby." Callahan intentionally meets the challenging gaze of Francie and Honey's mother. "Welcome back."

Chapter Twenty-Five

Captain Rick, in a white cotton shirt with navy blue epaulettes, appears in the door and walks to the front of the boat. "Okay, folks, everybody take your seats. I'll sign you in." He makes a few notes in his black-bound log book before clanging the small brass bell on the wall. "All aboard for Timicau." He shifts the boat into reverse and expertly twirls the wheel. A whiff of diesel fuel fills the cabin, making Callahan feel a little nauseous as the little ferry slides out of its boat slip into Morgan Creek.

Ruby remains standing, steadying herself on the window molding with one hand, as she surveys the interior of the boat. Only after it turns north out of Morgan Creek into the Intracostal Waterway does she seem to decide to sit down. Ignoring the mostly empty benches that rim the cabin, she walks straight to where Callahan is sitting on the island in the middle. "Tell me where you come off," Ruby says as she drops to the seat beside her—she leans towards Callahan, her breath sweetly boozy—"trying to get my no-good, son-of-a-bitch step-son to marry you?"

Marry me? Pepper?

Callahan's dumbfounded. "I have no idea what you're talking about."

Ruby licks her lips and gazes at the roof of the ferry. Her legs are crossed at the knee, and the toe of the top cork-heeled black shoe is twitching up and down.

When Callahan doesn't speak further, Ruby becomes absorbed in examining a gold coiled cobra charm on one of the two charm bracelets that dangle from her right arm, the foot still moving in small, unhappy jerks. Then, her eyes raise, and she angles a toothy smile at Callahan, a smile that could once dazzle. "Well, I don't believe you, Miss Bookworm Banks, because Francie tells me Pepper's gone a bit sappy over you." There are rivulets of red lipstick in the deep wrinkles around her mouth. "You might find this hard to believe, but I still know what it takes to land a man." She looks Callahan up and down as if her gored denim skirt and sleeveless white blouse are a G-string and a pair of pasties. Her voice takes on a hard edge "And I smell it in another woman when she's on the make."

Callahan resists a fierce impulse to defend herself.

There are things to be learned from a conversation with Ruby Dade.

She tries for a casual disinterested laugh. "Well, that's all news to me, Ruby, but what difference would it make if it were true?"

"It would make a hell of a difference." Ruby's lined eyes radiate dislike. "Because, just like your innocent little mama before you, you would be trying to lay claim to that which is not rightly yours. That which should belong to me and mine."

Is all this venom because Lila testified against her in that child custody hearing almost twenty years ago? John warned Mother that Ruby would hold a grudge forever.

Callahan modulates her voice to an appeasing, chatty tone. "You're barking up the wrong tree if you're worrying about *my* taking more than my share of Timicau. Have you *been* out there lately?" She cuts her eyes towards the far side of the ferry where the Peacocks and Annie Applegate are so engrossed in examining bird pictures in a large textbook that they seem oblivious to the ferry's newest passenger. "We're being invaded by complete strangers, though I do still see your brother out there from time to time."

Ruby stiffens. "Juby Roy? I don't claim that ornery bastard as kin. He's only my half brother, anyway, and he's always been mean as a striped snake." She opens a black crocheted purse in her lap, takes out a packet of gum, pops a new piece in her mouth, and angrily snaps the purse shut just as the ferry hits the wake from a passing barge and rocks violently.

When the boat stops bobbing, Ruby goes on. "And for your information, I know as well as you do what's going on out on Timicau. Since Francie got her own house, I can come whenever I take a notion to. John and Pepper spent nineteen damn years keeping me from my rightful home, but when Pepper built Francie's house, he lost that op-por-tu-ni-ty." Ruby says the word in five distinct syllables, her chin raised in clear defiance. "There's no legal way Pepper Dade can ban me from the island now that my daughter owns her own property out there."

Callahan nods, trying to appear agreeable. "It must be great to finally be able to come back." She has a pretty good idea Pepper thought long and hard before building Francie her own house.

A squadron of pelicans, looking sagacious as always, appears at the level of the boat's leeward window, flying in formation. She longs to be away from this unpleasant woman, up on top with Harry and his brothers, watching the birds. With effort, she returns her focus. "Pepper's really not my boyfriend, Ruby, but I have gotten to know him better, and I honestly don't believe he'd hold anything against you this long." For some reason, those diesel fumes are really making her queasy today.

Ruby's jaw sets. "Well, you believe wrong. He does, and I've always known why." She begins to chew furiously, noisily snapping the gum in the back of her mouth. "He blames me for getting in a family way with Francie, that's why. Blames me just like John had no part in it at all. And resents John marrying me to give Francie a father, instead of marrying your bitch of a mother."

Callahan bites her lip to keep from responding.

The man was too moral for his own good. What could John have seen in her?

Ruby places a clammy hand, gnarled fingers, blood red lacquered nails, on Callahan's arm, and Callahan has to resists an impulse to jerk away. "You see, I never was good enough for him. Even though I graduated first in my class of seventy five from Miss Aubrey Mulholland's School of Secretarial Science, I still wasn't good enough to be Mr. Pepper Snooty Dade's step-mother." The boat hits a series of small wake-made waves and rocks rhythmically. Ruby's black-brown eyes simmer with anger, her fingernails tightening into the flesh of Callahan's forearm. "Pepper wanted John to marry Lila, not me. And when your mother finally got the chance to get even, she stabbed me in the back and testified against me so John could take away my precious little girls."

"I see." Callahan feigns an itch to scratch on her shoulder to remove her arm from Ruby's grasp. She's chewing the inside of her lip now, having real trouble keeping her anger at Ruby in check. "Maybe we should leave Lila out of this. I'm not exactly over losing my mother yet. I'm sorry about what went on between you two, even you and Pepper, but I've not been a part of any of it." Shifting her weight in the seat to distance herself, Callahan stretches her legs, forcing a conciliatory smile towards the brooding woman. "I know for sure that Honey has missed you and longs to know you better."

Ruby looks blankly away, still angrily snapping her gum. Callahan racks her brain for more conversational grist, wants to keep Ruby talking. "What are you and Francie up to today?"

"I've brought out some herbs for her garden." Ruby points to a cart full of potted plants on the back of the boat. "At least Pepper let her move my camellias to her new house. I nursed those puny things for ten long years." More gum-chewing, boat-rocking silence.

Callahan tries again. "Is that a wedding ring you're wearing? I hadn't heard you'd remarried."

Ruby extends her bony left hand. A very big diamond engagement ring and a wedding band encrusted with diamonds sparkle mightily in the overhead cabin light. Ruby's smile is genuine this time, a smile of beauty queen proportions that stretches her aging skin to its limits. "I snagged me a good one this time." She holds up her hand and twists it under the light. "Barney L. Slocum. He's filthy rich and making more every day. Johnny-on-the Spot. You've probably heard of it. The biggest portable toilet business in the county, and there's building going on all over Charleston." Ruby nudges Callahan with an elbow, a secretive expression crossing her face. "Every carpenter that takes a crap in this county is shitting money into the pocket of Barney L Slocum." She returns her left hand to her lap, fingering the rings before turning to Callahan. "Say, have you heard any more about what happened to that dead Victoria woman? Did she drown herself or did somebody on Timicau do her in?"

"I don't think they know." Glad to be away from the hot topics of Lila and Pepper, Callahan allows herself to relax a little. That queasy feeling just won't go away.

"She was a looker that one. Francie suspects Pepper. Says it was probably the only way he could get shed of her. Francie says he ended things several months ago, but she cried her way back. Was determined to marry the asshole or die trying." The makeup decoupaged on Ruby's face cracks into a sneer. "Guess it turned out to be the latter, didn't it?"

Chapter Twenty-Six

Callahan's relieved that the ferry bumps against Timicau's dock at that moment because she can think of no tactful response to Ruby's cruel comments about Victoria.

"Well, if it's not His Nibs, hisself." Ruby points a red-nailed finger out the window towards the end of the pier to their right where Pepper's Boston Whaler bobs at the end of its rope in the *Aggie's* wake. Pepper, his bare back to them, is sitting on the pier near his boat, a small paintbrush in his right hand. He's been painting something on the boat's bow. He has a firm, friendly-looking back, the sprinkling of freckles across both shoulders adding an appealing, boyish quality.

Just right. I've never liked overly muscular men.

"Look at him. Typical." Ruby's lips curl in disdain. "Acting like I'm not even here. Pepper's got such a stuck-up nose, he'd drown if it went to raining out there. He gets busy as a cat covering crap whenever I show up."

As if he could even know she's on the ferry.

The minute the boat Captain steps on the dock to tie up the ferry, Ruby stands, her face hardening in determination. "Don't mind me." She pushes past Callahan, tripping over one foot and dislodging a sandal strap.

Ouch!

Ruby looks right, towards Pepper, eyes narrowing. "I'll be heading the opposite direction from that one. I'll not waste one more ounce of my precious breath on the likes of Pepper Dade."

Is she talking to me or to herself?

The minute Captain Rick gives the thumbs-up, Ruby's out the door. Through the window, Callahan sees her take a hard left and hurry up the dock–purple and red skirt swishing–towards Francie, who's waiting there in a pair of astonishingly tight yellow short shorts.

Ruby's afraid of Pepper. Why?

Captain Rick squats on the dock in front of the ferry, tying up the lead rope, but his head jerks right when he spots Francie, his eyes moving up the long, tanned legs to the obnoxiously tight shorts. To his credit, Callahan thinks, he self-corrects fast, quickly looking back at the rope in his hands as he wraps a dexterous figure eight with only one more sideways glance as the swishing skirt and the twitching, yellow derriere disappear under the shelter roof at the top of the pier.

Feeling suddenly sick now, Callahan tucks her pinky toe back under its sandal strap, stands, and heads for the door, her head swimming.

Maybe lunch didn't agree with me. Something's definitely not right.

She pauses, steadying herself on the door jam, realizes she's been ignoring a dull, persistent ache in her belly through this whole conversation with Ruby. Low in her abdomen, it's a pain that calls for a heating pad or the warm sand of north beach. Feeling too queasy to make polite conversation with the Peacocks, Annie, Harry, or his brothers, she deliberately hurries out the door before they have time to reach her, nodding to Captain Rick as he passes her pushing Ruby's cartful of herbs up the dock.

When she steps unsteadily out behind him, there are at least fifteen turkey vultures riding a thermal high in the sky overhead. She straightens her back against the deepening pain. "A kettle of vultures." The collective term for a gathering of such ominous black birds has always delighted her.

This pain isn't getting any better. I need to get home fast.

"Callahan Banks." It's Pepper's buoyant voice right behind her. His lips brush her cheek, his clean soap smell too strong today. Her stomach lurches. "You're here." His hand squeezes her elbow as he turns her around and steers her towards his Whaler at the far end of the dock.

She lets herself lean in to him, grateful at this point for his support, though he's clearly taking her the wrong direction. He seems inexplicably delighted to see her.

"If things get any better for me today, I'm going to have to hire someone extra to help me enjoy it. Thanks for leaving the message on my cell this morning, but you talked so fast I didn't have time to get it out of my pocket and answer. I've tried calling you back several times. Did your night really go alright? No problems, no visitors? I'm glad you're here because I'm working on something I want to show you."

They've reached his boat at the end of the pier. She's feeling too ill to attempt telling him about her electric toothbrush or folded toilet paper mysteries, too sick to even speak. The sun is ferocious. Stepping away, he directs her attention to the boat's bow. Without his support, she totters, almost falls, but he doesn't seem to notice.

"I've finally found a name for my boat. Boats need to be named for something permanent and amazing." His teeth flash a teasing smile which she observes though a shimmering haze that surrounds Pepper, the boat, and even a shrieking sea gull overhead.

She's covered in a full-body, clammy sweat and is horribly thirsty. Maybe she'd feel better if she could have a drink of water or put on a hat, any hat.

He's stenciled nine or ten letters, on the Whaler's bow. They're hard to make out in the heat and the haze. Two of them, she can read because he's filled in their stenciled outlines with black paint, a "C" and an "A." The same black paint that's smeared across the knuckle of the index finger he's using to point out the letters. Another wave of nausea washes over her. She swallows twice, willing herself not to vomit.

Her mouth's too far from her brain to form words. Her head's a spinning top, or is she fixed and the world spinning? Now, the dock is rocking. Probably the Applegates and their guests disembarking from the *Aggie* at the other end.

Is that distant yell a triplet?

"Callahan!"

No, it's Pepper.

She wishes she could answer him.

Too far away.

"Callahan, you've gone pale. Are you alright?"

Now, not only can she not talk, but she can't identify the plane she's meant to stand in or how to maintain her relationship to it.

Am I leaning at an angle or standing straight?

She realigns just the position of her head relative to her body, but the gray-green sea and a delicious coolness come into alarming and sudden focus. So she adjusts course in the opposite direction, too abruptly. She feels herself catapult forward towards the boat whose name now further disorients because it's Lila's favorite nickname for her, "The Callie B."

Chapter Twenty-Seven

"Hurry up, Dickie. Come'n look. She's deader than that crushed pelican Dad found."

"I don't think so. Her tongue's not hanging out like Ralphie when the mailman hit him. Mama, do you have a mirror? You hold it up in front of the dead guy's mouth, and if it doesn't steam up, you know for sure. It's the best way to tell till they get stiff."

"She is *not* dead. Mama, tell Tom and Dickie. She's not." The loud, protesting voice ebbing into Callahan's returning consciousness is familiar. Something warm and insistent is probing her wrist. Far away, the lapping of small waves. Nearby, the smells of soap and something fishy. And heat, heavy, moist heat. So much sun and heat.

"Neato. Finally, I get to see a real dead person like Dad works on, and I even sorta knew her."

"Mama, make Tommy stop calling Callahan dead!" Harry sounds close to tears. "Here, feel right here." More wrist probing. "That's her heart pulse. And look at her going up and down. Breathing means she's definitely not dead."

A sticky hand, cooler than the previous one, lightly squeezes Callahan's wrist. "Nope, can't feel a thing. Too bad, Harry. You'll never see your girlfriend again unless she's like Jesus."

"Callahan's not my girlfriend. You shut up, Dickie!" The 'shut up' is so ear-splittingly close that Callahan wills herself awake to save her own eardrums.

"That's enough, boys." A soothing woman's voice.

Annie Applegate.

"And, Harry, you know that 'shut up' is unacceptable. You're right, though. Callahan probably fainted in all this heat. She should be fine."

"Whew!"

Callahan's awake enough now to appreciate Harry's concern.

"It's a good thing Pepper was there. If he hadn't a-grabbed her, she was gonna bash her head open on his boat."

Definitely Harry speaking.

Even in her altered state of consciousness, Callahan's amused.

I'm lying on the pier.

She savors the dampish wood under her legs.

My *head and shoulders are in somebody's lap.*

"Look, her eyelashes are fluttering. I think she's coming to."

Pepper's voice.

It rumbles through her as he speaks.

Pepper's lap.

She's having trouble willing herself back. The sun's too hot, the world too bright for her heavy uncooperative eyes. But she forces them to open, bright sparkles dancing before her as things gradually come into focus.

"Hurray! Hurray! See, Callahan, you're not dead, are you?"

She musters a feeble smile for Harry as she takes in the worried faces hanging above her. She has the impression that this must be how the world looks to a goldfish from inside its bowl. Those are Harry's nut-brown eyes close above her to her right. And Annie's matching ones, looking relieved behind his, and the other two triplets on her left side, frowning in obvious disappointment.

I think I was more interesting dead.

Captain Rick's standing back a few feet and...

Who are those people? Oh, yes, that professor and his wife-twin, their pupils swimming in seas of over-wide white scleras, the classic sign of alarm in a primate.

And right above her is Pepper's face. He's supporting her upper body with his left arm and pressing a damp handkerchief to her forehead with his other hand. His anxious look is impossible to miss, even as spacey as she feels.

"Hi," she says to the face and sort of to the rest of them, too. "Looks like I needed rescuing. What happened?"

"You passed out and damn near killed yourself. That's what." Pepper's voice is low and concerned. "Don't talk, just rest." He leans forward and wipes the entire surface of her face with that wonderfully cool cloth.

It's disorienting to Callahan that even at a time like this, she's attracted by his smell and taken in by his biceps flexing above her as he moves the cloth around her face. She's also very aware that she's leaning against his bare chest. For a minute there, when he leaned over with the handkerchief, she thought he was going to kiss her and was actually disappointed that he didn't.

"Thank God, you're alright." He hands the damp cloth to Harry, who takes it to the edge of the dock, leans over, dips it in the water, and brings it back dripping water. Pepper wrings it out—his chest hair tickling the back of her neck, his smells so intoxicating—and begins wiping down her arms.

Ummm, delicious.

Then, he's mopping her face again.

"I'm okay now. Tell me what happened?" Callahan struggles to sit, but Pepper holds her against him.

"Give yourself a little time, Callahan. It was a pretty scary fall. I was showing you my boat's new name when all of a sudden, for no reason at all, you just pitched forward towards the water." He's holding the damp handkerchief to the back of her neck now. "Out of the corner of my eye, I saw your knees buckle and somehow managed to grab your arm and keep you from falling in. You were already gone, completely passed out, dead weight." He returns the welcome coolness to her brow. "Feel good?"

"Mmm, it does. So good." She gives herself permission to lie back, protected there, relishing his closeness, his scent, and, best of all, the sensation of his bare chest intimately pressed against her back.

෨෨

Pepper draws the curtains open to the lengthening shadows of early evening. "Light's getting so low out there you can't tell a turkey buzzard from a red-tailed hawk."

Callahan comes awake in the dimness of her own bedroom.

"Well, Miss Banks, here I am again, back in your house for another sleepless night, undoubtedly relegated to Lila's room yet again. But I wouldn't feel comfortable leaving you till I'm sure you're alright."

Callahan pulls herself up in the bed, groggy from so little sleep last night and the long nap Pepper insisted she take after the episode on the dock today. "What's that?"

He places a tray across her lap. "It's dinner. Vi's sent it. I called Twelve Oaks, and she took pity." As he talks, his eyes are scrutinizing her face. "Chicken salad, cucumber soup, and homemade biscuits. Plus her green beans. Nobody does green beans like Vi. You *look* better. How do you feel?"

"I feel…good. In fact, great. Those biscuits smell divine." Pepper does, too. She realizes she's had a heightened sensitivity to smells all day long. She takes a biscuit and reaches the knife for the pat of butter, stiffening in anticipation of more early-day belly pain. But, no pain.

What's going on?

"Why do you think you fainted, Callahan? Probably you were swooning in delight over my boat's fabulous new name, right?"

She shakes her head in a resolute left to right motion.

"No? Well what is it then? Woman troubles? Are you sick, or did somebody slip you a mickey?" Pepper tucks a tendril of hair that's hanging half-over her left eye behind her ear. "You still feel a little warm."

She's finding everything about him appealing today except for this boat-naming issue, which she needs to put the kabosh on sooner rather than later. The way his perspiration-damp, close-cropped curls frame his forehead. The slight scratch of his roughened fingers against her ear. Even the way the corners of his eyes wrinkle in approval as she wolfs down Vi's delicious meal. "I really feel perfectly fine now. I was getting a bellyache after lunch, and when I got off the Aggie, I went all woozie and light-headed. But it's gone. No sickness or woman troubles, and I can think of no one who would have slipped me a mickey except the villainous Irene Pasquini or her evil little dog. Because lunch at Morgan Creek with them is all I've eaten today." She washes down a bite of chicken salad with a swig of tea and samples the cool cucumber soup. "And with regard to the swoon, Mr. Dade. Please tell me you weren't permanently painting my name on your boat today. Because I would hate it if you did something like that without asking my permission."

He looks bemused. "We'll talk about the boat's name later. I've gone so far as to prepare a speech for you on that subject, which I will deliver when you feel better. For now, let's just be sure you're okay. Why were you having lunch with Irene?"

"Good question. I'm the one who went to lunch, and I still don't know why. She called and invited me first thing this morning. Said Cole was coming to talk with Robbie, and she needed some girl time." Callahan remembers Pepper cautioning her to trust no one.

Surely he'd not include someone as benign as Irene Pasquini?

"She told me you'd been a God-send yesterday, Pepper. So that's where you were. What were you doing?" Callahan takes a bite of the green beans and then another, relishing their old-timey taste. Vi cooked them in a heavy pot for hours. Callahan knows the process. Loaded them with fat back and salt, and she wishes she had at least three more helpings on her plate.

"I stayed with Robbie to give Irene a break yesterday because Cole asked me to. He was short handed and didn't want Robbie left alone till he woke up, and they got his statement. I hear that happened late this afternoon."

Callahan finishes the last bite of her beans and sops up the pot liquor with her biscuit. "Yes Irene said he was lots better. I'm surprised they thought he needed protection, though."

"Cole was being extra cautious because they still don't know if he was pushed or fell."

She finishes sipping the cup of soup. Pepper picks up the tray and sets it on the bureau. He's wearing a blue knit shirt and clean white shorts. "I trust you're done eating?" There's a sense of mischief about him. His mouth twists into a grin. "So how much better are you? Are you better enough for company?"

Her eyes widen when he kicks off his leather moccasins, and slides under the sheet beside her. Before she can protest, he's captured her face between his hands and is pulling her to him. His breath is minty. His body smells man-clean. She gasps when his mouth goes to hers, the strength of her desire taking her breath away.

She returns that kiss, and another and another, the gentle intimacy of his touch slowly reducing her to a mindless fog of pleasure and long-ing. Moisture, wet and insistent, wells between her legs. Hunger for him fills her throat and swells her lips. She's riding a wave of physical longing so intense that she knows she will not turn Pepper Dade away this night.

"I have wanted you"–his lips tease the taunt skin over her clavicle– "since you were so young that it was an imprisonable offense for me to even think that way. No kidding, Callahan." He's stroking the curve of her waist, then the rounding of her buttocks. "You're unlike anyone I've ever known, elusive, independent, a beautiful wild creature I never dreamed I could make my own."

She shudders, shot through with a white lightening of pleasure, when finally they do consummate that thing between them which must have begun a very long time ago. Afterwards, he holds her in silence for long minutes, holds her till she feels the tickle of his breath against her cheek and hears the deeply contented sighs of his sleeping. Still she stays in his arms, her flesh fomenting new desire even as she basks in the aftermath of being so richly sated.

Later, slipping quietly out from under the weight of his arm, she props herself on an elbow and takes advantage of his sleeping to study him. She wraps the ringlet of curled hair above his ear around her finger, and kisses it. She takes in the clean-cut, boyish contours of his face, notices his surprisingly long eyelashes, so blonde that their length is barely discernible. She kisses the corner of his mouth on that place that crinkles when he's amused. Pepper doesn't move. He seems dead to the world. She admires him from different angles, still reveling in the power of her body's release. Such deep satisfaction after such long anticipation, until, suddenly, the biologist in her connects the dots of her day in a frightening, yet exhilarating insight.

That belly pain has to have been the pain of Mezzerschmitz. How hot I felt when I fainted. My basal body temperature elevated. And, of course, my heightened sense of smell, my ravenous desire for Pepper, my inability—in fact my disinterest—in resisting him when I knew I should. I was biologically primed to mate on this day. And procreate?

Callahan trembles. Is it surprise, fear, or maybe even delight? She doesn't know, but she's very sure of one thing. She's now a boat sailing uncharted waters because she ovulated today, and for the first time in her life, she used no birth control at all.

Chapter Twenty-Eight

SATURDAY, JULY 11

Callahan awakes to the piccolo melodies of a shy painted bunting in the woods and the occasional dissonant croak, like a misplayed cello string, from a frog in the pond below.

She did not ask Pepper to leave her bed last night. She stretches in quiet satisfaction, remembering their sleeping, waking, making love and sleeping again. She's never experienced such raw attraction for a man. Never wanted and had him, only to immediately feel the hunger return.

Insatiable may be the operative word here.

Nor has Pepper—or so he says—experienced such. He's upstairs in the kitchen now. She can smell bacon cooking and hear the occasional click of utensil against plate. She's still unable to believe what's transpired in the last twelve hours.

Boy, if I could get pregnant the first time, I wonder how much the odds increase after two more? Do I care?

Feeling luxuriously indolent, she stretches her naked body under the sheets, extending each arm, each leg, then sliding a flat palm across her belly as she tries to picture what could be occurring inside of her.

It's the only time in her well-orchestrated life that she's done something so spontaneous and potentially life wrecking.

"Good morning." Pepper's deep voice holds a tenderness that's new. He's standing in the door from Lila's room, holding a coffee cup, a dishtowel tucked in the front of his white shorts. He's barefoot and shirtless, and just the look of him there reduces her to jelly all over again.

She tries forming her face into a non-sappy smile. "Good morning, yourself. Wow. How do you go about returning to the real world after a night like last night?"

"I don't know. That kind of chemistry is scarce, but I have an inkling there's plenty more where it came from." He tilts his head and studies her, appearing both bemused and contented. "How about a properly served breakfast on the upstairs deck? The bacon's only a little bit burned, and on my third try, I actually got the bread toasted to perfection under the broiler."

"Broiler? Why not the toaster?" She sits up.

His eyes go to her breasts. "You know, Callahan, all those years I watched you growing up, I tried to picture what was going on under your tee shirt, but even my excellent imagination didn't do you justice. You're the most beautifully natural woman I've ever seen. Oh, the broiler?" Like her question just got through to him. "Because, I couldn't find a toaster."

She stifles an urge to pull the sheets up under her chin, enjoying it just a little that she's rattled him.

"I could forego the bacon"—a smile plays across his lips—"if you'd let me under those covers again." He shakes his head. "But, I probably shouldn't. I've got some things I want to talk to you about, and I need to be at another closing on the mainland at eleven."

"What time is it now?"

"Eight thirty. Is that early for you to get up when you're on vacation?"

"No." She does pull the sheets up now, natural modesty getting the better of her. "It's actually kind of late. Let me throw on some clothes, and I'll be right up."

He brings the coffee cup to her in bed. "I'm going to start eating so I'll have time to make the nine-thirty ferry. Come on up whenever you're ready." She notices that he's remembered she likes her coffee with cream.

The table on the upper deck is set with bright yellow mats, mismatched cutlery and paper napkins. He stands when she reaches the top of the stairs and pulls out a chair for her. "Do you comb your hair?"

"Do I comb my hair? What a strange question. Of course I do. Why?"

"I was just wondering how it worked with you. It has been my experience, that the women in my life decline some of my better invitations because it might mess up their hair. One woman or another, trying to keep the hair on her head in place, has been interfering with my plans for years." He sits down and butters a piece of toast. "Francie and"—his face clouds—"Victoria, for example, would never consider going out in my boat, too windy. You passed the boat test with flying colors Sunday night when you survived the dolphin drenching in such good spirits. I studied you in the moonlight last night when you fell asleep...after our second encounter." He gives emphasis to "second" with a teasingly raised eyebrow. "And I said to myself, 'this is a woman who would never compromise what she wanted to do because of her hair. Seems to me, you can just shake your head, and it goes back to looking the same. Good, I mean, the same, good. So I was just wondering." He radiates good-humored approval as he hands her a glass of orange juice.

There's an up front quality about Pepper that both surprises and delights Callahan. "Uh, well, you're definitely right that I don't much care about how my hair looks, but don't get too besotted here. I brushed it just now before I came up. I do it at least once a day, every morning." She serves herself scrambled eggs and bacon from one of Lila's chipped yellow pottery platters and starts eating. "Not bad. Vi must have given you cooking lessons."

"Point proved!" He slaps the teak table with the flat of his right hand. "A once-a-day-hair-fixer is a rare and endangered species among twenty-first century women, and I've also noticed that you don't paint your nails and spend the rest of your time trying not to chip them." He takes her left hand to his lips and kisses it, the tone of his voice going serious. "So much is happening so fast right now that I'm having trouble sorting where to begin. I don't have a lot of time. Today's kind of a complicated closing. It's Teelia Moultrie. You've probably heard of her, the Charleston socialite?"

Callahan hasn't, but just nods.

"It's a puzzle to me why," Pepper says, "but she's decided to buy the lot next to Francie's. We go back twenty plus years, Teelia and I, to deb ball days when I was her escort. She's divorced now and has a miserably unhappy teenage son who seems convinced that moving out here will solve all his problems. Anyway, it's an emotional decision for her to sell her Sullivan's Island home place, and I need to be on time, so think I'll just dive in. About no condoms…"

Startled, she looks up from her plate. "You're wondering if I'm on the pill or something?"

"Not exactly. I wanted you to know that I always use a condom, always except last night. So you're in no danger of getting an STD from me via Vicky via J.P. via Francie, whatever."

Whoa. I hadn't even thought it through that far yet.

"But that's not the only reason I brought it up. You can't have known this, but I've watched and wanted you for a very long time. So last night when you didn't seem to mind, I gave myself permission to, well, to enjoy the moment with you." His eyes are riveted on hers. "So I wanted you to know that you don't need to worry about diseases *or* about getting pregnant either."

His face darkens, the firm lines of his mouth growing set. He rubs his ear. "Because I can't have kids, Callahan. I got the mumps on a sailing trip to the Caribbean with Daddy when I was eight. They tell me there's very little chance I'll ever be able to father a child. It's important to me that you know this up front. I want to be brutally honest with you because I want this thing between us to deepen and last."

I wanted to get pregnant!

She only knows it now that it's not possible. Disappointment, heavy as a soggy beach towel, snuffs out the titillating anticipation she's been experiencing since last night.

I wanted Pepper's child.

She forces herself to rally for his sake. He's still holding her hand tightly, and she squeezes his back. "It's okay," she says, "though strangely enough I wasn't protected in any way either, and I've never done anything so remotely stupid in my whole life. So your mumps may have just saved me from a calamity." She releases his hand and looks straight into his sad blue eyes. "I think Lila's death and my getting to know Harry Applegate have altered me in ways I'm not even fully aware of yet."

"It wouldn't be a deal breaker, then, Callahan?"

She feels the tension in his question. "A deal breaker? What deal?"

He looks abjectly miserable, all of the light drained from his face. "I'm doing this all wrong." The ear rub again. "I'd always thought that when I came to this moment, I'd plan it and make it the best ever. My not being able to have kids. That wouldn't be a deal breaker for you if we were to...get together?"

He takes a big breath and sighs it out. "I *was* painting your name on my boat yesterday, which I've deliberately never named. It was to be my entree into asking you to be my wife. I've never been surer about anything in my life. I've known a thousand women, but you're the first and only woman I simply don't want to live without."

Honey's cautions about not getting attached to Pepper flash into Callahan's consciousness.

He's saying he wants to marry me in almost the same sentence he's telling me his old flame is moving out here on Timicau.

Callahan has no idea what to make of all this except she knows she's never seen Pepper looking so flustered.

"I'll give you all the details, anything you want to know about the Dades, me, my foibles, my fuck-ups, all of that. I love you, Callie Banks. I haven't had much time to show you yet, but I'm prepared to spend the rest of my life doing it."

Callahan's shocked speechless for long seconds, then musters a reply. "Pepper, think about it. We hardly know each other. We've spent only those few evenings together since I got back."

"I know. I know." He nods. "You need time. I'll give you all you need, but, Callahan, I'd adopt children. I'd do most anything to make it alright for you. I've dated a shit load of women, so when I find the right one"–he grins beguilingly—"and she's a-once-a-day-hair-comber, I know it's right. Forgive me for being such a klutz, but my emotions have pretty well overtaken my reason since you came back to the island."

Feeling real compassion for him now, she touches, then strokes, his cheek. "Last night was the most remarkable sex I've ever had. But sex is sex, and I'm a funny loner kind of person. I don't even know if I'd want to be married, and I surely don't know you well enough to say yes."

He leans back in his chair, like what she's just said is a relief to him. "So that's not a no, right? It's what, a stay-tuned, maybe?"

She can't help herself. She leans across the corner of the table to where he's sitting and kisses him. He needs to be kissed, and she feels tension drain from him when she does it. "Let's leave it this way," she says, post kiss and re-kiss. "It's not a no. I've decided to take a sabbatical, and I'll be here for sure till second term in January. Let's pass more time together and see what develops."

"Okay, I can live with that." He stands and begins clearing dishes with a more normal Pepper-gusto. When she follows him into the kitchen, he sets the coffee pot on the counter so near the toaster that Callahan laughs. He looks up, surprised, then looks chagrined when he spots the old chrome pop-up device. He shrugs. "Guess I was looking for one of those mini-oven things instead of this old fashioned kind."

The kitchen clock says nine twelve. He has a fifteen-minute golf cart ride to the nine thirty ferry. "Pepper, you need to get out of here. Do me a favor, though, will you? Don't put my name on your boat right now, okay?"

She can tell he doesn't like it, but he nods agreement. "Before I go," he says, "I want to tell you that I was almost convinced until yesterday that Francie was somehow involved in the deaths on the island. It was an awful thing to contemplate, that my crazy-ass little sis could do such things." He begins pulling a blue polo shirt on over his head as he talks.

"When Robbie Pasquini came to," Pepper says, his head emerging, turtle-like, through the neck of the shirt, "he remembered nothing about his fall, but he did know what he wanted to tell Cole. The day that Vicky died, Robbie saw her down on the beach with JP, watched them have sex and all. Later, he also remembered he'd seen Francie down there with Vicky." Pepper tucks his shirttail in and slips his feet into well-worn leather moccasins. "See, Callahan, what made it all so suspicious was that Francie didn't tell Cole when he interviewed her the first time that she'd seen Vicky on the beach that day. Cole felt like Francie could have a real motive to harm both JP and Vicky if she'd seen JP cheating on her with Vicky. And we all know about Francie's temper."

Pepper checks his wristwatch. "Walk me down to the bottom of the steps. I'm running out of time, and I want you to hear the rest of this. Cole called Francie in and questioned her yesterday morning–probably the reason Ruby was headed out on the ferry to see her later in the day.

Once Cole talked to Francie, though, and checked out her story, he saw he was wrong."

Pepper's at the bottom of the stairs. He unlocks the lock, hands it to Callahan, and slides the door open. "Francie told Cole the minute he asked that she *had* been on the beach earlier that day, taking a walk, and had stopped to talk to Vicky for a few minutes but hadn't considered it important enough to mention. Turns out–and Robbie was able to confirm this–that Francie saw Vicky over an hour before Vicky had her little liaison with JP down there. In fact, when JP and Vicky were hooking up, the ferry records show that Francie was on the boat, headed to the mainland. So, case closed."

Pepper brushes Callahan's cheek with his lips and climbs into his golf cart. "Thank God we can mark her off the suspect list. I'll call you as soon as this closing's over. This time please keep your door locked and your cell phone on."

As she waves to his disappearing cart, she wonders if he now has the right to ask these things of her. When he disappears behind the trees at the end of the path, she continues to stand there with the lock in her hand, feeling becalmed, like great gusts of wind have filled her sails and are now gone. She never did tell Pepper about the signs of an invader in her house night before last. She makes a mental note to do that.

When she finally turns to go up the stairs, her sense of being suspended in a vacuum still overwhelming, something pink and sparkly on the ground to her right catches her eye. She walks to it, reaches down, and picks up the peach-colored, sequined, flamingo earring that Francie was wearing over a week ago when she came to report Victoria's death.

Funny, you'd think I'd have spotted it here before today.

Chapter Twenty-Nine

Callahan refastens the lock and climbs the steep steps to the upper deck, dipping her head to avoid a large spider web at the top. She drops Francie's earring in a teak bowl on the deck table and checks her watch. Ten o'clock, a long delicious day stretching out ahead.

What to do? Go through Lila's letters? Begin to clean out her closets? Go through all the financial records Pepper gave me?

Nothing quite appeals. She decides to wash the breakfast dishes. Fills the right sink with warm sudsy water, the left with clear, all the while chewing at her lip uneasily.

After such a night, it's no wonder that I'm unsettled, but I refuse to let myself get into the habit of missing Pepper Dade. The man's so all-consuming I lose the capacity to be the main character in my life every time he comes around.

She cuts off the water and puts platter, dishes and glasses along with the cutlery in the right sink to soak. Then, collects soapy water in the frying pan, absent-mindedly scrubbing dried egg off its bottom, her confused inner world a-swirl like the water in the pan.

Do I actually believe that he's always used condoms except last night? I probably do because he told me about it after the fact, not before. But why in the world did I let this happen?

She rinses the fry pan in the left sink, having her hands immersed in the steamy water, calming, somehow, and places the pan on a counter top dishtowel.

What about his certainty that I'm "the one?" It's a stretch to believe that. And his assurance that I don't need to be worried about getting pregnant? My body last night didn't read it that way. So subconsciously, I was hoping to get pregnant?

Hardly aware of what she's doing now, she continues washing and rinsing, the spatula, the knives, the forks, a serving spoon, in a contemplative rhythm she finds soothing.

And what about his sterility story? Do I believe that, too? I shouldn't. Men are infinitely devious when it comes to sex. Lila learned that lesson the hard way.

Callahan places the clean dishes in the drainer, lays a tea towel over them, and walks to the center of the kitchen where she stops and stands. Stranded, aimless. Feeling so unsettled she doesn't know what to do next.

What is the matter with me?

She tunes into her body, the rigid muscles at the back of her neck, her eyes straining to pick up any movement as if, independent of her, they're looking to find and protect her from danger.

I actually don't feel safe here now that Pepper's gone. I used to be afraid when he was here! It's like I'm being stalked by a predator I can't even name.

That same heightened wariness she experienced the night before last when someone had been in her house has returned two-fold.

I still don't know who got in here or how or why.

Instinctively seeking grounding in normalcy, she looks for old Albert on the point across the pond where he usually lies, soaking up the sun's early rays before it gets too hot. And sure enough, he's there, his massive body fully stretched to absorb warmth, the muscular girth of him always astounding to view when he's totally out of the water. But seeing Albert today brings no reassurance. Anxiety continues to niggle at Callahan like sand in a shoe.

And you can't do a thing till you shake it out.

She resolves to take action, some action, any action, to break the grip of apprehension.

I shall become Callahan Drew, instead of Nancy, and solve "The Mystery on Timicau Island." Would that I were as proficient a detective!

She pours herself a fresh cup of coffee and grabs legal pad and pen before heading out to a porch rocker. Since childhood, Callahan's depended upon her own wits and instincts to sort things.

No time to stop now. I'll write down everything that's happened in this last week since I got home and give my very excellent brain a chance to make some sense of it.

She leans back in the rocker to collect her thoughts. On the first line of the pad, far left, she writes and underlines the day she came back to Timicau Island.

THURSDAY, JULY 2

Arrive on island little before noon, drop things in house, unpack groceries and clothes, eat peanut butter sandwich and take walk on beach. Think I hear woman crying up near pergola at Francie's and see man talking to female in bright blue bikini. Some time after midnight, go to beach for another walk. Realize turtle nest is hatching. Kill several ghost crabs. Wait for hatchlings to reach water and walk home.

On the right side of the page under the caption OBSERVATIONS, Callahan writes:

Tide at its ebb at one am. No signs of other people or footprints. Victoria's body must have already washed out to sea on outgoing tide that afternoon or night, because for her to wash in on incoming tide Friday morning, she would already have to be out there. (Unless somebody took her body out later and dumped it.)

Check when Pepper left Victoria and Timicau that morning. Was it Pepper I saw up there under the trees making her cry, or JP? When did Mr. Pasquini see Victoria with JP? Pepper says Francie was gone by then so must have been the afternoon. Interestingly, Francie told me next day, Friday morning, she was hurrying to meet JP for a "nooner." Mr. P reports that JP had sex with now-dead Victoria the day before, on Thursday. Some kind of callous and amoral people, these are.

Callahan stops writing and rocks for a moment, searching for other details she may be missing. Finding none, she enters the date for Friday. Already, her anxiety levels are lowering.

FRIDAY, JULY 3

Yoga on porch at ten a.m. when Francie arrives. Says Pepper and Nadine discovered Victoria's body washed up on beach. Told to show up at Twelve Oaks for Cole's interrogation at one p.m.

High tide stranding Victoria's body on beach would occur near time Pepper found her.

Francie wearing flamingo sequined earrings like one I found by house today. F flustered that morning, in a big hurry to meet JP.

Francie also wearing mosquito-netting outfit, including "helmet." How could earring fall out if head swathed in mosquito netting? Unless it got stuck on outside of helmet when she put it back on and fell off down there. Why didn't I see it before today then?

Callahan chews the cap of the pen, can think of nothing further, so fills in the rest of the details for Friday:

Chat with Pepper at Twelve Oaks.

He doesn't seem upset enough.

Then Honey, Mrs. Pasquini, Vi and Cole. Mrs. P. mentions using new binoculars on second floor platform of their under-construction house. Pepper asks if she's seen anything interesting with them.

Don't think she answered his question.

Varina, clearly angry at Pepper for some reason, says that all women who come and go at Twelve Oaks eventually will suffer.

Does Vi know more than she's saying? What did Pepper think Mrs. P. saw with binoculars or was he just being conversational?

Cole also asks me that *s*trange questions re: whether I think Francie and Pepper are sexually involved.

The better I know Pepper, the less sense that question makes to me. Wonder why Cole asked that. Did Francie actually meet JP on Friday after she left my house for the "nooner?" She told Cole later that afternoon after my interview with him, she couldn't find JP for Cole to talk to him. Does that mean she never met him when she left my house, couldn't find him later that afternoon, or just didn't want Cole to interview him? Another possibility: Was JP already dead on Friday? The last people to see him alive—except the murderer, assuming there was one—were probably Robbie Pasquini with the binoculars and Victoria down on the beach Thursday.

Across the pond, Albert's tail suddenly thrashes, and with the surprising speed an alligator can muster, he disappears back into the water. Callahan's stomach knots in new angst. She looks for what might have spooked him, sees nothing.

Curious. That's not a typical water entry for Albert.

Momentarily unnerved, Callahan gets up and goes to the kitchen for the can of wasp spray, uncaps it, brings it back with her, and sets it on the picnic table.

At least, I'm armed.

Feeling a bit silly, yet reassured, she begins the summary of her third day.

SATURDAY JULY 4TH

To mainland in morning for milk. Meet Annie Applegate and triplets on ferry back to island. Annie says insider Charleston gossips report Pepper no longer going with Victoria when she died. Which could explain Pepper's not seeming so upset. Still...

Ask Pepper about this.

Preliminary autopsy results show no water in Victoria's lungs. She didn't drown even though she washed in from the ocean. She's diabetic and could have gone into a coma and then been washed out to sea.

Is there a way to check blood insulin levels after death? Find out about that. We still don't know for sure if V. was murdered or just died on the beach and was carried out on high tide.

Someone—think it was Francie—calls boat Captain to ask if anyone's seen JP Saturday because he was supposed to pick up a drill at the Pasquinis and hasn't been there.

That night, after I turn down Pepper's invitation for Fourth of July boat ride, Pepper shows up at my house anyway. Warns me not to go to the north end of the island by myself. At first, when JP disappears, it looks like he may have killed Victoria and fled.

But if he is the murderer, who would kill him and why? I have a feeling what happened up there at Ruby's studio on Sunday may be the key to solving this whole mystery.

SUNDAY JULY 5

Go to Ruby's shed anyway, early in the morning. Dust on front porch rockers disturbed, but Francie says she was there looking for JP day before. Prints from Mr. Hob Nail Boots in pluff mud down by old rowboat

Whose boat is that? I need to ask Pepper if it's his? I assumed it was.

Front door bolts not closed like they usually are on shed door.

Did Francie not close them?

I can't get the door to open at all. Have feeling somebody inside holding it. I bolt door shut.

So anyone in shed couldn't get out the door.

When Pepper and Dr. Applegate go there looking for Harry later that day, window in shed is broken out.

Pepper told me that. I should have asked him whether the bolts on the door were open or still thrown.

On way back, swing by Mrs. Pasquini's. Francie's there acting uncharacteristically friendly and nervous. Pumping Mrs. P for something. Don't know what. When I look back at Ruby's shed, rowboat is gone from dock.

Lots to try to understand here.

Shortly after I land at Mrs. Pasquini's, Harry drives north and stops at osprey nest where he has vantage point of nest and shed. Sees two men carrying something big covered in white from shed out to the boat. They spot and chase him.

Probably because they didn't want him to witness what they were doing. Who was in that shed, and what were they carrying out? Bet they were there earlier when I was.

It had to be JP's body covered with a sheet or canvas, and I bet one of the men carrying it was Juby. Maybe the same men pushed Robbie off the platform of his house because they suspected he'd seen them, too. In truth, though, the body—if it was a body—was probably moved Sunday, long before Robbie got there the next day. Either while I was on my way back from the shed to Mrs. Pasquini's or shortly after I climbed up. Because the boat was there when I was at Ruby's and not when I looked down from the Pasquinis' less than an hour later.

Callahan's eyes widen as she makes another connection and writes on:

So could that be why Francie was so nervous and why she was up there with Mrs. Pasquini? Did she know the men were moving the body and want to be sure we had no chance to observe it? How could Francie be mixed up in this if she was off the island when V. was killed? Surely the two deaths are connected. And if Juby's as much a part of this as I'm beginning to suspect, what was he doing hiding behind the sand dune, watching Harry and me that day? Francie's involved in this. I'm sure of it now, but how and why?

Concentrating on possibilities, Callahan stares blankly into space, her eyes unseeing for long minutes as the large banana spider at the top of the stairs weaves an intricate new addition to her web, her long, jointed yellow legs strumming the threads with intricate precision. The web stretches a full four feet from rafter to hand rail now, but Callahan's so absorbed in analyzing what she's written on her legal pad that it takes her longer than usual to notice that the web is periodically bouncing in a way unrelated to the spider's activity. It's bouncing because one slender tendril of the web is attached to the screen support at the handrail. A fist of fear clenches Callahan's heart.

It's bouncing because someone's quietly and stealthily walking, step-by-step up my stairs, someone who shouldn't be there because I closed and locked the lock at the bottom this morning. This time, I am very sure of it.

Chapter Thirty

Callahan's fear morphs into anger when the net-swathed figure of Francie Dade carrying a large wicker picnic basket, a white Coach purse slung over one shoulder, emerges panting from the stairwell. She's several inches too tall to avoid the spider web and apparently so vision impaired by her mosquito net helmet that her head is entangled in the sticky strands before she notices it.

"Ewwwww! Ewwww! Gross!" She drops the picnic basket and frantically waves her arms. "God, Callahan, why would you leave such a disgusting thing in your house?" She stumbles across the porch, jerks the net helmet off, and shudders.

Staying seated, Callahan slides the legal pad under her legs and sits on it so Francie won't see what she's been writing. "The spider web's not *inside* my house. It's on my deck, and I leave it there because I enjoy watching her work. So Francis, what brings you out here, both unbidden and unannounced, this lovely summer morning? And, by the way, how did you get in?"

Ignoring both questions, Francie walks back to the top of the stairs, ducks under the spider web, and collects her basket. She carries it to the picnic table, deposits it there, and begins unzipping her body suit, pausing mid-zip, when her eyes fall on the flamingo earring on the teak tray. "Well here it is! What in the world are you doing with my favorite earring? I've looked everywhere for this thing."

"You may have to answer that one for me since it was at the bottom of my steps. Any chance you came for a visit when I wasn't home and lost it there? And by the way, there's a lock on my door for a reason. How'd you get in, and whatever made you think it would be OK?"

Francie shrugs and goes back to extricating herself from the mosquito netting. She's wearing all white today, tight white tennis shorts, a sleeveless scoop-necked tee shirt of cotton so fine that the dark outlines of her large nipples are visible beneath the rhinestone word "FUN" emblazoned across her chest. Several diamond tennis bracelets stack up her right arm. "I just entered your birthday numbers in different orders till the lock popped open." The jump suit drops to the floor. She steps out of it, picks up the earring and shoves it into her short's pocket. "It wasn't rocket science. I went to your birthday parties for years." A sudden smile pierces her face, evil, somehow, in its intensity. "You don't seem to appreciate how hard I have been trying to be a good neighbor, Callahan. Take today. Look! I brought you a picnic lunch." She gestures towards the wicker basket. "In the past, I maybe wasn't always the friendliest person, but I've reformed." The cruel force of that smile again. "Better late than pregnant as Mother Ruby always says."

"A picnic?" Callahan knows she looks puzzled. In her wildest dreams, she can't picture Francie Dade taking time to prepare or share a lunch with her.

"Peanut butter and jelly." Francie takes a step towards her, the deep V of her cleavage and her heavy sweet perfume uncomfortably close. "Don't you remember you told me at my house it was your favorite?"

Callahan rocks backwards to distance herself from the smell. "I guess I do, but it's a little too early to eat. It's only eleven o'clock. Why didn't you call?"

Francie plops into the rocker nearest Callahan. "I did call, on your damn cell. And, as usual, you didn't answer. Had a free day, so I took a chance, packed this up and came out. You got any ice tea in the fridge?"

She's stood up and is headed for the kitchen by the time Callahan nods yes.

When Francie nears the spider web hanging lopsidedly from the ceiling, she points at it. "I am tuckered out from the heat and that climb and battling that awful thing." Her hair's loose to her shoulders today, its professionally streaked blonde tresses held back from her face by a rhinestone head band that sparkles like "FUN" across her chest.

When she emerges from the kitchen with two glasses of ice tea, she hands the chipped glass to Callahan and gulps half of her own before walking to the picnic table and setting it down beside the wasp spray. She pulls a red checked table cloth from the basket, slides tea glass and wasp spray to the far end of the table to clear a space for the cloth, and lays it on the half of the table nearest them. Humming something dissonant, she produces and places napkins, silverware, paper plates and a Tupperware box of chocolate chip cookies that Callahan recognizes as Vi's. Next, a blue crockery bowl of sliced cantaloupe–also recognizable from Vi's kitchen–and a smashed peanut butter sandwich on unappetizing white bread wrapped in plastic wrap. Francie peels back the plastic, rather gingerly Callahan thinks, and places the sandwich on a plate.

"There." Francie's deep sigh drops her bosoms.

"So where's your sandwich?" Callahan's fairly sure that everything *but* the peanut butter has come from Vi.

Francie picks up her tea and takes another sip, tennis bracelets jingling against glass. "I hate peanut butter, plus I'm on a low-carb diet. All set now." Her voice falsely cheery, she motions Callahan to join her at the table. "Picnic time!"

Callahan doesn't move.

"Callahan, what are you, ungrateful or something?" An angry undertone in Francie's voice triggers something self-protective in Callahan.

I'm not eating her food.

"You go ahead, Francie. Pepper made me a huge breakfast this morning, and I'm just not hungry. Thanks for coming out, though.

Have you heard how Mr. Pasquini's doing or if they have any leads on JP?"

"So the son of a bitch finally got into your bed." Francie's neck and the bare skin above "FUN" are turning a splotchy, spectacular shade of red.

Like a lizard in rut. Boy, something's upsetting her. Pepper and me?

"Callahan, I'm going to have to ask you to eat some of this lunch. You're pissing me off. I've gone to an awful lot of trouble."

On impulse, Callahan points at the cantaloupe. "How about just a little bit of the cantaloupe, then. It looks ripe to perfection." Her heart rate has accelerated, she notes, the sound of her pulse hammering in her ears.

Francie scowls. "No cantaloupe till you've had your peanut butter and jelly. That's what *I* made. I got fresh ground peanut butter from Whole Foods and even begged Vi for some of her raspberry jam. Thank God she still helps me with food or I'd starve to death. So I must insist you at least try it. I suppose Pepper's talking marriage now?"

Callahan ignores the demand that she eat the sandwich and the question about Pepper. Sipping her own tea, she continues to rock, enjoying watching Francie squirm as she makes small talk.

Sitting beside the table, facing Callahan, every move Francie makes conveys increasing irritation. Her legs are crossed at the knees. The top foot in a white low cut tennis shoe with rhinestone insets pumps impatiently. She tosses her hair from left to right, then right to left, scowls, drums red fingernails on the table and responds to Callahan's chatty questions with monosyllabic answers. She does occasionally take a sip of the tea that's left in her glass but makes no effort to taste the food or hold up her end of the conversation.

I guess she hasn't quite gotten neighborly chatting down yet. She's the one who was in my house the other night. I'm sure of it. She got in today because she'd already figured out the combination for the lock earlier. But why?

Out beyond the porch over the pond, thick storm clouds, like torn, dirty dust rags, are beginning to darken the sky. Francie's face, too, is growing darker. Callahan's experienced Francie's notorious short fuse so many times that she's hardly surprised when Francie abruptly stands, grabs her large leather purse, and stomps inside the house.

"I'm going to use your bathroom. I'll be back in a minute."

The banana spider, already repairing her web, has attached a new string of silk, her jointed legs strumming as deliberately as a classical guitarist.

So why is Francie here at all?

A fly that must have come in with Francie sails into the upper undamaged quadrant of the web and is trapped. Darting across her web, the spider abandons her repair project to enmesh her captive in silk. Clearly doomed, now, the fly never-the-less continues frantically bobbing up and down. Callahan's so drawn into the drama that she fails to notice that Francie's come back out on the porch behind her until she smells Francie's heavy sweet perfume unexpectedly close.

Without warning, Callahan's head is wrenched against the back of the chair and something drawn so tightly across her neck that she begins to choke. Gagging violently, she windmills her arms, to free herself, but a second and then a third cord are yanked across her wrists and attached behind her back to the cord holding her neck against the chair's back. To move either arms now has the affect of tightening the cord binding her throat. "Francie," Callahan gasps the words in a raspy whisper. "What are you doing? Is this some kind of a joke?" Francie moves in front of her, a raging madness flaming her eyes. Desperate now, Callahan aims the toe of one free foot towards her captor, almost overturning the rocker as she pulverizes Francie's shin. Francie's nostrils flare. She picks up a straight leg chair by the nearby picnic table, raises it above her head, and smashes it full force against the front of Callahan's leg, a blow so stunning that Callahan's immobilized by pain. Immobilized long enough for Francie to wrap two more long bungee cords around the bare, bruised, surface of Callahan's lacerated legs, link them together, and stretch them tightly against the wooden supports under the rocker. "That oughta do it." There is seething hatred in the look she gives Callahan.

Lunging in the rocker is futile now, though Callahan tries, struggling to move a few times more. Francie responds by brutally jerking the neck rope so hard that it breaks the skin, and Callahan feels the warmth of blood dribbling down her collarbones. She gags, heaves, and coughs uncontrollably. Her breath falters, her vision shifting in and out of focus, till, somehow, she leans back in the chair enough to slightly slacken the pressure.

Every move I make only tightens this neck cord.

"God damn it, will you sit still!" Behind Callahan, Francie's shrill voice. "I hadn't planned to choke you to death, Callahan, but you're one person I actually might enjoy killing that way."

Kill me? Francie's the killer? I thought her incapable of something like this.

Callahan's reluctant to move at all now, the bungee at her throat so tight she's becoming light headed. She watches, almost from a distance it seems, as Francie busily reinforces ties on her right wrist and forearm with a red bungee wrapped around the rocker's wooden armrest. A blue bungee's next added to her left forearm, the thin cord stretched so taunt it cuts into the flesh of her wrist. When Callahan shifts her weight slightly to test for give in the neck bungee, her suspicions are confirmed. The neck cord is cross-attached to both arm bonds behind the chair.

Francie's reinforcing the bungees that bind her right foot and leg to the front of the rocker now and cross tying the cords behind the chair's back to the left leg in a way, Callahan remembers, that American Indians used to torture settlers, only minus the chair. Each leg and each arm, when moved, tighten against the others and deepen the strain

at the bungee cutting into the flesh of her throat. In less than five minutes, Francie's managed to completely immobilize her.

"Francie, why are you doing this?" Callahan can barely eke the
whispered words out through the pressure on her larynx.

Francie's laugh from behind is deranged. "Because, my ever-the-
intellectual friend, no one—least of all you—will keep Francis Dade from
that which is rightfully hers!"

Callahan's hopes are dimming. She casts longing eyes on the wasp
spray far away on the picnic table, realizing that she's completely at the
mercy of this woman who's already been willing to kill others though
Callahan can still make no sense of it.

I'm as suddenly and hopelessly trapped as that poor, hapless fly.

Chapter Thirty-One

And now Francie moves in front of her, her chest heaving, her perfectly lined red lips set in cruel determination, as she jerks bungee after bungee of different lengths, widths and colors from the big designer purse. Callahan's astounded at the strength and fury of this woman she was enjoying toying with only minutes ago.

Francie's no longer Francie. She's a crazed Barbie doll, a knot of the coifed blonde hair loosed from its sparkly band sticking up from her head at a rakish angle, the mascara under her right eye smudged down to the circle of blush on her cheekbone as she straps Callahan ever tighter into the rocker.

"Why are you so angry?" Callahan's voice comes out hoarse and distorted under the pressure on her neck.

The brown eyes narrow, but Francie doesn't speak, her expression hard and unfathomable.

"Francie." Callahan wills her weak voice to sound sympathetic. "Francie, I would never do anything to usurp your position on this island."

"You're god damned right you won't. The island's meant to be mine, all of it, and when I marry your precious boyfriend, it will be."

"My boyfriend? Who? Pepper? He's your brother!"

Francie steps back now and surveys her handiwork, arms folded in front, fists clenched. Apparently assured that Callahan can't move, she seems to calm a bit. "He's not my brother, Callahan." Her voice is low with derision. "You're as dense as poor John. Ruby was already knocked up when she seduced John. She just made sure that she fucked him enough that he'd believe the little bun in her oven was his. Mother-love, you see? She got herself a proper father for her precious, about-to-be-premature, little me."

Her cool ironic tone and pitiless smile are bone chilling. She picks the white leather purse up from the floor, snaps it closed, carries it to the picnic table and brushes unseen dirt off its bottom before setting it down.

"John and Honey never figured it out, but Pepper finally did. For which I am grateful because he now understands that he's fair game for me to pursue." An unhinged giggle issues forth. "I think he built me a house because he knew he'd weaken, us all living together, and eventually I'd get him to fuck me, just like Ruby did his old man. And with the same results." Here she mimes the spraddle-legged, leaned-back walk of a very pregnant woman.

Then, straightening, Francie runs a hand through her hair, smoothing the errant piece back into place. "And you know what else?" She poofs up the left side of her hair, then the right and readjusts the sparkly hair band. "As long as I don't have sluts like you and Vicky in my way, it can and will happen again."

Again? Does that mean she's already slept with him?

Callahan's reminded of Cole's question but also wonders why, if Francie's been intimate with Pepper, he didn't tell her about the effect of the mumps.

Francie turns from the table and walks in front of Callahan's rocker, pinching her on the cheek in a gesture that seems almost playful until she squeezes hard. "How could you think I'd be willing to accept one little third of this island when it was the Dades who drove my people off it to start with? And nobody but Juby's ever had the balls to stand up to them and their money. Too bad you won't live long enough to see it happen, Callahan, because one night after a couple of martinis, Pepper's going to get a hard on for this glorious body of mine"–she strikes a pose like Bacall in a doorway and puffs out her breasts–"and the rest will be history."

Callahan's wrists and ankles ache from the pressure of the tightly drawn cords. She reminds herself not to be distracted by pain, fear, or by Francie's chatter.

Concentrate, Callahan. Use your wits. Is there any way to get out of this chair? You can stall, for one thing. Time is your friend till you find a better solution.

"So, Francie." Callahan tries sounding chatty and unconcerned though her throat burns like acid's eating it under the chafing cords. "Let me assure you I'd never marry Pepper or any man. As far as I'm concerned, he's all yours. I'm like Lila in that way."

Francie's fists clench again, her face growing red. "Well, you're fucking him, aren't you? And fucking leads to complications like little Francies. Besides, he's crazy about you." She shakes her head distractedly. "No, you have to die. I left those warnings in your bathroom to scare you off the island at least two days ago. You've run out of time, and, besides, I've never liked you anyway. My own daddy thought more of you than he did me. It's why I've decided to experiment with a little different technique on you, Callahan." Francie's voice is as flat and detached as if she's placing a pizza order.

She purses her lips and smiles ruefully. "Even Vi and Wallace are getting starry eyed, hoping Pepper will marry their little island urchin."

Urchin? Me? How dare she? Stop, Callahan. Don't be distracted. Think. Keep her talking.

"Well, even if *I'm* not around, what about Honey? She is John's daughter, too. Right? And entitled to her third of the island?"

Francie sighs mightily. Her nipples are noticeable under her thin cotton tee shirt.

It's like she's getting off on thinking about killing me.

"Yes, Honey will have to die, eventually, but I'll take her last after I get really good at this. I like her the best, and, after all, she is my sweet little half sister. I tried to warn that stupid bitch Vicky that she and her little Yorkshit terrier would be better off staying away from Pepper. If she'd paid any attention to me, she'd be alive today. And her little dog, too." Francie pauses, her eyes brightening. "You never got to meet little Buster, did you, since I rather effectively used him to practice my injection technique on over a year ago."

When Francie walks behind the rocker, her voice trails off into the kitchen. "Pepper told Vicky they had no future, but she wouldn't take no for an answer. Then, last month they started fucking like gerbils again, and I had to consider the possibility that *she'd* get knocked up or he'd take her back just for the sex."

Callahan hears the refrigerator open and the click of an opening ice tray. Then, the sound of the fridge door closing, and Francie's voice coming closer. "I couldn't risk him getting entangled with her before it was my turn."

She really doesn't know anything about what the mumps did to Pepper.

The casual way Francie talks about ending people's lives–including her own–horrifies Callahan. Her throat's bone dry now, her tongue swollen over-big in her mouth, but she's determined to keep Francie talking. "So did you use that old standby, the peanut butter sandwich?"

Francie walks back to the deck with a full glass of ice tea, and her lip curls in a sneer. "At least, you're not as dumb as Vicky, but it's still too late, Callahan. You know, you all have always underestimated me. 'Francie, the dumb blonde. Francie the nympho.' I know how people talked. But I have an advantage nobody took into consideration, and that's my mama and her plants. Ruby's taught me all she knows: herbal remedies, hallucinogens if you want to trip out, pain relievers, uppers, downers. Even with your big university degrees, I bet you don't know about that bush right there in your own back yard." She points to an oversized, shiny-leafed bay below the porch. "When you boil its leaves, you get an amazing pain killer. Turns into a popular little product called acetylsalicylic acid. Aspirin!"

Francie sits down in the rocker beside Callahan, talking faster and more animatedly now. "I've got poppies and a cactus in my garden that drug lords would kill for. And, then, I've got my all-time favorite plants. My castor beans, which, once you grind them into a dry paste, make one of the deadliest poisons in the world, an efficient little powder called ricin. Remember Honey's fat old cat, Colonel Mustard? Everyone mourning over his heart attack? I just let him sniff a couple of grains of my homemade powder that day after he peed all over my new bedspread. Nobody even suspected clueless, little Francie. Plus, unless you know to look specifically for ricin, the cause of death continues to be a mystery." Francie rocks quietly for a minute, obviously enjoying the chance to brag about her exploits.

Fighting panic that's coming at her in waves now, Callahan continues to rack her brain for new topics, new questions. "JP? How about JP?"

"That son of a bitch, that no good cheating son of a bitch!" Francie stops rocking. "He got what he deserved, his own private last supper while Cole was still trying to track him down for an interview. I decided not to tell him to contact Cole after I heard from Irene what he and Vicky had been up to. I just promised JP the best blow job of his life if he'd meet me at Ruby's cabin for a nooner and a picnic last Saturday."

It's impossible for Callahan to move her head, but she forces her eyes left towards Francie in an effort to appear accepting and interested.

Francie's smile turns almost sweet. "I kept my promise, too. Gave him one of my better ones, even if it had to be his last. I drugged his fried chicken so he fell asleep right afterwards, and then I shot him up with ricin. Because of his size, I knew it would take a lot. Ricin works faster if you sniff it or inject it than in food. I did hate to lose that man, though, with the size of his dick and all."

Francie's face has taken on a contemplative look, her eyes rolling up towards the ceiling as she recalls the details. "Killing's like everything else. You get better with practice. See, the first time, I didn't stay to tie up loose ends. I left the poisoned pimento cheese sandwiches for Vicky that Thursday and made sure I was long gone from the island before she even ate them. Actually, I expected her to last a couple of days because she'd eaten the poison, not sniffed or been injected with it. Figured she'd die in town, and they'd think it was the flu or something. Maybe her diabetes messed it up. Still, as long as nobody knew I'd been with her on the beach, there was no way of tracing it to me. Except that horny Pasquini creep spied on them and ruined it all." She lowers her eyes and begins rocking faster. "When I heard he'd been up there with his binoculars watching JP fuck Vicky, I knew I had to do some damage control. Because if Vicky told JP I'd brought her lunch or Mr. Pasquini saw me bring it..." She shrugs her shoulders in a helpless way. "Also, I hadn't factored in JP being a cheating bastard. That's another reason he had to die." Unprompted now, clearly enjoying telling the story, Francie continues. "I did Pasquini last. I had to wait till he came up his new staircase alone Monday morning looking for JP. A well-placed shove was all it took."

Silence falls upon the porch for a minute. Thickening clouds on the horizon flicker with occasional lightening. The even thud of Francie's rocking and the heavy familiar scent of her perfume make the moment seem almost companionable.

Unless you're the mouse, and the cat has plans for you. Time for more questions.

"So was it JP's body down there at Ruby's shed Sunday? His body that Harry saw them moving?"

"Yeah, it was him. My Uncle Juby and one of his buddies took him out in the inlet and dumped him so he'd wash out to sea. They were actually surprised he turned up on Sullivan's a couple days later, you know, that the sharks hadn't gotten him first. You and that Appplegate brat almost ruined that whole thing. They had to break the shed window, climb out, and unlock the door after you locked them in. Why in the hell would you do a stupid thing like that?" Francie's face goes stormy. "That's another reason I'm looking forward to killing you, Callahan. You're always showing up on this island in places where you're not wanted."

Francie talks on as dispassionately as if she's discussing a new lipstick color. Callahan's very sure now that she's dealing with a full-blown psychopath.

Which means there's nothing I can say to appeal to her feelings because psychopaths have zero capacity for empathy.

Callahan knows she's running out of options though her brain still spins, seeking the one inspired idea that—so far—hasn't come.

"Francie, can I ask you another question, since I clearly won't be around to testify against you?"

"Sure, why not?"

"How come JP had water in his lungs if you poisoned him on Saturday and didn't dump him in the ocean till the next day?"

"Oh, that! I messed up by letting Vicky die on the beach. So after I drugged and injected JP, I just waited. It took most of the day, but he finally started choking and gasping—probably his heart going nuts. Then, I brought in a couple of buckets of ocean water and poured it over his rotten cheating face so it would look like he drowned. See, Callahan, you're going to be even more interesting because I've decided to be sure you die more slowly and study you. You know, like a science experiment, after all I've learned doing Vicky and JP." She stands and rubs her hands together. "Let's see how many hours you'll last." Francie's nipples are clearly erect now.

Callahan hears fear drumming in her ears.

Francie walks to the picnic basket, extracts and puts on a pair of plastic gloves before picking up the peanut butter sandwich from the shiny red paper plate. She turns to Callahan. "Disposable, see? I burn all evidence and touch nothing without plastic gloves." Using a plastic knife, she cuts the sandwich into tiny pieces. "I was expecting you to be a little more cooperative so the only ricin I brought today is already in the sandwiches."

It's while Francie's cutting and terror's rising in Callahan's chest that she has a flashback to Harry's answer when she asked what he'd do if the "bad guys" caught him. His big smile. The cocky tilt of his head. "I'd just holler bloody murder."

Holler bloody murder? The odds of someone's being in hearing distance are slim to none. But something spooked Albert before Francie got here. Someone near enough to hear me?

Resolving to use the only part of her anatomy that Francie has not disabled, Callahan opens her mouth and screams. Over and over, as loud as she possibly can. "Help! Someone, anyone. Help me! Francie's trying to poison me!"

Scowling angrily, Francie hurries back across the porch with the sandwich pieces on the plastic plate. "Will you shut the fuck up." Her face is flushed with rage. "There's nobody out there to hear you, anyway."

Callahan closes her mouth and locks her jaws. Francie tries stuffing a piece of the sandwich in with her right hand, her left one still holding the plate. One-handed, though, she can't pry Callahan's pursed lips open enough to shove the small piece in. Her eyes narrow. She transfers the sandwich piece to her left hand, rears back her right hand, and viciously slaps Callahan across the face. "Now open your goddamn mouth."

Time detaches for Callahan, the drums replaced by ringing in her ears from the force of the blow. She clenches her teeth again and tightens her lips, even more determined to hold Francie off for as long as she can.

The slap may sting, but it still bought me time.

Francie sighs like an over-wrought mother and goes back to the picnic table with the plate.

In the seconds while Francie's gone, Callahan gasps for air and yells again, snapping her mouth closed and locking her jaws when Francie returns holding only one sandwich piece in her gloved right hand.

"You have just seriously pissed me off, Callahan. I told you to stop yelling." Francie walks behind her and with no warning, violently jerks the bungees tighter against her neck. Jerks them so tight that Callahan fears her airway may be obstructed. Panic rises in her chest. Unwilling to open her mouth with Francie so near, she begins sniffing air rapidly in through her nostrils, hoping that some small amount of oxygen will make it past the bungee and down into her lungs. Already, she's growing dizzy.

I can't hold out much longer.

In front of her, the blue vein in the middle of Francie's creamy white forehead has begun pulsing. Francie's using both hands this time to pry at Callahan's mouth and hold the sandwich piece. When it slips from her fingers and drops to the floor, she swears. "Well, shit, I'll put an end to this." Clearly frustrated now, Francie spins back towards the picnic table.

Grateful beyond measure for a chance to breath through her mouth, Callahan gasps air into the back of her mouth and, hopefully, down the swollen passage of her trachea.

Francie comes back carrying the plastic knife. She stabs the blade between Callahan's lips and pushes it between her teeth, using it as a lever to open Callahan's mouth with her two extra big thumbs.

Oh, God.

Callahan remembers Lila's words now. "People with big thumbs are capable of greatly selfish acts."

It's only a matter of time till she gets the poison in. Should I spit it right back at her or act like I'm swallowing it but not do it? Does it have to be swallowed to work or is a taste enough to kill me?

Callahan can feel her jaw muscles tiring even as she continues to clench her teeth.

Keep holding. Keep holding on.

Suddenly, the knife breaks in half, its broken plastic end gouging the inside of Callahan's lip. She tastes her own blood.

Another reprieve.

Francie explodes in profanity. "How in the hell am I supposed to make this look like an accident with just my two hands and one broken knife?" Her face brightens then, as if she's just answered her own question. "Wait a minute. You have a kitchen full of shit I can use. I'll be back. Hang on, Callahan." There's an optimistic trill to her voice.

Callahan gulps air while Francie's gone. The cord around her neck and the swelling beneath it seem to be closing down her airway. She's too oxygen-starved now to try to scream, too dizzy to think straight.

This time, Francie brings a pair of pliers, a stainless steel cutlery knife, and—most horribly—a good-sized wooden-handled paring knife back out to the deck.

"Now, then." Francie's over by the table where she's placed the new utensils. Her voice goes up a note to reasonable. "You have a choice here, Callahan. Either you be a good girl and open your mouth or"—her voice lowers menacingly—"I'll be forced to cut it open for you!"

Callahan closes her mouth and clamps her teeth together once again. She's close to blacking out now, her head throbbing, her vision moving in and out of focus.

I'll let her cut me up if I have to and it buys time.

Francie has a piece of the sandwich in the pliers in her right hand when she approaches Callahan and—mercifully for the moment—the stainless steel cutlery knife in the other. She has no trouble slipping the cutlery knife between Callahan's lips, but this time she targets an upper molar, positioning the knife's narrow end against it. "Now, we'll just give it a pry." Francie's voice, all business, is beginning to fade farther and farther away. "Just a little pry…"

Even though she knows she's close to blacking out, Callahan remains intensely focused on clenching, clenching, clenching her teeth. So it takes her a long minute to recognize the sound as the crack of a rifle from down by the pond when she hears it.

Francie still stands before her, but her big thumbs have slackened and her expression no longer menaces.

She looks surprised.

A small red hole appears on top of the pulsing blue vein, then grows larger and redder. Francie's hands fall away, and the knife and pliers drop to the floor as the hole–almost in slow motion it seems to Callahan–enlarges and reddens.

In a determined move, Callahan forces her chin to her chest and in so doing slackens the pressure on the throat bungee. She gulps air, her vision gradually clearing until she recognizes that it's blood leeching over Francie's glamorous features, into the startled brown eyes, and down over the sparkly white FUN tee shirt, which is slowly turning red. Francie staggers backwards, falls, and drops with a heavy thud onto the wooden floor of the porch.

Chapter Thirty-Two

The thirty or more night herons across the pond have all gone squawking and airborne in response to the rifle shot. She's aware of their protests, even as her eyes stay fixated on Francie's face, its perfectly arched brows and startled expression slowly disappearing under an uneven film of clotting blood, some of which still oozes from the wound in her forehead and puddles on the floor.

So he shot her from clear across the pond. If I hadn't yelled, he wouldn't have known what was going on here.

Thunder rumbles menacingly in the skies above her. Callahan's body begins to shake, the bare skin under the bungees burned raw from chafing. Her teeth chatter. Her lacerated lip and battered legs throb. Tears flood her face in an exhausting autonomic nervous system release she has no capacity to control. And yet, in spite of her body's responses, there's a new and growing apprehension.

Only one person on Timicau could have made a shot like that at such a distance.

She soon hears the thud of his footsteps on the lower stairs. The footsteps continue up her stairs now, heavy-booted.

Hobnail-booted.

Ponderous and slow. So slow that it seems an eternity till Juby T. Roy, his heavy old rifle slung over one shoulder on a weathered leather strap, emerges from the stairwell and walks into her line of vision.

"She were my own flesh, Miss Callahan, but I couldn't let her go on with it no more." His voice is raspy as she'd always imagined it would be. He speaks to her as if they'd talked before. "She were my own flesh, and I did hate it, but it were too much of enough."

He walks across the porch towards her, the band of his misshapen, felt hat stained with sweat, its brim half obscuring his unshaven face. His scent is old and musty, like sun-starved dirt under porches. This is the first time she's ever had more than a few fleeting seconds to glimpse this man who's been the stuff of her nightmares. When she actually did see him on the island, always in the dense cover of the maritime forest, he disappeared in an instant and never spoke a word.

He's much shorter than she remembers him, no taller than five-foot-eight, and below the hat brim, she sees the knobby, bulb-tipped nose and sun-darkened face of a man grown old.

How long has it been since I last saw him? Fifteen years at least.

Still, she'd recognize him anywhere from his hunched, steady gait and the almost feral energy he exudes.

He's a private creature, like a hermit or a troll, only at ease when he's alone. Amazing he's come up here today.

"I owe you my life, Mr. Roy." She can barely whisper the words. "You know that, don't you? There's no way I can thank you for what you've done."

He nods his agreement. "I did have to save you. Weren't the first time neither. I tuck you on fer my responsibility when you was just a little thing. Too young to be where you was at. Too wild to know better." She catches a stronger whiff of him now, the earth smells mixed with pluff mud and coon fur, rotting tree bark and salt air. Captured scents she, herself, carried home here to Lila's little tree house after a day in the woods, only to have them scrubbed away in the nightly bathing ritual.

His shirt, a tattered grey-brown faded camouflage pattern, is limp with sweat. His pants, faded cargo pants, seem like the same ones he wore all those years ago. And he is wearing heavy discolored lace-up boots, boots which she's quite sure have hobnail bottoms.

When he reaches her chair, he pauses, removes his hat, and holds it in his left hand. His black-dark eyes are flat and milky with developing cataracts, his thinning, gray hair plastered to his head, and he looks miserably sad. "You don't need to be afraid of me none. I always looked after you even though I come to hate your mama." His gnarled right hand, splotchy with age marks, goes to his hip to remove a huge knife from the leather holster hanging from his belt. "She talked against Ruby in the court, you know, but I ain't held what she done against you, Miss Callahan."

He's standing before her now, holding a massive hunting knife, the edge of its blade sharpened to shiny silver, but Callahan feels little fear. Limping, he walks behind her. She can see his outline in her peripheral vision if she tilts her head against the restraining bungees. When he raises the knife, her blood momentarily runs cold, but all he does—the sound of his breath heavy as he works—is set about carving through the bungee cords across the back of the chair. One at a time they fall to the deck, until, suddenly, she's freed. Her legs are so bruised and weak she doesn't think she'll be able to stand. Her right hand is totally numb. Her neck...

"Miss Callahan, I'm going to have to take and go now. You tell The Law there's no use of them a-hunting me, for I'll see that they never take me in for what I done here. T'wouldn't be just anyway. What I done had to be done. And you'll be alright come a little bit."

He turns and walks away from her, the empty leather knife holster slapping against his upper leg, the knife still in his right hand, the gun still slung over his shoulder. He pauses when he reaches Francie's body on the floor by the picnic table, stares down at her for a good minute before putting his hat back on and reholstering the big knife. "Poor young 'un. She was such a purdy thing, but she never could learn nothing worth knowing."

I've stopped shaking.

Callahan tries to rise out of the chair, but her legs are too numb. "Please, Mr. Roy." Her voice is so weak she's not sure he'll hear her. "Before you go, may I ask you something?"

He looks over his shoulder towards the impoundment, is clearly becoming uneasy. Then, he moves with remarkable quickness to the top of the stairs where he pauses to answer her question though she hasn't yet asked it.

"Yes'm, it were me behind the dunes that day when you and the boy was looking at them jelly fish. I been watching you pretty close since I heard what Francie and her mama was up to."

"Well, then"–Callahan can stand now, and she walks across the porch gingerly, extending her hand to him–"that requires a second thank you."

He seems discomfited by her closeness but does take her extended hand into his own calloused one when she reaches him. "No need a-thanking me, Miss Callahan. There ain't that many of us left, you know? Them which loves this island the way we does. Them what's not afraid to go out in the wild. I weren't going to let Francie take you from us. Seems like she couldn't help herself no more. Somebody had to stop her. Much as I wish it weren't me, it's still good I hear'd you a-callin."

She pats his hand, nods agreement, and then drops it, her heart swelling with affection for this strange and solitary old man.

He turns and makes his way down the first flight of stairs. A tremendous streak of lightning illuminates the sky shortly followed by booming thunder.

Callahan knows the storm's about to hit. "Juby." She surprises herself by hurriedly calling his name.

He pauses on the first floor landing, turns to look up at her.

"I'm sorry for calling you Juby. It just slipped out because I've heard you called that for so long. Could I ask you one last favor since you've granted me so many today. I know you're around here a lot, hunting snakes and gators and coons, living off the land the way you were brought up to. Now that I've gotten to know you, I'll be grateful when I sense that you're about. But would you be so kind as to not kill the one big old gator on our pond. I love him so."

"Albert? That ain't no problem. We was young'uns together, that gator and me. It's against Nature to kill yer friends. I'll keep an eye on him for you, Miss Callahan. I will."

He turns into the lower stairwell and is gone. Within seconds, the rain does come, a deluge so driving and hard that even the steps under the roof and the decks are quickly flooded.

I wonder how far he got before the storm hit, where he'll find shelter.

Callahan hurries upstairs to escape the drenching rain that's slanting under the eaves. She runs past Francie's body on the deck and into the house where, shaken and shocky, she drops into the first chair she reaches and remains there, watching the storm runs its course. Gradually, the pounding rain dilutes and then washes away the blood on Francie so that she begins to look more herself, Francis Dade, staring open-eyed and surprised, with only that small red perforation in the middle of her forehead.

When the thunder is through rocking the house, and the lightning has slashed and cleansed the sky, a single painted bunting begins its golden trill, and Callahan knows it's time—past time—to call Cole and Pepper. She dials both on her cell but reaches neither, so leaves the same grizzly message. Then, she takes her cell phone, two compresses for her bleeding legs and a dry Turkish towel to the swinging porch chair where she waits at the far end of the deck, away from Francie's body and the remains of the poisoned sandwich which now lies mushed and soggy on the table.

Swinging may be one of the most soothing of all pastimes.

It's only when she's sat swinging a good long while, the sweltering heat of the day returned and making its way into the cool of the rain-drenched porch, the earth steaming its vapors away out beyond the porch, that Callahan remembers the last thing Juby said and smiles,

How in the world did Juby T. Roy know we call the old gator Albert?

Chapter Thirty-Three

It's seven pm. Cole's gone. He's taken Callahan's statement, surveyed the rain-washed crime scene and, with the help of his two deputies, removed Francie's body, purse, peanut butter sandwich, and all the bungee cords for evidence. Pepper, mercifully involved in yet another closing on the mainland, was spared viewing Francie's body, thanks in part to Cole's deliberate haste.

Callahan and Pepper are once again alone, seated at the picnic table on the deck. He's not a foot from where Francie's body lay, eating pork chops, turnip greens and macaroni and cheese as if nothing has changed.

Thank heavens for Vi. Life has to go on, and even though it hurts to swallow, having something good to eat makes things a bit more bearable.

Pepper's been here about an hour, but he's still looking green and incredulous, green as the four stripe-tailed yearling gators, each about twelve inches long, lying on a floating log in the pond below them. He seems unable to believe what Callahan's had to tell him about the distorted thinking that led Francie to believe she could seduce Pepper, kill the competition, and have it all.

"Callahan, I never laid a hand on Francie. It was like living with a direct descendant of Vlad the Impaler to even share a house with her. I was twelve when she was born, so I never knew her as an adult. Honey had tried to tell me, but it took moving back into Twelve Oaks after Daddy died for me to see it was an impossible situation. You never knew what screwy thing she'd be planning next. How she could think I'd want to sleep with her…" His voice trails off, his eyes polished with unshed tears.

He's clearly been blindsided by this though he says he suspected Francie had serious psychiatric problems.

"I couldn't even love her like a sister, Callahan, never felt the warmth I did for Honey. I blamed myself for that till about a year ago when I read a random article in *The Wall Street Journal* about personality disorders, and I realized that, for Francie, everything would always have to center on her. That's when I knew I had to get her out of our house." He stabs a pork chop and cuts a piece off of it. "Francie was the whole reason I was forced to develop the island. I hate doing it, but she insisted on her third of Daddy's estate right after he died, and I didn't have any way to come up with that kind of cash. Still, in my wildest dreams, I didn't think she could be a sociopath or a psychopath or whatever she was."

He stands up and heads for the kitchen. "Boy, I'm whipped as a rented mule. Do you care if I pour myself a little of that sour mash I brought your mama?"

She watches him at the kitchen counter as he drops three ice cubes into a short bar glass and fills it with whiskey. She touches the raw skin on her wrists and tries to stretch out the ache in her legs. Every inch of her feels whipped as Pepper's "rented mule."

Pepper seems to notice. "Callahan, would you let me pour you a drink, too? With all you've been through, a shot might do you good." When she doesn't protest, he adds ice cubes and fills a second glass, carries them back to the table, and hands her one.

"I never drink anything but wine." She takes a sip and wrinkles her nose. "It tastes like medicine."

"Just sip it slowly." It's the first glimmer of a smile she's seen on his face tonight. "It's too strong to drink fast. Takes time to develop a taste for whiskey."

She eats a bite of macaroni and takes a sip, noting with pleasure that Albert has appeared in the middle of the pond. The four babies quickly slide into the water. She's never seen Albert eat his offspring like textbooks report male alligators do, but she's seen him grab them on numerous occasions and shake them violently before throwing them in the air and back into the pond. There's a warm glow in her belly from the bourbon. "Did I tell you, Pepper, that Juby knew Albert's name? That's got to mean he's been so close to the house that he's listened to Lila and me talking. It makes me wonder what else he knows about us."

Pepper's wearing khaki slacks and a blue and white checked shirt that make his eyes extra blue. He's staring at her like he hasn't heard a word she's said. "I can't believe how close I came to losing you, Callahan. I had an idea Ruby and Francie might be mixed up in this, but it never occurred to me Francie would come after you." He shakes his head ruefully. "I'd have never forgiven myself."

He didn't *hear a word I said.*

Callahan takes the last bite of her pork chop and then another sip of the bourbon. She really does sense something inside relaxing. "Pepper, I hope Cole won't try too hard to catch Juby. I think Juby was right. He did what he had to do. He didn't kill JP. He did help Francie dispose of him, but he also saved my life."

"I doubt if Cole will do much more than close this case as fast as he honorably can do it. There's no way to prove Ruby's had any part in it, though you can bet she did. And Juby would be next to impossible to find, the way he lives. He's a true survivalist. Even more importantly, Callahan, you still don't know what an amazing thing that old codger did for you today. Cole was completely aghast when I spilled the beans to him this afternoon."

An unusual carefulness in Pepper's voice peaks Callahan's interest. "Whatever do you mean?"

Pepper looks at the ceiling for a minute, his thick blond lashes accentuated by the intense slanted light of the early evening sun low on the horizon.

He's trying to decide whether to tell me something or not.

"I come from a family that does have its idiosyncrasies." He lowers his eyes to hers and sets his mouth. "But I want you to be a part of it, warts and all. And I can't help what Ruby did." He takes her hand and squeezes it. Her skin's so raw she feels the imprint of his signet ring as pain. "Callahan." Pepper shakes his head, his eyes moving to the far horizon. "Juby didn't just kill his niece today. When he sighted that gun on Francie's forehead and pulled the trigger to save you"–his eyes return to her face, misery and compassion radiating from them–"Juby Roy killed his only daughter."

Chapter Thirty-Four

TWO MONTHS HAVE PASSED
SEPTEMBER 25

Someone has tightened a tourniquet around her heart. Callahan actually feels like her heart has ceased beating.

This can't be right.

She draws in a shuddering breath and, seeking brighter light, hurries from the bathroom towards the front deck where a late morning autumn sun still sits low enough in the sky to peek under the eaves. With trembling hands, she raises the three inch white plastic wand to the light and reexamines the two circles on its side, each bisected with a horizontal line. Fingers fumbling, she again unfolds the instructions that came with the wand, sure she'd misread something on the page when she was in the bathroom. "A false negative is possible"–this last line on the paper stands out because it's written in bold-faced type–"but not a false positive. When your specimen produces a horizontal line in both circles, pregnancy is assured." Her arrested heart begins racing wildly.

But Pepper is so sure he's sterile.

She staggers backwards into a rocker and collapses. Sits there for long minutes, letting the news sink in. She wasn't concerned when she missed her period in July because going off birth control pills had left her with abnormal cycles before. When August came and went with still no period, she'd wondered, but dismissed her concerns because of what Pepper had told her. The queasy mornings and late afternoon exhaustion of these last two weeks, though, finally made her face this possibility. So yesterday, she bought the pregnancy test-kit and used it this morning, just to assure herself she wasn't pregnant.

So, I'm assured, but not quite in the way I expected. What am I going to do?

༐

She's at north beach now, lying face-up on a beach towel, having fled her house for the whispered assurances of the lazy surf. The sun's directly overhead, it's buttery light illuminating bits of clinquant sand. The scattered clouds overhead are all cirrus, lacy as petticoats. The surf is calm. A few sandpipers, stutter-stepping after a receding wave, are the only other movements on the beach. It's a peaceful, perfect fall day except nothing about Callahan's inner terrain is either peaceful or perfect.

I feel like I'm at the North Pole with my compass needle spinning. Why didn't I believe my instincts that first night with Pepper? I knew I'd ovulated that day.

A sea gull shrieks right over her head, momentarily startling her. She clearly remembers sensing her pregnancy that early July morning, then completely ignoring her intuition after hearing Pepper's reassurance.

Good God, I've had at least one glass of wine most every night since with Pepper! Have I done something to hurt my baby? Our baby.

The seagull shrieks again and dives towards the ocean. It's the first time Callahan's faced the fact that this baby is not hers alone. When Pepper learns she's carrying his child, everything will be different. He's spent the last two months trying to talk her into marring him, but now...

He'll go ballistic. Maybe I shouldn't tell him.

She feels a sardonic smile cross her face.

He'll know soon enough whether I tell him or not.

She does a mental calculation, remembers attributing the snug fit of her jeans yesterday to the indolence of the summer past.

I'll be showing, at least for him in the bedroom, within weeks.

She shifts positions, half-sitting to watch a squadron of pelicans that appears in their classic V formation on the horizon. She's taken, as always, by the unstudied perfection of their aeronautical maneuvers, all the more remarkable because they're so awkward on land. She scoops up a handful of warm sand and trickles it over the bare skin of her still-flat belly and on to the black surface of her bikini bottom, feeling a nascent joy as she wonders if the little creature within her is aware of the sand's warmth or movement. She's moving surprisingly fast toward acceptance, she realizes, actually feels giddy with excitement as she thinks about the days and months ahead.

Wouldn't Mother be excited! I'll have to get on the Internet and see how far the baby's already developed.

She pictures and instantly loves the curved little tadpole swimming safely within her in a fluid not unlike the ocean lapping at her feet. Then, calculating, she realizes that at ten weeks her baby's probably not a tadpole at all, but tail-less and well enough developed to look very much like a fetus.

Darn! I've already missed a lot of time when I could have been tracking its development inside of me.

She lies down on her back again and heaps more sand, handful after handful, upon her belly till it's covered. She's sure that any baby of hers will understand that she's welcoming it in the best possible beach-like way. One particular grain of sand, shiny and lots larger than the others catches her eye as it falls. She pushes up to her elbow, picks it off her belly, and slants it toward the sun, enjoying the reflection of first the blue sky, then the aqua ocean, then again, beige sand as she shifts its angles.

William Blake, she's reminded of that wonderful quote. *To see the world in a grain of sand and heaven in a wild flower, hold infinity in the palm of your hand and eternity in an hour."*

The astonishing irony of what's gone on in *her world* the last six months and what changes now lie ahead strikes her.

My mother and Pepper's father loved each other, but too late. Lila would never trust another man so John couldn't get her to marry him, let alone carry his child. Now Pepper's convinced he loves and wants to marry me, and here I am carrying a child he has no idea he can even have. But do I love or want to marry him? In fact, do I want to marry anyone?

Her mother's admonitions about independence and self-sufficiency are rooted in her psyche. Callahan realizes that finding her own life may require her to exorcize at least some of them.

So can the circle of all this misdirected love ever close into something named family? Or will we just keep turning the pages of our lives, writing each other out of the script, generation after generation?

Her head's spinning.

And what about work? I told the College of Charleston I'd be available in January. Will they let me come later? Will I want to come later and leave my baby?

There are so many questions to answer and such big decisions to be made that Callahan lies back on the warm sand and, seeking wisdom beyond herself, positions herself to meditate.

෴

And that's where Pepper finds her at least forty-five minutes later, startling her to consciousness with a yell from the cart path on the dunes above the beach. "Here you are! I had an idea I'd find you here when your golf cart wasn't at your house or the dock."

She sits up, feeling calmer and anchored into herself from the meditation. "Hey." She's excited he's here, she realizes, seeing him with new eyes as he jogs the length of the path down to the beach towards her.

He's the father of my baby, remarkably handsome, solvent, eligible, interesting, seemingly in love with me, but for a lifetime? How does a person ever get brave enough to commit to sharing her whole life with another person?

He arrives breathless and animated, Nadine loping beside him. "I've got a surprise for you. Varina just told me about it this this morning, and I couldn't wait for you to see it."

Brushing the sand off her belly, Callahan stands to meet them. She reaches to pet Nadine just as Pepper scoops her up in an embrace, followed by a greedy kiss. She does love the taste and smell of him.

His eyes are twinkling. He reaches into his pants pocket and produces what appears to be a very old brown velvet ring box. "Open it."

Uneasy, Callahan takes the box as Nadine abandons them to chase the sandpipers at the water's edge.

"It was Mother's." Pepper's usually good at hiding what he's feeling, but today he's clearly excited.

She gasps when she opens the box, gasps at the sheer beauty of the engagement ring it holds. Clearly very old, it's the most beautiful one she's ever seen. Two perfectly matched large diamonds in an ornate but elegant platinum setting are circled by six smaller ones, all of which catch the sun with a sparkle considerably more impressive than her William Blake grain of sand.

"I want you to take it." He speaks before she can, lifting her chin with his thumb to raise her face to his, earnestly staring into her eyes. "I know you're not ready to commit to marriage yet, but this was my mother's. I didn't know about it till today. I want you to have it because I love you, Callahan, and one day before too long, I hope you'll wear it as my wife."

"Whoa! This is a lot to take in. Think I'd better sit down. Come join me." She brushes the sand off the towel to clear a place for him. It's when she's lowered herself to her beach towel, giddy from his kiss, his presence and this offer of Mignon's beautiful ring, that inspiration strikes.

This is too perfect.

She closes the box with a snap and, without hesitation, places it in a zippered compartment of her beach bag. "That ought to keep the sand off it. My gosh, Pepper, it's the prettiest ring I've ever seen. Thank you. I accept it."

His jaw drops. She knows he's astounded she's taken it so readily.

"And here's what I'll do." She smiles up at him. "I will think long and hard about becoming your wife, but I'd ask you to let me keep the ring anyway, whether we marry or not. Keep it in escrow for your child."

Pepper's mouth closes, and his brows drawn together. Then, he does that endearing thing he does when he's confused. He tugs at his ear. "Child?" Pain joins confusion on his features. "Callahan, honey, don't you remember I can't have a child?"

"I do remember." She's loving this. "But I can no longer say that I believe you because—guess what?—I am at least two and a half months pregnant. I have no idea why it happened, but this is no Ruby-thing. You're the only man I've been with in the last six months, so best I can tell, you'll be a father in less than seven months, whether you thought you could be or not."

If Mignon's diamonds could shine in Pepper Dade's eyes, that is the quality of light that fills them at this moment. He looks at her with incredulity, wonder and utter joy. "My God," he says. "You're serious, aren't you?" He rubs that ear again. "You're really serious. You've got to marry me now, Callahan. It's an answered prayer, a gift from God. I can't believe it. You and I, we're having a baby."

Chapter Thirty-Five

THANKSGIVING DAY

Callahan's been in the bathtub much longer than it takes her to bathe. She's due at Twelve Oaks in less than an hour for an early afternoon feast, but still she remains submerged. Soaking, marveling at the roundness of her formerly flat belly, and mulling things over. Just about all of her burning questions have been answered in these last two months since she found out she was pregnant.

All except for the big one. Do I marry him or not? I have to sort that one out all by myself.

A bar of soap that's delicately balanced on the edge of the tub breaks loose and falls into the bath water with a plop, like a yellow slider turtle off a log into the pond. It brings Callahan back. Noticing her waterlogged skin, she pulls the plug, stands, steps out, reaching for a towel. Her eyes fall upon the cracked silver mirror she moved to her bathroom counter from Lila's box only last week.

She's felt surprisingly at peace about her mother since that day when she read all of Lila's letters in one sitting and later pinned Pepper down about all he knew. Callahan finishes drying herself, hangs the towel on a wall peg, and steps into clean underpants, stretching them to accommodate her expanding girth. She fastens her bra on the last clasp and studies herself with the eyes of a scientist in the full-length mirror she added to the back of the bathroom door only yesterday.

There's no denying it now. You're a gestating mammal in every physical detail.

She laughs, delighted. On a whim, she picks up Lila's mirror and carries it with her into the bedroom where she flops down on the bed. It turns out that Lila was considerably more complicated than she'd ever imagined, her mother's early-learned distrust of men so scarring that she never fully believed a man again. It was Curly, Lila's father, who cracked the face of this mirror into its three splintered sections. Cracked it across Lila's nose.

The only thing she had left from her mother, and he broke her nose with it the night she told him she was pregnant with me. Called her a slut like her own mother, who'd abandoned them, and threw her out of the house. No wonder Lila hated Curly, my dad, Reggie, and all the painful memories that mirrors evoked.

Sipping wine, Lila had told Pepper all this over a series of starlit, rocking-porch nights. "I actually started bringing extra good wine to keep her talking."

Pepper had seemed willing—no anxious—to share all he knew with Callahan that night last week when she mustered the courage to ask him about Lila. A very wet Nadine, fresh from a beach walk, had beat Pepper up the steps and launched herself joyfully into Callahan's disappearing lap. Emerging from the stairwell seconds later and seeing them entangled in the rocker, Pepper proclaimed, "the most affectionate creature in the world is a wet dog." As if to emphasize Pepper's point, Nadine slathered more dog kisses across Callahan's face. Callahan laughed and took a quick breath, forcing herself to blurt out the question that had long been on her mind. "Pepper, would you be willing to answer something really personal about my mom? I know you were very close to her, but were you, you know, sexually involved?"

A curious expression crossed his face as he walked across the porch towards Callahan. He grabbed Nadine's collar and pulled her off. "You must not have known Lila as well as you think you did. I'll tell you the truth. I'm as susceptible to temptation as the next man, so I can't say I wasn't interested. Some women, regardless of their age, remain eternally sensual. But she'd have no part of it." He began rubbing Nadine with an old towel they kept folded on a porch chair for that purpose. "So I learned just to be glad for her companionship and wisdom. I found her endlessly complex, interesting, and fun. But I'd bet you a side of beef that the *only* sexual relationship she ever had after you were born was with my daddy. They did have that between them and a deep affection, for which I've always been grateful."

"Even after he married Ruby?" It was slowly beginning to dawn on Callahan how much she did not know about her mother.

"It wouldn't surprise me because they were going strong right after he and Ruby were divorced. Could be another reason Ruby and Juby disliked her so much. Best I can tell, Lila pretty much did what she wanted to do. She seemed willing to face the consequences, but I don't remember her ever having to. Daddy used to worry her to death about turning you loose on the island when you were little, but look how you turned out. I think she was wise in a way few women are."

Feeling tears well in her eyes as she remembers Pepper's words, Callahan realizes she's been stroking the nubby texture of the old white spread on Lila's bed, something that brought her comfort when she was a little girl.

Mother only let me know what she wanted me to know, no more.

When she cleaned out Lila's bedside table, Callahan found an envelope holding five scraps of paper, each with a quote written in her mother's large loopy handwriting. She reaches for that envelope on her bedside table now, opens it, and rereads the quotes which have probably given her as much insight as she'll ever have into what made her mother tick.

In black ink: Rachel Carson: "Those who dwell among the beauties and mysteries of life are never alone or weary of life."

In brown ink: Henry David Thoreau: "The question is not what you look atbut what you see."

And three more quotes without attribution in blue ink:

"Expect nothing. Blame no one. Do it anyway."

and

"We don't see things as they are. We see things as *we* are."

and

"Judgment is a self-deception and act of sabotage, both for the victim and the one who initiates the action."

My mother chose to be without judgment, of herself or others except, maybe, for the two men who betrayed her. She spent her life trying to "see" more clearly, dwelling amid the beauty and mystery here. And Carson was right, she never wearied of it. But she was cut off from people, refused to share more of herself than she was comfortable sharing. It's easier to judge no one, if you allow no one close enough to affect you.

Callahan remembers Lila's tale about the dolphins delivering her into the waiting arms of her mother on the sandbar north of Timicau.

I knew it was her fairy tale, a way of keeping me from knowing some unhappy truth, yet for many years I actually let myself believe it. By protecting me from the truth, did she—did we?—miss the chance to know each other better? And did she overemphasize the importance of my being independent at the expense of true intimacy? Do I?

Callahan places the envelope with its quotes back on the bedside table on top of the latest Peter Matheson books she's been reading. "He was happy and unhappy all at once. He was in love." That Matheson quote's has been so on point these eight weeks since Callahan told Pepper about her pregnancy. She's been endlessly conflicted, happy beyond anything in her life experience, then terrified because she's allowed Pepper to get closer to her than she ever has another man.

Maybe even Mother. So is this love?

He's been her supporter, her teacher, her cheerleader, so many roles, so much growing interdependence.

Still, each time I share an iota more, it makes me jumpy as a frog pond. I think I've been programmed, Lila's warnings trumping my feelings each time I even consider marrying Pepper. Though, truthfully, the last few weeks have been such a blur, it would have been hard to decide anything.

Early on, Pepper was absorbed in planning Francie's private funeral service and in finding a place for Robbie Pasquini to live nearby while he recuperated. In the past few weeks, he's been sorting through the estate implications of Francie's death. To his great credit, he's continued to treat Francie, in death, as he did in life, like she really was his half sister, a blood relative with an inheritable interest in the island, but he's having second thoughts about that now.

Three weeks ago, Ruby and her husband, the porta-john magnate, moved into Francie's house, sparing Vi the care of the seven cats, but creating almost daily complications for Pepper. Juby, of course, has not been seen since the shooting, though Cole really has tried to track him down. Ruby's twice regaled Callahan on the ferry with venomous stories about Juby, even going so far as to confirm that he was Francie's biological father. "He started diddling me when he was fourteen, and I was eleven. Pretty soon, it just got to be recreational for us, if you know what I mean, until I got in a family way. I gave that man the skinniest years of my life and, then he wouldn't give me a plug nickel when I needed help. And he never done a thing for Francie once she was born except to kill the life out of her at the end."

Callahan reminds herself not to forget what Juby said about Ruby that day on the porch after he cut her loose. "When I found out what she and her mother was up to..."

So what else were they up to? How much did Ruby really know?

Ruby's culpability can't be proved, but her presence on the island is disquieting, nonetheless.

On another note–Callahan sits up in the bed–*what in the heck am I going to wear?*

Finding clothes that fit her new proportions has lately become the challenge of the day. She's told only three people besides Pepper about her pregnancy, but Honey's going to be at dinner today, and Pepper's asked that she be told. Callahan heads for her closet where several elastic topped skirts and loose-fitting tops, the kind Pepper describes as "blouses made by aborigines," have become the staples of her wardrobe. She smiles to herself.

His humor makes him fun to be around.

The "aboriginal blouse" she drops over her head's a blue flax over-shirt. She steps into a beige skirt, pulls her hair back at the nape of her neck in a band and adds a turquoise necklace. Then, picks up the Mexican mirror to take a peek. The mirror, though, reflects only a fractured and distorted view, here a nose, there a necklace.

It's really useless if you want to see the whole picture. Maybe that's why I bought the new mirror. Am I ready to see the whole picture at last?

Once dressed, on impulse, she walks to the nightstand and takes the brown velveteen box out of the drawer. It opens with a snap, diamonds sparkling wildly in golden sunlight through the bedroom window. She's not yet even given herself a chance to experience the sensation of the thing upon her fourth finger.

An experiment. If I try it on, it will be an experiment only. How do people begin to know if they can make a marriage out of a love affair? Do we have enough in common?

He loves football. She doesn't even understand it. They do enjoy fishing together and have in common a fierce protective love of the island and its creatures.

Are our differences too great? Our ten-year age difference, our interests? This Child. We'll have this child in common regardless of what I decide. I enjoy the way he expresses himself, look forward to talking to him at the end of the day, like getting his take on politics and local news, though I often disagree with him. He's a good person, a moral man, not a driven intellectual but sharp and smart and quick on the uptake. Is that enough?

Callahan sits back down on the bed, recalling the one occurrence that's most unnerved her as she's tried to come to terms with this pregnancy. Harry Applegate! The second person, besides Vi, with whom she discussed her pregnancy was his mother, Annie. On the ferry, about two weeks ago, Annie took one look at Callahan from the opposite side of the boat, stood up and moved to sit beside her. "I do not mean to pry, Callahan, honestly I don't, but I know women, and you are clearly working on adding to the population of our island. You want to tell me about it? It's such a magical time."

Someone else being that direct, I'd have resented it.

But the good sisterly heart of Annie Applegate had shone through in her chocolate brown eyes, and her ready smile drew Callahan to her. Callahan had longed for a confidante, another woman with solid good judgment, close to her age who'd been through it all, and then there was Annie. By the end of the ferry ride, information was flowing freely. Callahan never intended to hide the identity of her baby's father though she realized later she probably owed Pepper some input on that decision. Annie seemed perfectly delighted until Callahan said she had reservations about marrying.

Annie drew back, folded her arms, and cocked her head. "Why in the world wouldn't you marry him? He seems mature enough to be a wonderful father, and he's clearly crazy about you. What's holding you back?"

The answer slipped through Callahan's lips before she could stop it. "My mother."

"Your mother?" Annie's eyes clouded in confusion. "But, Callahan, your mother's been dead for over six months, hasn't she?"

"She has." Callahan swallowed a lump in her throat. "She is dead, but she wouldn't want me getting married. She never did, and I don't think I'd know how to be married."

At this, Annie threw her head back and laughed out loud. "Why, darling," she said, "getting married is like learning to swim. You take a big breath. You hold your nose, and you jump. And when you come to the surface, you start kicking and thrashing till you get some idea about what keeps you afloat." She patted Callahan's arm with chubby warm fingers. "And then, you go from there. I've always preferred the sidestroke, but Wharton thinks the crawl's the only way to cross a pool. From then on, you trust yourself to get better at it, and–with a little bit of luck–you do. Callahan, nobody in the world knows what they're doing when they decide to get married. If they think they do, they're either deceiving themselves that love is enough, or they're lying to you." She raised her voice and belted out. "Marry the man."

At which time, Harry, cheeks red, purple baseball hat askew, entered the cabin from outside. "What man? Who's getting married?"

"Can I tell him?" Annie asked before Callahan could answer.

"Sure, why not?"

"Callahan and Mr. Dade are having a baby, Harry, and she's trying to decide whether to get married."

Harry stopped dead in his tracks in front of her, his nose wrinkled in puzzlement, his penetrating dark eyes narrowed. And what he said at that moment, doggone him, keeps coming back to Callahan. "Boy, you'd be really stupid not to marry Mr. Pepper. I wouldn't want to grow up without my daddy."

Callahan's pulse races each time she recalls Harry's words.

I wonder what my life would have been like if I'd had a father.

Callahan stands now, knowing she needs to leave at once if she's not to be late for dinner at Twelve Oaks, then pauses. Instead of closing the ring box and putting it back in the drawer, she takes out the ring and–for the first time–slides it on to her fourth finger. It's a perfect fit. She imagines the gentle energy of John and his love for Mignon, all a part of this beautiful ring. Pepper's mother is the only other woman who's worn it, and now Pepper wants it to be hers.

What if Harry and Annie are right, and Lila a little wrong? Maybe, just maybe, I can try this for a day, for a Thanksgiving dinner, for as long as it takes to cross a pool with the sidestroke, and then again another lap, until I can see where it all leads.